A FOOLISH GAME: A REGENCY ROMANCE

LAURA BEERS

A Foolish Game: A Regency Romance
By: Laura Beers

Text copyright © 2020 by Laura Beers
Cover art copyright © 2020 by Laura Beers
Cover art by Blue Water Books

❀ Created with Vellum

MORE ROMANCE BY LAURA BEERS

The Beckett Files
Regency Spy Romances

Saving Shadow
A Peculiar Courtship
To Love a Spy
A Tangled Ruse
A Deceptive Bargain
The Baron's Daughter
The Unfortunate Debutante

❧ I ❧

London, 1813

Lady Isabella Beauchamp had the misfortune of being born a girl. This was something she was quite sure about. She wasn't truly free to be who she wanted to be. Society had such stringent restrictions about how a lady should behave. It was exhausting to pretend to be something she was not. She wanted to experience adventure and the rush of excitement, she decided, as she raced her horse through the fields surrounding her townhouse.

But that was impossible. For she was a lady, the daughter of a marquess. Just because he was deceased did not change the fact that Society expected certain things from her, as did her family. They were constantly chiding her for her unladylike behavior, and she found it to be rather irksome.

Why couldn't her family understand that she was unable to conform to Society's ridiculous expectations of her? Why wouldn't they let her be who she was meant to be, even if it meant she was destined to become a spinster?

Glancing over her shoulder, she saw her brother, Everett, the Marquess of Northampton, gaining on her, leaning over his gelding's neck, apparently coaxing a little more speed from the horse.

She tightened her hold on the reins, leaned lower in her side saddle, and urged her horse faster, feeling alive as the wind blew through her blonde hair that had scandalously fallen from her chignon. The pounding of Maximus's hooves beneath her were rhythmic, and she knew she would never tire of that sound.

As she approached the iron fence surrounding the back of their property, she drew up her mount then wheeled the white gelding around to face her brother.

"I win again," she announced proudly.

Everett reined in his horse. "That you did."

"They should call you 'The Marquess of Lost Races'," Isabella quipped.

Chuckling, he replied, "You are truly awful at giving nicknames."

"Perhaps, but that makes it no less true."

"I must acknowledge your exceptional riding skills," Everett said, adjusting the reins in his hand. "You have managed to beat me in every race I've challenged you to."

"I would have beaten you even more soundly if you had let me ride astride," she remarked confidently as she tucked her hair behind her ears.

Everett eyed her with disapproval. "You are in London now," he chided, his voice taking on a stern edge. "You can't ride astride. It is simply not done."

"I think it is rather ludicrous," she admitted. "After all, I will stay on our lands and—"

He cut her off. "No, absolutely not. And, frankly, I tire of repeatedly having this same conversation," he stated in an irritated tone. "Nothing you say will change my mind."

Isabella opened her mouth and closed it, forcing herself to bite back the angry retort she wanted to make. She knew there was no point in arguing. Her brother could be just as stubborn as she was.

She leaned forward and rubbed Maximus's neck. "Understood," she muttered.

"I am not a heartless monster," Everett sighed. "After the Season concludes and we return to our country estate, then you will be free to ride astride again."

"I suppose I can manage to wait that long."

"That is assuming you haven't found yourself married by the end of the Season," Everett added with a grin.

Isabella stiffened. "I can assure you that won't happen."

"Your aversion to marriage is starting to become rather troublesome," Everett commented.

"I am only eighteen years old," she contended.

"True, but you aren't even entertaining the thought of allowing someone to court you," he observed knowingly.

Her horse pawed at the ground as if sensing her growing irritation. "Why should I?" she countered. "I have no desire to be trapped in a loveless marriage."

"You won't feel trapped if you marry the right person," he said gently. "I certainly don't feel that way with Madalene."

Isabella shifted her gaze away from her brother's, her eyes scanning the green fields. "You were lucky," she remarked. "Madalene fell from a tree into your coach, and it was practically love at first sight."

"Both of those things are true, but it doesn't diminish what I am trying to tell you."

"Which is?"

"You need to become more serious about choosing a suitor."

Isabella met his gaze with determination. "No," she asserted. "I have no intention of marrying this Season, or the next. Maybe I won't marry at all. I'd be perfectly happy to spend the rest of my days living contently as a spinster in a small estate."

Everett gave her an exasperated look. "Do be serious, Isabella."

"I am being serious."

"You would willingly forego marriage to become a spinster?" he asked in disbelief.

With a shrug of one shoulder, she replied, "The thought of being alone doesn't frighten me."

"It should."

She paused, unsure of how to make him understand. "*If* I do decide to marry, it will only be for love."

"As well you should."

Tightening the reins in her gloved hand, Isabella said, "But love is not possible for everyone. I fully acknowledge that I have a peculiar personality. A trait that many gentlemen of the *ton* are not willing to overlook."

"Not only are you the daughter of a marquess, but you have an impressive dowry—"

She spoke over him. "I want a man that will love me above all else and not because of my lineage or my dowry."

Everett's voice softened as he spoke encouragingly. "You deserve that, but you have to give your suitors a chance. You may find some of them are tolerable."

"Most of the men that have come to call on me are boring and pompous."

"Just promise me that you will try."

Isabella glanced up at the clear, blue sky as she attempted to delay her response. She really didn't want to make a promise to her brother that she had no intention of keeping.

Everett must have understood her reluctance to respond because he surprised her by changing the subject. "How are you faring now that Charlotte has left on her wedding tour with Hudson?"

"I must admit that I am rather melancholy," she replied, "but I hope they have a wonderful time in Scotland."

"They both seemed so happy on their wedding day."

Isabella smiled at that thought. "They were. I have never seen Lottie so happy. I don't think she could have stopped smiling even if she'd wanted to."

Everett nodded. "I thought the day I married Madalene was my happiest day, but every day, my love for her grows stronger. Now, whenever I am with her, my heart overflows with joy."

"I am happy for you," Isabella said. "For both of you."

"Will you be attending the theatre with us this evening?"

Isabella stifled a groan. "I suppose I have no choice. Mother will be insistent that I attend, no matter how much I protest."

"What an unfortunate life you lead," he joked. "We force you to attend theatres, balls, and soirées with us."

"Isn't it, though?" she replied, smiling.

"Come," Everett said, turning his horse towards their townhouse. "We'd better hurry back before it gets too late."

"Do we have to?"

He nodded. "Yes, I have a meeting with my steward today."

"Can I stay and ride alone?" she asked hopefully.

"Absolutely not," he answered. "It isn't safe to ride alone."

"But—"

He spoke over her. "Even on our lands," he asserted.

"I used to ride alone all the time in the woods surrounding Miss Bell's Finishing School."

"That is very disconcerting to hear," he said. "That was not a wise thing to do. After all, there are unscrupulous people everywhere."

In a smug tone, she replied, "I have no doubt that I could outride anyone who intends to do me harm."

"That is not the point."

"Then what is?"

He watched her closely as he paused, his expression growing solemn. "It is time for you to start acting like a proper lady."

"Aren't I?"

"No, you're not," he responded with a shake of his head.

"I'm trying, Everett."

"You need to try harder."

Her lips curled downward in frustration. "You cannot possibly comprehend all the restrictions that are placed on me because I am a lady."

"I understand—"

She cut him off. "No, you don't! I have to dress a certain way, think a certain way, behave in a certain way, and for what?" she asked, tossing her hand up in the air. "To make myself noticeable to potential suitors by pretending to be something that I'm not. It is ludicrous."

"I know it may be difficult…"

"No. I tire of this game," she replied, speaking over him. "It is a game I am not willing to play anymore."

Everett looked at her with a baffled expression. "What are you saying?"

Squaring her shoulders, she replied, "I am going to start playing by my own set of rules."

"If you do so, you will be shunned by Society."

"Then so be it."

"You can't possibly mean that."

"I do," she replied firmly.

"Why don't we return to the townhouse," Everett suggested, turning his horse to face her. "We will continue this conversation at a later date."

Her horse whinnied, drawing her attention. "My opinions won't change on the matter," she informed him. "I can be so much more than what Society expects me to be; what *you* expect me to be."

"I have no doubt, but you must think of your reputation," he pressed, "of our family's reputation."

"I understand that's what you want, but I can't keep living a lie."

Everett sighed. "I don't want you to, Isabella, but sometimes duty comes before our own wants." He glanced towards the sun. "Can we finish this conversation later? I do need to meet with my steward soon."

"All right," she replied, adjusting the reins in her hand. "I'll race you back to the townhouse."

Without saying another word, Everett turned his horse and kicked it into a run.

Isabella urged her horse forward, knowing it wouldn't be long before she overtook her brother. This was a race she would easily win.

Isabella reined in her horse in front of her four-level townhouse and dismounted as Everett's horse came to a stop on the gravel courtyard.

"I won again," she announced victoriously as she handed off the reins to an awaiting footman.

Everett shook his head good-naturedly. "Well done, Isabella," he praised as he dismounted.

"Thank you," she replied, following him up the stairs.

The ebony door to the townhouse opened, and their tall, balding butler stood to the side and greeted them.

"How was your ride?" Howe asked, glancing between them.

Everett started to remove his gloves as he replied, "It went well."

Howe closed the door and turned to face her. "Your mother is requesting your presence in the drawing room."

"Did she state why?" Isabella inquired.

"Lord Westinghouse and Lord Donald Scarsdale are here to call upon you," Howe informed her.

Isabella glanced at the open door of the drawing room on the opposite side of the entry hall. "And my mother is currently entertaining them?"

"Yes, milady."

"How long have they been waiting?"

Howe glanced over at the longcase clock positioned near the staircase. "No longer than ten minutes." He directed his next comment to Everett. "Lord Donald also requested to speak to you privately after he meets with Lady Isabella."

"I expected as much," Everett remarked as he extended his gloves towards the butler. "This is the third time he has called upon my sister."

Isabella met her brother's gaze and asked, "You don't think he would truly offer for me, do you?"

Everett bobbed his head. "I do."

"But we hardly know each other."

Her brother looked amused. "You danced a set together at Lady Huffington's ball, and he has come to call on three separate occasions. What did you anticipate was going to happen?"

"Lord Donald is pleasant enough, but it is much too soon for me to even consider the thought of matrimony," she declared. "What will you tell him?"

Everett gave her a reassuring smile. "That the decision is yours, and yours alone."

"Thank you," she murmured.

"Now, go entertain your suitors," he said, pointing towards the drawing room door. "You mustn't keep them waiting for too long."

She placed a hand on her hip. "I must admit that I don't want to encourage them."

"Then don't," Everett responded. "After all, you are a beautiful young woman, and I have no doubt that you will have a continuous stream of suitors vying for your attention."

"Because of my beauty?"

He nodded.

"But I am so much more than that," she protested. "I have my own opinions and ideas."

Everett placed a hand on the sleeve of her grey riding habit. "We both know that, but the majority of men become distracted by a woman's beauty."

"Do you think Lord Donald is only interested in me because he thinks I'm beautiful?" she asked.

"I'm not sure," her brother replied with a shrug. "That is something you will need to discover on your own."

"But how do you recommend I go about that?"

Lowering his hand to his side, he said, "I don't know, but you are quite clever. I have faith that you will find a way to discover the truth."

An ingenious thought came to her. One that would no doubt test Lord Donald's intentions towards her.

She turned towards Howe. "Can you inform them that I will be down shortly? I would like to change first."

"Why not just entertain them in your riding habit?" Everett asked.

Placing a hand up to her chest, she feigned outrage. "I can't possibly meet potential suitors wearing a riding habit. What would they think of me?"

Everett eyed her curiously. "What are you about, sister?"

"Nothing," she insisted, walking over to the stairs. "I just would like a moment to change into something more appropriate."

"Suit yourself," Everett said. "I will be in my study."

Isabella hurried up the stairs and headed for her bedchamber. She flung open the door and her lady's maid gasped as she looked up from organizing her dressing table.

"Good heavens. You startled me," Leah declared, bringing her hand to her chest. "Is everything all right?"

Stepping into the room, Isabella closed the door behind her.

"I need to change," she informed her. "Lord Donald and Lord Westinghouse have come to call."

Leah walked over to the armoire in the corner. "Would an afternoon dress be sufficient?"

"I was thinking of something different."

"Oh?" Leah asked, turning to face her. "What were you thinking, milady?"

Isabella removed her riding gloves as she said, "I want to wear the gown that I wore to Lady Buxton's masquerade ball."

"The peacock dress?"

She nodded.

Her lady's maid frowned. "But, why?"

"It has come to my attention that Lord Donald is going to ask my brother for my hand in marriage, and I want him to see me for who I truly am."

Leah had a puzzled look on her face. "Is your intention for him to think you are mad?"

Isabella shook her head. "I want to know if he is able to look past my appearance and see if he is truly interested in me as a person."

"Your logic may be faulty, but I am beginning to understand your motivation behind it," her lady's maid said as she walked over to the door. "Allow me to retrieve the peacock dress. I will be back shortly."

A short time later, Isabella exited her bedchamber in a rich blue gown with hundreds of peacock feathers sewn into the skirt. She headed towards the drawing room but stopped just outside of the open door.

From her position, she could see the dark-haired Lord Donald sipping his tea as he conversed politely with her mother on the settee. The fair-skinned Lord Westinghouse was standing at the window, his hands clasped behind his back, and he was looking out towards the gardens.

Isabella placed her hand to her stomach as she took a deep

breath, garnering strength. It was time for her to discover the truth about Lord Donald.

"Good afternoon," Isabella said as she walked into the room. "I apologize for the delay, but I wanted to change out of my riding habit and into something more appropriate."

Lord Donald placed his teacup onto the table as he simultaneously rose from the settee. "Not at all." He froze, his eyes perusing the length of her. "You are looking... uh... particularly lovely today," he stammered.

"That is kind of you to say, Lord Donald," she replied as she came to stand next to her mother, who was frowning at her. "This is one of my favorite gowns."

Unclasping his hands, Lord Westinghouse turned from the window to face her. "I take it that you are fond of peacocks."

"Very much so," she replied enthusiastically. "I have a peacock morning gown, peacock nightshirt, peacock bonnet, peacock fan, and peacock shoes."

Lord Westinghouse lifted his brow. "I had not realized that so many articles of clothing could incorporate peacock feathers."

"Oh, yes," she gushed before turning her attention towards Lord Donald. "Are you a fan of peacocks, as well?"

Lord Donald smiled indulgently at her. "I am."

"How wonderful," she replied. "I have been pleading with my mother to acquire a peacock for me as a pet."

"Why would you wish for a peacock as a pet?" Lord Westinghouse asked.

"Because I believe peacocks are among the most fascinating and beautiful creatures on earth," she stated. "Furthermore, we would have an enormous supply of feathers that would come in handy when I ask the dressmaker to create more peacock gowns for me."

"You require more gowns that include peacock feathers?" Lord Donald inquired with a knitted brow.

"But, of course," she replied. "May I ask what your favorite thing about peacocks is?"

Lord Donald's face went slack, clearly not anticipating the question. "I suppose I like their feathers."

She nodded encouragingly. "Did you know that peacocks are not born with their fancy tails?"

"I had not realized that," Lord Westinghouse said, his bored tone belying his feigned interest.

"It is true," she continued. "They look rather ordinary after they hatch, and it is only after six months that the males begin to distinguish themselves."

Lord Westinghouse muttered, "How interesting."

"Isn't it though?" she responded. "I find it intriguing that only the males have bright, bold feathers." She sat down on the settee. "I can share with you all kinds of facts about peacocks. I have loved them since I was a little girl."

Lord Donald's eyes shifted towards the open door. "Is that so?"

"It is," she replied. "If you are interested, I have a few books in our library about peacocks that I could lend you."

"That is not necessary," Lord Donald said.

"Did you know that peacocks cannot fly long distances?" she asked. "Even though they can fly, they spend the majority of their time on the ground."

Lord Donald looked tense, like a trapped animal. "I... uh... did not know that."

"Then you must read the book," she said, her hands waving excitedly in front of her. "I should warn you that it goes into great detail about their mating rituals."

Her mother's head snapped up. "Isabella!" she warned. "That statement is too crass to cross a lady's lips!"

"My apologies," she replied, glancing between the two gentlemen. "Would either of you like to hear the peacock's crow? I have been perfecting the sound for years."

Lord Donald put his hand up. "No, thank you." He again glanced towards the open door. "I regret to admit that I must cut this meeting short."

"Perhaps you will call on me again, and we can speak more of our love for peacocks," she suggested hopefully.

Tugging down on his ivory waistcoat, Lord Donald looked like he had just swallowed something very sour. "Yes, well, we shall see."

Lord Westinghouse spoke up. "Allow me to walk you out, Lord Donald," he said, his voice clipped.

As they exited the drawing room in only a few strides, Isabella rose and rushed over to the door. She saw both gentlemen hurrying towards the main door, not bothering to wait for the butler to open it for them.

After the main door was closed, her mother spoke up from behind her. "Do you want to explain to me what you think you were doing?"

Isabella turned around to face her mother. "I wanted to see Lord Donald's true intentions towards me."

"By wearing a peacock dress?" Mary questioned, crossing her arms over her chest.

She nodded. "If Lord Donald had any real affection for me, he would not have been scared off by a mere costume."

Her mother's frown lessened. "You do have a point, but you could have gone about it differently."

"Howe informed me that Lord Donald asked to speak to Everett privately after he spoke to me," she revealed. "I have no doubt that he was going to ask permission to court me."

"Would that have been so awful?"

Isabella smoothed out the feathers on her gown. "Yes, it would have been dreadful. Lord Donald hardly knows me, and I would have rejected his offer of courtship."

"I daresay that you didn't give him a chance," Mary said.

"He seemed like a nice enough man, and perhaps, in due time, you could have developed true affection towards him."

"I refuse to settle for anything less than love."

Mary's tone softened as she approached her. "I wouldn't expect you to, but I worry that your expectations might be a bit too high when it comes to suitors."

"I don't believe that to be the case," Isabella replied.

A smile came to her mother's lips. "Where did you get the ridiculous notion to wear a peacock dress to meet your suitors?"

"From Penelope," she admitted.

"Penelope?"

Smiling, Isabella shared, "When Penelope first met Nicholas, she wore a hideous orange gown and big, round spectacles and pretended she was partially blind."

Her mother shook her head. "Where did you learn all those facts about peacocks?"

"From Charlotte," Isabella revealed. "She would share the most random facts that her grandfather had taught her about birds over the years."

"I should have known," her mother remarked. "Can you truly impersonate a peacock's crow?"

Isabella laughed. "No, but I was prepared to make one up if the situation warranted it."

"Dear heavens, child," her mother responded, smiling, "whatever am I going to do with you?"

"It might be best if I go and change out of this costume," Isabella said, looking down at her dress. "It is rather uncomfortable to wear."

"I can only imagine, my dear."

As Isabella exited the drawing room, she felt a twinge of sadness that she had been right about Lord Donald. He had only been interested in her appearance, and not her. Would she ever find someone who would love her for the peculiar person that she was?

2

Lord Ewin Colborne was bored. Completely, utterly, and irrefutably bored. He glanced down at the empty glass in his hand and grimaced. For the past three months, he had filled his time with gambling, drinking, dinner parties, balls, and every other tempting indulgence that London had to offer during the Season. But it hadn't made him any happier. He still found himself miserable, and no matter how many soirées he attended, it wouldn't change that fact.

"Are you even listening to me, Ewin?" his friend, Oliver Braggs, asked.

Without bothering to glance up, Ewin replied, "No."

"I assumed as much," Oliver sighed. "All right. Out with it. What is wrong?"

"I'm bored."

"Then let's go gambling."

"Not interested," Ewin said. "Besides, a gambling hall is the last place I should be right now. My funds are dwindling as we speak."

Leaning back in his chair, Oliver placed his arm onto the table and suggested, "We could go riding in Hyde Park."

15

Ewin glanced over at the window, noticing for the first time that the weather had changed. "No, it is raining. That would be a rather foolhardy thing to do."

"We have done it before."

He looked at his glass on the table and pushed it away. "That didn't make it right. And, if I recall correctly, we were rather drunk that day."

"That we were." Oliver chuckled. "Do you want to go place a bet in the betting book?"

Ewin shook his head. "We have already placed a ridiculous number of bets in that book, including who could drink the other one under the table."

"Which you've won on multiple occasions, I might add," Oliver pointed out. "You need to cheer up, mate. We are at White's, and we are going to have a jolly good time. Should I order you something else to drink?"

"No," he replied. "I'm tired of being drunk most of the evenings and sleeping off the effects the next morning."

"Then what would you care to do?" Oliver asked.

His eyes scanned the sparsely populated card room, knowing it was only a matter of time before White's would be completely full, and gentlemen would be turned away at the door.

"I don't know," Ewin replied. "I might just retire for the evening."

Oliver's brow lifted. "But it is still early."

"I care not."

"Are you feeling all right?"

He let out a deep sigh. "I'm tired."

"Perhaps I should fetch a doctor for you," Oliver responded, shifting in his seat.

"I have no use for a doctor," Ewin replied with a shake of his head. "I'm just tired of my life."

"Meaning?"

Ewin huffed. "I woke up this morning on the sofa in my

drawing room because I was so drunk last night that I didn't have the energy to walk up the stairs to my bedchamber. Every morning, I have a pounding headache until I drink at least three cups of coffee, and only then, can I start piecing together what we did the night before."

"I must admit that I am not a fan of coffee," Oliver remarked.

"Neither am I, but it is the only thing strong enough to ease my headache," Ewin admitted. "After my headache has abated, I take a hackney over to White's to meet you, and we start the same blasted cycle over again."

"Then let's change up our routine," Oliver said. "We could always start drinking later in the evening."

"That is just it," Ewin expressed. "I'm tired of drinking. These past few months have been a haze, and I have become the type of person that I have always loathed."

"What type of person is that?"

"Slothful. A drunkard," Ewin answered. "I'm wasting my life, Oliver."

Oliver's smile vanished. "What is it that you want to do with your life?"

"I don't know," he replied honestly, "but I can't keep going on the way that I have been."

Leaning forward in his chair, his friend lowered his voice. "If you recall, you started drinking because you wanted to have a good time, and to prove to your father that you didn't need or *want* him in your life."

"That is all true, but there must be another way."

"I'm listening."

Ewin smoothed out his long sideburns. "My father still has not relented his position on Lady Rebecca and has cut me off. But I would rather chew glass than move back into Stanwich House and be under my father's oppressive rule again."

"Why not just marry the chit?" Oliver asked.

Ewin shuddered. "I would rather die."

"Surely Lady Rebecca isn't that bad?"

"She is a shrewish young woman who is only interested in marrying me because I'm a duke's son," Ewin explained.

Oliver lowered his voice as he leaned over the table. "You could always marry Lady Rebecca and take a mistress. It is more than perfectly acceptable to have that arrangement amongst the members of Society—"

"Absolutely not!" Ewin declared, cutting him off. "When, and *if*, I do marry, I will take the vows of matrimony seriously."

Oliver put his hands up in front of him. "I was merely making a suggestion."

"I know, and I am sorry for lashing out at you," Ewin responded. "I just need to find a purpose for my life; a reason to move forward."

"Your grandmother did leave you an inheritance."

"A *small* inheritance," Ewin corrected.

"Regardless, you could take that money and purchase a modest estate in the country."

"I have thought of that, but that would require me to leave London."

"May I ask what is keeping you here?" Oliver hesitated before adding, "Aside from spending time with your favorite mate."

Ewin chuckled. "You make a good point. I believe I will contact my solicitor about purchasing an estate."

Oliver bobbed his head approvingly. "Excellent," he said. "I believe my work here is done." He rose and tugged down on his ivory-colored waistcoat. "I am off to the gambling halls. Unlike you, I do not have the same aversion to spending money right now."

Ewin gave him a mock salute. "I wish you luck this evening, and I do appreciate your advice."

"Next time, it will cost you," Oliver joked, smirking. "I didn't study philosophy at Cambridge for nothing."

As his friend walked away from the table, Ewin's gaze returned to his empty glass. He needed to do something with his life, or his father would be right about him.

Ewin refused to accept that he was a failure. He would do whatever it took to prove his father was wrong about him. But where should he even begin? Even if he did manage to secure a modest estate, he knew nothing about the intricacies of running one.

He was so lost in his thoughts that his mind barely registered the voice of another friend.

"I didn't expect to see you here," Everett commented.

Ewin glanced up and saw the familiar faces of Everett and Nicholas, the Duke of Blackbourne, standing next to the table.

"It is good to see you both." Rising, Ewin pointed towards the empty chairs. "Please join me."

As Nicholas sat, he asked, "Why are you hiding in the corner of the card room?"

"I wasn't hiding," Ewin replied. "In fact, you just missed Oliver. He was on his way to a gambling hall."

"Why didn't you join him?" Nicholas inquired.

Ewin shrugged. "Not interested. Frankly, I am tired of losing money at those gambling halls. I'm terrible at cards."

Everett spoke up. "Gambling has never appealed to me."

"Likewise," the duke said. "My wife does a good enough job of spending my money."

Chuckling, Ewin remarked, "I promise I won't tell Penelope you said that."

"Please don't," Nicholas responded, smiling. "I'm afraid I would never hear the end of it."

"How is Penelope feeling?" he asked.

"She is home resting."

"And your son?"

Nicholas puffed out his chest in pride. "He is well," he replied. "Jacob is a little over a week old now."

"This is the first time that Nicholas has ventured out of his townhouse," Everett shared. "I was regaling him with stories about Isabella."

"What did Isabella do now?" Ewin asked curiously.

Everett smirked. "She changed into a peacock gown to greet Lord Donald and Lord Westinghouse. My mother informed me that Isabella kept rambling off facts about peacocks and even asked Lord Donald what his favorite fact about them was."

"I'm afraid to ask why she did this," Ewin said, chuckling.

"Isabella wanted to dissuade Lord Donald from offering for her," Everett explained.

"I take it that it worked."

"Splendidly," Everett replied with a nod. "Lord Donald and Lord Westinghouse couldn't seem to leave the townhouse fast enough."

"May I ask where she got a peacock gown from?"

"It was a part of a costume that she wore to Lady Buxton's masquerade ball," Everett shared.

Amused, Ewin said, "Your sister's antics never cease to amaze me."

"Her aversion to matrimony is rather irksome," Everett confessed. "She refuses to even give her suitors a chance to get to know her."

"She is still young," Ewin defended.

Everett humphed. "All she cares about is riding horses and driving me mad."

"Isabella has always preferred spending time with her horse than with other people," Ewin commented. "She has been that way since we were young."

"True, but I thought she would have grown out of it by now," Everett said. "I worry that she will fall out of favor with the *ton*."

"Impossible," Ewin declared. "She is a beautiful young woman, and I have seen how the gentlemen swarm around her at every ball."

"That is true, and it is a bloody nuisance," Everett muttered. "I wish I could end this madness and just arrange a marriage for her."

A waiter came by and placed three glasses of port onto the center of the round table. "Is there anything else I can get you?" he asked politely.

"No, thank you," Everett replied, sliding a few coins across the table.

Nicholas reached for a glass and took a sip of his drink. "We all know that Isabella would never agree to an arranged marriage. She wants to marry for love, just as her friends have."

"I know, but she is going about it all wrong," Everett contended.

A thought occurred to Ewin. Perhaps he could help Isabella and help himself at the same time. After all, spending time with Isabella sounded much more appealing than continuing as he had.

Swirling the liquid around in his glass, he said, "I can help with that."

Everett looked at him with a baffled expression. "In what way?"

"I have grown up around Isabella, and I believe that I could find her a suitable match."

"But why?" Everett asked, eyeing him critically. "What do you hope to gain from this?"

Placing his glass onto the table, Ewin replied, "Nothing. I just want what's best for Isabella. She deserves to be happy." He paused. "Besides, it might alleviate my boredom."

Everett looked unsure. "I still contend that it is an impossible feat. I have never met a woman more particular about her suitors than my sister."

"I think you should let Ewin try," Nicholas remarked. "After all, what is the worst that could happen?"

Leaning back in his chair, Everett studied him for a moment

with a furrowed brow. "If I agree to this, then no rakes, fortune hunters, or dandies shall come anywhere near my sister."

"Agreed," Ewin replied. "Isabella is too good for the likes of them anyway."

Everett began drumming his fingers along the table. "I propose a wager, then," he announced.

Ewin's brow lifted in surprise. "I thought gambling didn't appeal to you."

"Placing a bet in White's betting book is hardly the same as visiting a gambling hall," Everett contended. "Besides, this arrangement could benefit both of us."

"I'm listening."

Everett glanced over his shoulder before saying, "If you are able to do the impossible and have Isabella agree to a courtship with a suitable suitor by the end of the Season, then I will pay you ten thousand pounds."

"Ten thousand pounds?" Ewin repeated in astonishment.

Everett nodded slowly. "But if you lose, you walk away with nothing."

A smug smile crept into Ewin's expression. "Are you sure you want to make this bet?" he asked. "It hardly seems fair."

"It is," Everett replied. "I would pay anything to ensure that my sister was happy."

"Then shall we go and make it official?" Ewin suggested eagerly as he rose.

Everett stood and asked, "Are you sure you can find a match for my sister? After all, she might not even be willing to go along with this scheme."

"I will get Isabella to come around," Ewin responded confidently.

Everett chuckled. "I have no doubt that this Season will be anything but ordinary."

"Blasted needle," Isabella mumbled under her breath as she pricked herself with the needle for the tenth time this afternoon.

"Mind your language, dear," her mother chided from the settee across from her. "It isn't proper for a lady to use such offensive words."

Isabella lowered the white handkerchief to her lap and asked, "Why do I have to stitch my initials on handkerchiefs anyway?"

"So you can give one to a special gentleman as a token of your affection," Mary replied.

Glancing down at the handkerchief in her hand, Isabella remarked, "I daresay that I lack the patience for needlework. It is boring and repetitive."

"You just need more practice," Mary encouraged. "It is considered a grand accomplishment for a lady to produce beautiful stitch work."

"Why?" Isabella questioned. "My lady's maid can handle all the needlework for me."

"What if we searched for a printed pattern in the Ackermann's Repository to create something together?" her mother suggested. "That would be fun, wouldn't it?"

Isabella shook her head. "Frankly, that sounds dreadful."

"There are certain expectations placed upon a lady," her mother responded. "Proficiency in needlework is one of those things. Didn't Miss Bell teach you that?"

"She tried, but I often skipped my morning embroidery class to go riding in the woods," Isabella admitted.

Her mother frowned. "That is disconcerting. Your riding abilities will not help you become noticeable to potential suitors."

"I have been trying to tell you that I am not interested in marriage," Isabella stated. "I refuse to be confined by the limitations of matrimony."

Mary pressed the needle through her fabric as she said, "You say that now, but you will eventually find someone you won't want to live without."

"I disagree," Isabella replied. "The only thing I can't live without is Maximus."

Her mother lowered her needlework to her lap and sighed. "I won't always be around, and I want to ensure that you will be well taken care of."

"My brothers will see to that."

"I am not talking about your material needs, my dear," Mary clarified. "I want you to discover the happiness and joy of being with the man that you love."

"But why is it so important to you that I marry?" Isabella pressed.

A pained look came to her mother's eyes. "Because I was never blessed to fall in love."

"Did you not ever love Father?"

Mary shook her head. "No, it was an arranged marriage. But we never suited, not even in the beginning. I later learned that your father never stopped seeing his mistress, and he even brought her letters with us on our wedding tour."

"How awful," Isabella muttered.

"But as a dutiful wife, I had to appear blissfully unaware of the other woman that your father was keeping across Town."

Isabella had heard rumors of her father's other family, but she hadn't dared believe it. Until now. How could her father treat her mother so callously?

Mary's eyes turned pleading. "Promise me that you will open your heart to the possibility of love."

Isabella delayed her response for a moment as she saw how drawn and tired her mother looked. Her faded brown hair was styled in a chignon, and her blue eyes appeared too big for her pale face.

"I promise," she finally said.

A weak smile came to her mother's lips. "It pleases me immensely to hear you say that. I have been growing increasingly weaker, so I worry about your future."

"Have you told Dr. Grove about this?"

Mary nodded. "I have, but this is what happens to older people. Our bodies start to give out. My heart is struggling."

"Well, fight it," Isabella declared, her voice taking on a hint of a plea.

"I will, for as long as I am able to," her mother asserted.

Isabella fought back the tears forming in her eyes. "That is good. I don't know what I would do without you, Mother."

Mary's expression softened. "You are stronger than you give yourself credit for. I have no doubt that you will be able to carry on, and even thrive."

Before she could reply, Howe entered the room. "Lord Ewin Colborne is here to call upon Lady Isabella," he announced as he turned his gaze towards her. "Are you available for callers, milady?"

"No," Isabella rushed to reply, having no desire to meet with Lord Ewin.

Her mother laughed. "Yes, she is. Please show Lord Ewin in."

Howe tipped his head and departed from the room.

"I don't care to see Lord Ewin," Isabella protested. "He is infuriating, vexing, maddening—"

Mary spoke over her, the amusement evident in her tone. "Aren't you the least bit curious about why he has come to call upon you?"

"Most likely to torment me," Isabella muttered under her breath.

"You two aren't children anymore," her mother observed. "Those days are long past."

"Perhaps he just came to gloat…" Her words stilled when Lord Ewin walked into the room dressed in a blue riding jacket, buff trousers, brown waistcoat, and a white cravat. He was tall, slender, and broad-shouldered with tousled brown hair, and grey, thoughtful eyes.

Isabella had always found Ewin to be remarkably handsome, but she detested his flamboyant nature. It was just one of the many things she found irritating about him.

"Ewin!" Mary exclaimed, rising from her seat. "What an unexpected delight to see you."

Lord Ewin stepped over to her and kissed both of her cheeks. "It is always a pleasure to see you, Lady Northampton."

Her mother gave him a mock chiding look. "When did you stop calling me 'Mary'?"

He grinned. "My apologies. I will correct that most grievous error right now, Mary."

Mary smiled kindly at him. "Please have a seat," she encouraged. "May I offer you some refreshment?"

"I had been hoping to take a turn around the gardens with Lady Isabella," Ewin said, turning his gaze towards her.

"Why?" Isabella blurted out.

Ewin chuckled. "I see that you still don't mince your words, Bella."

Isabella stiffened at the nickname that Ewin had given her when they were little children. "My name is Isabella," she reminded him.

"I prefer Bella."

"Well, I don't."

Ewin smiled. "Pity."

Isabella placed her handkerchief onto a side table. "Why are you here, Ewin?"

Taking a step closer to the table, Ewin asked, "Whose initials are L.P.?"

"It is supposed to read 'I.B.'," she informed him.

Ewin picked up the handkerchief and looked down at it in amusement. "Your needlework is terrible, Bella."

"Thank you for that," Isabella replied. "Is there anything else you would like to criticize about me?"

Ewin shook his head as he placed the handkerchief back onto the table. "No, but I would like to comment on how lovely you are looking today."

Smoothing out her pale pink, silk gown, Isabella replied, "Save your flowery words for someone who believes them."

"Isabella," her mother rebuked. "You aren't being very kind towards your guest."

Clasping her hands in her lap, Isabella said in a bored tone, "I apologize, Lord Ewin, if I offended you with my harsh tongue."

To her annoyance, Ewin looked amused. "Would you care to continue this conversation in the gardens with me?"

"Would it get you to leave sooner?" she asked boldly.

With mirth in his eyes, he replied, "It would."

"All right," Isabella agreed, rising. "I suppose one turn around the gardens wouldn't be terrible."

Ewin extended his arm towards her, and she hesitated only for a moment before placing her hand on his arm. She knew if she had refused his assistance, then her mother would spend the afternoon lecturing her on decorum, and she truly did not want to have that lecture again.

As Ewin led her towards the rear door of the townhouse, he asked, "I haven't seen you since Hudson's wedding luncheon. How are you faring?"

"I am well."

He nodded his approval. "Have you been enjoying the festivities this Season?"

"I have."

A footman opened the door for them, and then discreetly followed them into the courtyard.

They stepped onto the footpath that led into the well-maintained gardens, and Ewin turned his gaze towards her. "I never answered your question about why I called upon you today."

"No, you didn't," she replied, suddenly feeling curious.

Ewin stopped and turned to face her, his Hessian boots grinding on the loose gravel. "You should know that your brother, Everett, has tasked me with helping to find appropriate suitors for you this Season."

Her brow lifted in surprise. "He has?"

"He is worried about you."

Isabella removed her hand from Ewin's arm and stepped back. "You do not need to concern yourself with that. I am more than capable of finding my own suitors this Season."

"I think you do need my help," he challenged arrogantly.

"And why is that?" Isabella asked, placing a hand on her hip.

He took a step closer to her, and she tilted her head to look up at him. "You tell me exactly what you are looking for in a suitor, and I will sift through the legions of gentlemen to find you the perfect candidate."

"But, why?" she questioned. "Why would you want to help me?"

"Because I care for you, Bella," he replied, his eyes searching hers.

Isabella paused, unsure of the game that he was playing. "You care for me?" she repeated incredulously. One thing she knew for certain was that Ewin didn't care for her. He only cared for himself.

"I do," he replied, "which is why I want to ensure that you are happy and well taken care of by an honorable gentleman. A man that will care for you as you deserve."

She pressed her lips together as she collected her thoughts. She had no desire to spend additional time with Ewin, nor did she want his help to find suitors. Frankly, she wanted nothing to do with this infuriating man.

"I must decline your offer. Even if I had any intention of marrying this Season," she hesitated, "which I don't, I still wouldn't accept your help."

"I'm afraid that isn't an option," he remarked.

"Pardon?" she asked.

"Why don't you create a list of attributes that you are looking for in a husband, and I will call upon you tomorrow to collect the list?"

She narrowed her eyes slightly. "Are you even listening to me?" she asked. "I don't need or *want* your help, Ewin."

Ewin shrugged. "Then don't make a list, because I already know you better than you know yourself," he said. "For starters, I know that you are looking for a man who has a love for horses."

"That is true, but—"

He interrupted her. "And apparently, peacocks," he joked.

His unexpected remark caused a giggle to escape her lips. "I had to do something to distract Lord Donald from offering for me."

"You did a splendid job."

"Thank you."

His eyes searched hers for a moment before he spoke. "You must trust that I have your best interests at heart."

"Trust is to be earned, Ewin," she stated matter-of-factly.

He took a step forward, reached for her hand, and brought it up to his lips. "Then I shall work hard to win your trust," he murmured, his warm breath against her knuckles.

Isabella found herself rooted to her spot, unable to formulate any words with Ewin standing so close to her.

Taking a step back, he released her hand, and grinned. "Silence is an admirable trait in a woman."

She opened her mouth to unleash her sharp tongue on him, but he spoke first.

"I shall call upon you tomorrow."

As Ewin started walking back towards the townhouse, Isabella shouted at his retreating figure, "I have no intention of making a list!"

In response, he waved over his shoulder without looking back.

Isabella found herself growing increasingly irritated, and she had to resist the urge to stomp her foot. How dare her brother recruit Ewin to help her find more suitors! Why was it so inconceivable to him that she had no desire to marry this Season? She was content with the way things were, and she didn't need a man to complicate her life.

It didn't matter how many suitors Ewin paraded in front of her. She would reject all of them!

❦ 3 ❦

"WHAT ATTRIBUTES DO YOU THINK I WANT IN A HUSBAND?" Isabella asked her sister-in-law, Madalene, as she sat in front of the writing table.

Madalene glanced up from her needlework. "Why are you asking me?" she questioned. "You are making the list for yourself. I already have a husband."

"True, and you found your husband by dropping down into his carriage," she said. "Perhaps I should write down that any potential suitor will need to know how to drive a carriage."

"I would assume most gentlemen of the *ton* know how to do that."

"Most likely," Isabella replied. "What about knowing how to climb trees?"

Madalene lowered her needlework to her lap. "Again, I must assume that most gentlemen would know how to climb trees."

Tapping the end of the feathered quill against her lips, Isabella mused, "I would want a potential suitor to enjoy Bath buns."

"Don't most people enjoy Bath buns?"

Isabella nodded. "Good point. But I don't think I could marry someone who *didn't* like Bath buns," she insisted. "I am going to add it to the list."

Madalene humphed as she placed her needlework next to her on the sofa. "May I ask what made it to your list?"

Isabella picked up the paper and read, "My future husband will need to be tall, have brown hair, can ride horses, enjoys naps, is able to read, and loves Bath buns."

"That is your entire list?" Madalene asked in disbelief.

"It is." Isabella lowered the paper down to the table. "Is it not sufficient?"

Madalene grinned. "You have been working on that list for nearly an hour, and that is all you've come up with?"

"Do you think I am being too specific?" Isabella asked.

Laughing, Madalene replied, "Your list is lacking in many regards."

"Meaning?"

Madalene rose and walked over to the writing table. "Have you ever met a gentleman who can't read?"

"I have never specifically asked someone if they could read or not," Isabella said. "I suppose I could start asking that question."

"The majority of the gentlemen of the *ton* have been educated at Oxford or Cambridge," Madalene reminded her. "I am confident that they can read and write in multiple languages."

Isabella bobbed her head. "You are right. I will cross 'is able to read' off the list."

"And why would you care if a gentleman enjoys naps?"

She shrugged one shoulder. "I like naps, so I just assumed my husband would like naps, as well."

With a smile, Madalene suggested, "It might be best if we focused more on attributes to start with. For example, do you want a husband who has a clever wit, is intelligent, honest, loyal, compassionate?"

"Yes, all of those things," Isabella replied.

"What about generous, empathetic, and is full of patience?" Madalene listed.

"Those are good, as well."

Madalene tapped the paper on the desk. "Then, go ahead and write them down."

Isabella nodded and added them to her list. When she was finished, she looked up and said, "I would also like a potential suitor to be able to keep up with me when I'm riding."

"That might be a challenge," Madalene remarked. "You are a superb rider."

"Do you think my standards are too high?"

Madalene shook her head. "Frankly, they are not high enough," she said. "You're looking for someone who will be your match, your partner in life. You don't want to settle for less if something is important to you."

"I like dogs," Isabella pointed out. "Should I write that on the list?"

Madalene laughed as she took a step back. "You are not looking for another version of yourself, especially since I don't think the world is ready for two of you," she joked. "What you are searching for is someone who will make you better when you are with them."

Leaning back in her chair, Isabella let out a sigh. "I don't know why I'm even bothering. I have no intention of marrying this Season anyway."

"You never know," Madalene started, "love has a funny way of creeping up on you."

"This is all your husband's fault, you know," Isabella complained, pointing the quill towards her sister-in-law. "I am mad at Everett for putting Ewin up to this in the first place."

"Why exactly are you mad at me this time?" Everett asked good-naturedly as he strode into the drawing room.

Isabella placed the quill next to the ink pot, then turned to look at him.

"Because of you, Ewin is going to start parading suitors in front of me. He wants to help me find a husband this Season."

Everett came to stand next to Madalene, and they exchanged loving looks. "Is that such a bad thing?" he asked.

"Yes!" she exclaimed, tossing up her hands. "I never asked for his help in the first place."

"Why should that matter?" Everett inquired. "Ewin has the time and resources to help you find an appropriate suitor. He is well connected in Society as the son of the Duke of Glossner."

"It matters not," Isabella declared. "As I have said on previous occasions, I have no desire to marry this Season, if ever."

"Then it shouldn't be an issue if Ewin introduces you to a few select gentlemen," Everett pressed. "Would it?"

"It will just be a waste of time."

"So be it," Everett replied. "It is Ewin's time to waste."

Isabella rose from her chair and walked over to the window. As she looked out towards the gardens, she asked, "Why don't you believe me when I say that I am content being on my own?"

Everett sighed. "I just want you to be happy."

"I am happy," Isabella contended.

"Are you?" her brother asked, his tone expressing his disbelief.

Isabella turned to face him. "I don't require a husband to be happy, Everett."

"I would agree, but I don't want you to end up as a spinster, either." He grew solemn. "I propose that we make an agreement."

"I'm listening."

Everett took a step closer to her. "If you truly make an attempt this Season to meet potential suitors, then I won't ask you to attend any social functions when we return home to our country estate this fall."

Her brow lifted. "You wouldn't make me go to the country dances?"

He shook his head. "Or to any house parties," he added. "You would have ample time to ride your horse on our lands and practice your needlework to your heart's content."

"I hate needlework," she muttered.

Madalene spoke up with a knowing smile on her lips. "That is because you don't practice it enough."

"That is not true," Isabella contended. "Mother makes me practice nearly every day for hours, and I am still awful at it."

Everett crossed his arms over his chest. "Do we have an agreement?"

Isabella shifted her gaze away from his as she delayed her response. She would be a fool if she did not accept Everett's offer. She hated attending country dances and house parties, and her brother was well aware of that. Furthermore, if she went along with his terms and spent the Season meeting with potential suitors, then she would be free to do whatever she wanted when they returned to their country estate. The only downside that she could see was that she would be spending time with Ewin, and that was most unfortunate. But it was still better than the alternative.

With her decision made, she announced, "I agree to your terms."

A look of relief flashed across Everett's face. "I am glad. I truly believe you are going to have an eventful Season. You might even find yourself having fun as you meet your suitors."

"I suppose that wouldn't be such a terrible thing."

Everett grinned as he uncrossed his arms. "And who knows?" he asked. "You might find that you favor one of them."

She shook her head vehemently. "I think not."

"Just don't rule it out completely," he advised. "I beg of you."

Isabella nodded. "All right."

"Good," he replied, turning back towards his wife. "Now it is time I take Madalene upstairs so she can rest."

Madalene smiled, and Isabella noticed the dark circles under her eyes for the first time.

"I would like that, very much," Madalene murmured as she placed her hand on her stomach. "I'm afraid I didn't sleep well last night."

As they walked out of the room, Isabella headed towards the writing desk and picked up her list. Her brother said she had to make an attempt to meet new suitors, but he didn't specify who the suitors had to be.

Reaching for the quill, Isabella decided she might as well have some fun this Season. And she was going to start by revising her list.

―――――――

Ewin sat in a filthy hackney as he headed towards Isabella's townhouse. He couldn't exactly determine where the pungent smell was originating from, but he highly suspected it emanated from the sticky floor.

It was a far cry from the conditions he was used to, but this was to be his life now. No more riding around in his family's posh coaches. His father had cut him off after he had refused to marry Lady Rebecca. But he didn't regret his decision, not once. He refused to marry someone that he didn't love, wholly and completely.

His father had laughed loudly at him when he had told him that. He called him a fool and told him to leave Stanwich House until he came to his senses.

That had been three months ago.

Ever since then, he had been living off the small inheritance that his grandmother had left him. He took up residence at the Albany and employed only a small household staff, including a butler, housekeeper, valet, and cook.

He knew that he needed to make a change in his life, or he would eventually run out of money. He could take his limited funds and buy a modest estate in the country, somewhere far away from his father, and start collecting rents from tenants. But he didn't want to leave London. Not yet, anyway. There was something keeping him here. Something truly important.

Isabella.

He had been in love with Isabella for as long as he could remember. Frankly, he couldn't remember a time that he *wasn't* in love with her. He found everything about her amusing, including her aversion to him.

That is why he'd jumped at the opportunity to be with her, even if it was to introduce her to potential suitors. He knew she wouldn't go along with any of them, but it would give him an excuse to spend time with her. That was something which hadn't happened in a long time, not since she went away to Miss Bell's Finishing School.

Since their country estates bordered one another, they had grown up together and had spent their youth getting into all types of mischief. But now, Isabella held only contempt for him. He didn't know why, but he was determined to find out.

The hackney came to a stop in front of Isabella's townhouse. He reached his hand out the window and opened the door, not bothering to wait for the driver to come down from his box. Once he stepped onto the pavement, he extended the driver a few coins and began walking towards the ebony-colored door.

After he knocked, he waited for only a moment before the tall, balding butler opened the door.

"Good afternoon, Lord Ewin," the butler said. "How may I assist you today?"

"Good afternoon, Howe." Ewin reached into his waistcoat pocket and pulled out his calling card. As he extended it towards the butler, he asked, "Is Lady Isabella available for callers?"

"She is," Howe replied, stepping to the side to grant him entry. "If you will remain here, milord, I will announce you."

As the butler headed towards the drawing room, Ewin took a moment to admire the ornate woodwork running the length of the ivory-colored walls, the mural painted in rich colors on the ceiling, and the numerous works of art hanging throughout the hall.

After a long moment, the butler stepped out of the drawing room and approached him with a solemn look on his face. "I'm afraid Lady Isabella is unavailable for callers."

"She is?"

Howe stopped in front of him and a minute smile was on his lips. "She informed me that she is available for callers, but she is unavailable to see *you*."

"I see," he replied, his eyes darting towards the open drawing room door.

"But Lord Northampton had informed me this morning that you were going to call and requested that I not turn you away, even at Lady Isabella's insistence," the butler informed him.

"I appreciate that, Howe."

The butler tipped his head. "I wish you luck with Lady Isabella, milord."

Ewin chuckled. "Thank you. I am going to need it," he said before he crossed the entry hall.

As he stepped into the drawing room with its green-papered walls, he saw Isabella sitting on the camelback settee reading a book. He took a moment to admire her without her knowing. Isabella was an undeniable beauty with her blonde hair, oval face, petite frame, and creamy white skin. He had been beguiled by her wide, expressive, blue eyes since they were little.

"What are you reading?" he asked, stepping further into the room.

She frowned as she closed the book. "I should have assumed it wouldn't be that easy to get rid of you."

He grinned as he placed his hands on the back of an uphol-stered armchair. "Everett informed Howe not to turn me away, even if you did."

"Pity," she replied, lowering the book to her lap.

"May I ask why you didn't want to receive me?"

"I have my reasons."

Finding himself curious, he asked, "Being?"

She met his gaze. "If you must know, I find you insufferable."

He chuckled. "Can you be more specific, Bella? Or do you have a problem with my entire person?"

"First, I have asked you, repeatedly mind you, not to call me Bella, but you blatantly refuse."

Shrugging, he replied, "I prefer calling you 'Bella'."

"Second, you are much too arrogant for your own good."

"I call it confidence," he said, offering her a dashing smile.

She pressed her lips together before saying, "Your smile does not disarm me, Ewin. I am well aware of the gentleman that you are."

He did not like the direction this conversation was heading, so he decided to change the subject. He pointed at the book in her lap and asked, "What are you reading?"

"If you must know, it is the *Grimm's Fairy Tales*," she replied, squaring her shoulders as if preparing to fight.

"What is your favorite fairy tale?"

She eyed him curiously. "Aren't you going to make fun of me?"

"No," he answered. "Why would I?"

"Because my brothers often tease me about my love of fairy tales. Relentlessly, in fact," she revealed.

He shrugged. "I see nothing wrong with reading fairy tales. I have often indulged in reading stories by the Grimm brothers."

Isabella watched him closely as if gauging his sincerity. "Thank you. I wish my brothers felt the same way, but Hudson insists that I live in a delusional world."

"You always have," he joked.

A hint of a smile came to her lips. "Besides, reading fairy tales is better than practicing my embroidery," she admitted, glancing over at the table where a handkerchief sat.

"I would have to agree with you there."

Isabella reached over and picked up the handkerchief. She held it up for his inspection. "You will be happy to know that I did manage to correct my initials. They now read 'I.B.' "

"Impressive."

Dropping the handkerchief back on the table, she huffed, "What an unbearable pastime."

"Many women enjoy needlework, my mother being one of them," he shared.

Isabella brought her gaze to meet his. "How is your mother faring?" she asked. "I haven't seen her in ages."

He cleared his throat. "I'm afraid I'm not sure," he replied. "I haven't seen her in over three months."

"Why?"

"My father and I had a falling out, and I am not welcome at Stanwich House anymore," he confessed.

Isabella gave him a timid smile. "I am sorry to hear that."

"What's done is done," he said, hoping to change the subject. "Have you had an opportunity to go riding today?"

A twinkle came to her eyes. "I rode through Hyde Park this morning with Everett."

"Did you beat him?"

"Of course," she replied, smirking. "Rather soundly, in fact. Was there any doubt?"

Ewin chuckled. "Not from me." He pushed off the chair and came around it. As he sat down, he asked, "Did you have a chance to prepare the list that we spoke about yesterday?"

"I did." She rose, walked over to the writing desk, and picked up a piece of paper. "I worked on it all day yesterday. Madalene even helped me."

"That's good."

She extended the paper towards him. "Here is what I am looking for in a potential suitor."

Ewin accepted it and glanced down at the long list. He turned the paper over and saw even more writing.

"This list is rather long," he remarked.

"I thought I should be as specific as possible." She returned to the camelback settee and sat down.

Glancing at the list, he started reading but stopped himself. He looked up at her in surprise and asked, "You are looking for someone who has an extensive knowledge of birds, plants, animals, archaeology, *and* architecture."

She bobbed her head. "Yes, I want someone who is highly educated and well read. That way we will always have plenty to converse about."

"Are you familiar with these topics yourself?"

"I may dabble in them."

He gave her a baffled look. "Since when have you been interested in plants?"

She shrugged. "They are pretty to look at."

"I see," he muttered. "And archaeology?"

She grinned. "I love touring ruins, and I want my future husband to join me."

He arched an eyebrow. "But you also want someone who isn't a loud eater."

"Yes, there is nothing more annoying than someone who

chews loudly," she replied, bobbing her head. "And I abhor gentlemen who talk while they are chewing."

"Duly noted." He turned his gaze back down at the list. "I am fairly confident that no gentlemen of the *ton* have a pet bear."

"I have often heard stories about how students at Eton would bring bear cubs in their dormitories to be their pets," Isabella said.

"I heard those stories too, but I never met someone who had one."

Waving her hand in front of her, she replied, "That was more wishful thinking on my part. After all, having a grown bear as a pet would be foolhardy. Perhaps it would be easier if you just found a gentleman who is knowledgeable about bears."

He frowned as he glanced down at the list. "You want a gentleman who is proficient at needlework?"

"Yes," she replied firmly, moving to sit on the edge of the settee. "And that is not negotiable."

Ewin took his other hand and placed his fingers to the bridge of his nose. This list was utterly ridiculous. Some of her requirements were impossible, starting with needlework. What gentleman would have ever bothered to learn that skill?

"Is there a problem?" Isabella asked sweetly.

Too sweetly.

The little minx. She knew exactly what she was doing.

He lowered his hand and smiled. "No problem," he stated. "I was just woolgathering for a moment."

"I'm glad," she said, letting out a breath of air. "I was worried that my list was too specific, and it would be impossible for you to pursue."

"No," he replied, folding the paper in half. "I may not be able to find a gentleman who incorporates *all* of your requirements, but I can try to find one that meets some of them."

Isabella smiled. "I look forward to it."

He tucked the list into the pocket of his waistcoat and rose.

"Thank you for your list," he said. "This will come in handy as I begin my search for your ideal suitor."

Her smile grew. "If I think of any more requirements for a potential suitor, I will let you know."

"Please do." He offered her a slight bow.

As Ewin walked out of the drawing room, he knew that Isabella was toying with him. But he refused to back down. Some of her requirements were absurd, but he would find a way to beat her at her own game.

4

ISABELLA HAD JUST TURNED THE PAGE IN HER POETRY BOOK when she heard a knock at her bedchamber door.

"Enter," she ordered.

The door opened, revealing her red-headed lady's maid. "I have come to dress you for dinner, milady," Leah said.

"Is it that time already?" she asked, turning her gaze towards the darkened window. "I'm afraid I lost track of time."

"That is quite a common occurrence when you are reading," Leah joked as she closed the door behind her.

Isabella smiled. "That is true."

Leah walked over to the armoire and pulled out a white dress with a pale pink overlay. "I thought you might like to wear this gown for the evening."

"It matters not what I wear this evening. I am only dining with my family," Isabella remarked with a wave of her hand.

"You'd best not let your mother hear you say that," Leah teased as she laid the gown on the bed.

Isabella lowered her book onto the chaise lounge and rose. "You are right. As my mother says, 'A lady must always dress herself with the utmost care'."

"That is sound counsel." Leah walked over to the dressing table chair and placed her hands on the back. "Are you ready for me to prepare you for the evening?"

"I suppose I must be," Isabella responded as she sat down on the chair. "I don't see why it is necessary to style my hair multiple times a day."

"Because, milady," Leah began, pulling out the pins in her hair, "you are constantly messing up my elaborate hairstyles."

"That is never my intention."

Leah let out a disbelieving huff. "You say that, but I am beginning to think you intentionally ruin your hair on your long morning rides," her lady's maid teased as she placed the long pins on the dressing table. "Would you mind if I use the curling tongs to create small ringlets around your face?"

"If you think that is best," Isabella replied, reaching for a bottle of lotion.

Leah walked over to the fireplace to retrieve the curling tongs. "I understand that Lord Ewin came to call on you today."

"Yes, much to my great annoyance." Isabella made a face. "I tried to send him away, but he insisted that he just had to see me."

"Did you give him the list?"

Isabella smiled as she rubbed the lotion on her arms. "I did, and he was quite dumbfounded by it," she replied. "I am confident that I won't be seeing Lord Ewin for quite some time."

"Why is that?" Leah asked, coming to stand next to her.

"Because he will be hard-pressed to find a suitor who meets very many of my requirements, much less all of them."

"I can only imagine. I truly doubt there is anyone who owns a pet bear cub."

"Precisely," Isabella said, "which is why I put it on the list."

Leah started curling Isabella's blonde hair, then asked, "Do you think Lord Northampton will be upset that you created an impossible set of requirements for Lord Ewin?"

"My brother only said that I had to make an *attempt* to meet potential suitors this Season," Isabella replied. "Besides, Ewin was the one who suggested I make a list in the first place."

"Are any of your requirements real?"

Isabella nodded. "My real requirements are interspersed throughout the list."

Her lady's maid was quiet for a moment. "May I ask why you hold such animosity towards Lord Ewin?" she asked.

"What makes you think that I hold animosity towards him?" Isabella countered.

Leah shrugged one of her shoulders. "It just appears that way."

Considering her response carefully, Isabella replied, "I suppose it is because he is not the same Ewin that I grew up with."

"In what way?" Leah asked, moving onto another section of hair.

Isabella sighed. "We used to have such fun when we were children, but we started growing apart when he left for Eton with my brothers. Now Ewin is conceited, arrogant, a rake…" Her voice trailed off. "Frankly, I hardly recognize him anymore."

"That is most unfortunate," Leah muttered.

"It is," Isabella agreed, "because we used to be the best of friends."

"If that was the case, then why do you suppose Lord Northampton enlisted Lord Ewin's help?"

"Isn't it fairly obvious?" Isabella asked. "Everett is determined for me to marry this Season, and Ewin is well connected in Society. Furthermore, Ewin is a good friend to our family."

"Do you truly believe your brother is trying to marry you off?"

"I do," Isabella stated firmly, "but he will be sorely disappointed at the end of the Season when I haven't selected a suitor."

"Perhaps you will meet a suitor who changes your perspective?"

Isabella met her lady's maid's gaze in the mirror. "I assure you that won't be the case," she replied. "I am not foolish enough to believe that love exists for everyone."

"That is a sad way to live, milady."

"I disagree," she contended. "I may adore fairy tales, but I know that not everyone has a hero waiting to save them. Sometimes, we must learn to save ourselves."

Leah stepped back and asked, "Are you pleased with your hair?"

Isabella took a moment to admire her reflection in the mirror. "I am," she replied. "Again, I must reiterate that you are immensely talented, Leah."

"Thank you, milady," her lady's maid said as she returned the curling tongs to the fireplace. "Now it is time to dress you."

A short time later, Isabella walked out of her bedchamber, dressed for dinner, and she headed towards the drawing room on the first level. She had just stepped onto the last stair when she heard the familiar voice of Lord Ewin drifting out of the drawing room.

Blazes! What's he doing here, she wondered.

She stopped just outside the door. As she peered inside, she saw Ewin standing next to Everett. They appeared to be engaged in an amusing conversation. Just then, Everett tipped his head back and laughed loudly at something Ewin had said.

Isabella took a moment and perused the length of Ewin. He was dressed in a black jacket, black trousers, a white waistcoat, and a white cravat. His hair was brushed forward and his long sideburns had been trimmed. He did cut a dashing figure. It was a shame that he was such an infuriating man.

Madalene's voice came from behind her, startling her. "Why are you spying on Everett and Ewin?"

Isabella spun around, bringing her hand up to her chest. "I wasn't spying on them," she protested.

"Then why are you loitering outside of the drawing room door?" Madalene asked in an amused tone.

"I was merely curious as to why Lord Ewin was here in the first place," Isabella replied. There. That was the truth. At least, the partial truth.

Madalene glanced into the drawing room. "Everett ran into him when he was leaving this afternoon and invited him to dine with us this evening."

"That was kind of him," Isabella muttered.

"It was, wasn't it?" Her sister-in-law brought her gaze back to meet Isabella's. "Are you ready to join them or would you prefer to loiter in the entry hall?"

"Do I have that choice?" she asked hopefully.

Madalene laughed. "I'm afraid not."

"Pity."

Her sister-in-law gave her a knowing look. "You should know that I find Ewin to be positively entertaining."

"That is because you have been around Everett too much," she teased.

Looping her arm through Isabella's, Madalene encouraged, "Come. Let's join them. I am famished."

As they stepped into the room, Ewin turned his attention towards Isabella, and she found herself meeting his gaze. His eyes were the most unusual color; a greyish-hazel, which always managed to draw her in. He briefly ran his eyes down the length of her, and she saw approval in them, making her feel beautiful. Which was odd. Why would she care if this man found her desirable?

She didn't.

"You are looking rather enchanting this evening, Bella," Ewin remarked.

Isabella forced a smile to her lips as Madalene dropped her

arm to go greet her husband. "Thank you, Ewin," she responded politely.

"You are welcome," he replied, maintaining her gaze. "Did you have a pleasant afternoon?"

"I did," she admitted. "I spent it reading."

Ewin took a step closer to her. "May I ask what book had you so riveted?"

"*The Rime of the Ancient Mariner*," she revealed.

" 'He prayeth best, who loveth best'," Ewin said, quoting Samuel Coleridge.

She stared at him in amazement. "You have read the book?"

"I have. I read it while studying at Oxford," he shared. "I did not take you for a lover of poetry."

Isabella nodded. "I have always enjoyed a wide variety of topics when I read, including philosophy and logic."

Everett interjected, "I would much rather have Isabella reading poetry than fairy tales. At times, I worry she already lives in a fictitious world."

Not taking offense at her brother's comment, Isabella shared, "I refuse to be confined to the restrictions that Society has dictated. Furthermore, I think it is foolish that certain subjects are considered taboo for ladies."

"I agree with you," Ewin responded.

Isabella blinked. "You do?"

"I would much rather converse with a lady who is well-read than a lady who only engages in polite conversation," Ewin revealed.

"I must admit that surprises me," she said.

"And why is that?"

Isabella pressed her lips together, carefully pondering her next words. She didn't dare admit that she had often been watching him at social gatherings and noticed he spent an enormous amount of time conversing with a variety of different ladies.

Realizing he was still waiting for her response, she replied, "I apologize, but I had just assumed you held the same general opinion as the rest of the members of the *ton*."

Ewin seemed to consider her for a moment before saying, "You will discover that I am unlike any other gentleman of the *ton*."

"How so?" she asked, surprised by the intensity in his eyes.

A slow smirk curved across his lips. "I guess you will have to find out on your own, Bella."

Her mood soured at the use of her nickname, and she shifted her gaze away from his, tired of this ridiculous conversation.

Fortunately, before she had to converse with him again, Howe stepped into the room and announced dinner was ready.

Isabella turned her attention towards her brother. "Is Mother not joining us for dinner?"

"No," Everett replied with a shake of his head. "She is not feeling well."

Glancing over at the open door, Isabella suggested, "Perhaps it would be best if I had dinner with Mother so as to keep her company."

"That won't be necessary," Everett stated as he started leading Madalene to the door. "She told me that she was retiring early and will most likely already be in bed. You can speak to her tomorrow."

Isabella nodded her understanding. "All right."

Ewin came to stand next to her and extended his arm. "May I escort you to the dining room?"

She worked hard to keep the annoyance she felt out of her features as she glanced down at his proffered arm.

"Thank you," she muttered, placing her hand on his arm.

Ewin chuckled as he started leading her into the entry hall. "May I ask what it is about me that you find so irritating?"

"Who says I find you irritating?" she asked, keeping her gaze straight ahead.

He glanced over at her. "You are a horrible liar, Bella. You always have been."

"Why do you say that?"

Leaning closer to her, he revealed, "Whenever you lie, you have a tell."

Isabella looked confused. "What's a 'tell'?"

"It's a facial expression you have whenever you're lying," Ewin explained with a grin.

"I do not!" she protested.

"You do," he replied. "You purse your lips."

Her steps faltered outside of the dining room, and she turned to face him. "I do?"

He nodded confidently. "You have done that since you were a little girl."

"I had no idea."

Ewin's eyes roamed her face. "I have made it a point to learn as much as I can about you, Bella."

"Why?" she found herself asking.

"Because you have always intrigued me," he revealed in a hushed voice.

Isabella found herself speechless at Ewin's declaration. What had he meant by that? But before she could ask, he led her into the dining room.

"Hudson used to sneak out to go hunting?" Isabella asked, surprised. "That sounds so unlike him."

Ewin nodded. "All the time," he replied, "but he somehow always managed to talk himself out of trouble."

"Now that sounds like Hudson," Everett remarked from the head of the table.

Isabella wiped the corners of her mouth with her napkin before placing it back on her lap. "Did you not lodge at Eton?"

"No, we did not. The Long Chamber at Eton was already full," Ewin revealed, "so we lived in a house near town. It was known as the 'Dame's House'. Our landlady, Mrs. Wallace, was responsible for us while we were residing with her."

"Did you sneak out with him, as well?" Isabella asked.

"Yes, but I was not as sly as Hudson was," Ewin shared. "Mrs. Wallace would report me to the headmaster, and I received a birching on the bare posterior on more than one occasion."

"Good heavens, that sounds horrible," Madalene said as she reached for her glass.

Ewin grinned. "Receiving the punishment wasn't the worst part," he admitted, placing his fork onto his empty plate.

"Truly?" Isabella asked.

"The fact that it was done in front of the other students in the library was much more devastating than the actual punishment," he revealed, leaning to the side as the footman cleared his plate.

Isabella gasped. "How awful," she murmured. "I must admit that I am grateful that Miss Bell was not a harsh disciplinarian."

Madalene laughed. "If that had been the case, then we all would have been in trouble the majority of the time."

"That is true," Isabella agreed. "Miss Bell was a very kind-hearted woman."

Ewin shifted in his chair to face Isabella. "How did you enjoy Miss Bell's Finishing School?"

A genuine smile lit up her face. "It was a wonderful experience," she gushed. "I was able to make many lifelong friends, including Madalene and Charlotte, who are now my sisters-in-law."

"Did you have to wake up at six in the morning and study till eight at night as we did at Eton?" Ewin questioned.

Isabella shook her head. "Heavens, no. We were required to wake up at an early hour, but just so we could ready ourselves for the day. After breakfast, we attended our classes, stopping only for a midday meal."

"That is assuming you went to your classes," Madalene remarked innocently as she smiled at Isabella.

Everett lifted his brow. "Did you not attend your classes?"

"I did," Isabella paused, smirking, "if the weather wasn't ideal for riding."

Frowning, Everett chided, "That was a rather foolhardy thing to do."

"No more than climbing trees," Isabella countered, turning her attention towards her sister-in-law.

Madalene laughed. "At least my climbing trees did not interfere with my course work."

"Good point," Isabella agreed. "Regardless, I learned the usual subjects. I am well versed in history, chronology, mythology, botany, geography, arithmetic..." Her voice trailed off. "Should I go on?"

"I must admit that list is impressive, but can you produce every kind of needlework?" Everett asked.

"You know perfectly well that I cannot." Isabella pressed her lips together before saying, "Needlework is the bane of my existence. Besides, I am not sure why it is so important I know how to use a needle and thread."

"Because you are a woman," Everett pressed, "and it is expected of you."

"Wouldn't it be wonderful if a woman was judged solely on her wit?" Isabella challenged.

Everett bobbed his head. "I won't disagree with you there, but we live in a society that values appearances and traditions."

"That is rubbish," she muttered.

Leaning back in his chair, Everett said in a firm tone, "I value duty above all else, and there are expectations that come with being raised in this family."

"And sometimes, people must question the foolish traditions of their father's," Isabella countered.

"Well, that person is not you," Everett stated.

Isabella arched an eyebrow. "Why not me?"

"Because, Isabella," Everett started slowly, "it is best to avoid battles that we cannot win."

Silence descended over them, and Ewin glanced at Isabella, her lips drawn together in a thin, disapproving line. He decided it might be best to broach another subject, one that would hopefully bring a smile to her face.

He cleared his throat. "Have you come up with any more requirements for your list?" he asked.

"No, I have not," Isabella said in a soft tone.

Everett spoke up. "What list is this?"

"It is a list that Isabella created for me to help her find the ideal suitor," Ewin replied. "Did you not know about the list?"

"I did not, but that is delightful news," Everett said. "I am glad to hear that Isabella is taking this seriously, considering we had an agreement."

Ewin glanced between them. "What agreement?"

"If Isabella makes an attempt this Season to entertain suitors, then she won't have to attend any social events when we retire to our country estate," Everett informed him.

"Is that so?" Ewin asked, turning his gaze towards Isabella.

Isabella shifted in her chair, keeping her eyes downcast.

"So what requirements is Isabella looking for in a potential suitor?" Everett asked eagerly.

Ewin saw Isabella close her eyes and let out a sigh. It was evident that she believed he would share the contents of the list with her brother and betray her trust. Well, that wasn't going to happen.

Meeting Everett's gaze, he replied, "Isabella's list was rather straightforward. She would like someone who can ride, is well-read, and is a superb dancer."

Isabella turned her head towards him, surprise on her features.

Everett smiled. "I am glad to hear that," he said. "There are many gentlemen of the *ton* who fit that description."

"That is what I thought, as well," Ewin agreed. "I already have a few gentlemen in mind that I think Isabella might approve of."

Chuckling, Everett remarked, "Frankly, I was worried that Isabella would give you an impossible list of demands."

Ewin smiled over at Isabella. "It is nothing that I can't handle."

"Good," Everett said, pushing back his chair. "Should we adjourn to my study for some port and give the ladies some time to themselves?"

"I think that sounds splendid," Ewin responded, rising.

As he extended his hand towards Isabella, she slipped her ungloved hand into his and allowed him to assist her in rising.

Isabella removed her hand from his but remained close. In a hushed voice, she murmured, "I would like to thank you."

"For what?" he asked.

Isabella glanced over at her brother as he assisted Madalene in rising. "For not tattling on me and sharing the contents of my list."

"You are welcome."

She bit her lower lip, drawing attention to her perfectly shaped mouth. "Why did you do it?" she asked.

He reached out and placed a hand on her shoulder. "Because we are friends."

"We are not friends," she retorted, shrugging off his hand.

"We used to be friends."

She nodded, her blue eyes watching him carefully. "But that was a long time ago."

Ewin wanted to ask her what had changed between them, what had caused her to become so distant towards him, but now was not the right time. That was a conversation better had in private.

He stepped back and confessed, "Nothing has changed for me, Bella. I have always considered you a friend."

Everett came around the table with Madalene on his arm. "Will you be joining us for a game of whist after our port?"

"I would be delighted," Ewin replied. "I haven't played whist in ages."

"Excellent," Everett said. "You can partner with Isabella."

Ewin nodded his approval. "It would be an honor."

❈ 5 ❈

THE HACKNEY JERKED TO A STOP OUTSIDE OF EWIN'S fashionable Albany apartment. After exiting the coach, he extended the driver a few coins before turning back towards the black, ornate gate that kept the Albany secure.

"Evening, Lord Ewin," a guard said as he opened the gate.

He tipped his top hat at him. "Good evening," he replied as he passed through the gate and headed into the courtyard.

The main brick building was set back from the street, and two parallel buildings framed the courtyard. Ewin crossed the cobblestones in a few strides and approached the main building. He hurried up the steps, opened the dark blue door, and walked down the narrow passageway until he arrived at his apartment. As he opened the door, he was immediately greeted by his aging butler.

"Evening, milord," the butler said as he crossed the entry hall.

Ewin removed his hat and gloves and extended them towards his butler. "Good evening, Cluett," he responded.

"Did you have a good evening?"

"It was most enjoyable."

Cluett smiled approvingly. "That is good, milord," he said. "Lord Dowding is waiting for you in your study."

Ewin stifled a groan. The last thing he wanted to do was talk to his brother at such a late hour. "Thank you," he muttered before he headed towards the front of his apartment.

As he entered the room, his tall, broad-shouldered brother rose from his chair. "There you are," he grumbled. "I have been waiting for nearly an hour."

"That is generally what happens when you arrive unexpectedly." Ewin decided it would be for the best if he left out the part about being unwanted. He wanted to attempt to keep this conversation civil.

"May I ask where you were this evening?"

Ewin walked over to the drink cart and poured himself a brandy, not bothering to respond right away. He swirled the liquid for a moment, took a sip, then replied, "If you must know, I was dining with Lord Northampton and his family."

"How is Everett?"

"He is doing well," Ewin replied, placing the stopper back on the decanter.

"And the dowager?"

Ewin frowned. "Sadly, Mary was not feeling up to dining with us."

"That is unfortunate." George walked over to the window and looked out at the courtyard. "I have heard that Everett's sister is quite the incomparable beauty."

"That she is," he replied honestly.

His brother chuckled. "I remember that chit. She was quite unfortunate looking in her youth with her pale skin and light blonde hair. She used to follow you around incessantly when we were visiting our country estate."

"The girl's name is Isabella," Ewin stated dryly, "and she is still a dear friend."

George looked at him curiously. "Have you bedded her yet?"

"How can you even ask that question?" Ewin asked, stunned by his brother's crassness.

"I take it the answer is no, then."

Ewin's eyes narrowed as he stared at his brother. "What is it that you want, George?" he growled. "I know you aren't here out of the goodness of your heart."

"I have come on Father's behest—"

Ewin cut him off, holding up his hand. "You have wasted your time, then."

"On my word, Ewin," his brother started, "you have thrown your tantrum long enough, and now it is time for you to accept your duty."

Pouring himself another drink, Ewin attempted to curb his growing anger. "I no longer have any allegiance towards Father."

"That is rubbish."

"Is it?" he questioned. "Father squandered the family fortune, and now he is marrying us off to pay his debts."

George walked over to the drink cart and reached for the decanter. "You must not look at it that way," he pressed. "Father arranged advantageous marriages for both of us. If you play your cards right, you could be a very rich man."

"That matters little to me. I refuse to be forever tied to Lady Rebecca or her disreputable father, Lord Frampton," he stated firmly as he walked over to his desk. "She is a shrewish young woman who is severely lacking in many regards."

As he poured himself a drink, George said, "You are going about this all wrong."

"Am I?"

His brother nodded. "Marry the chit, produce at least one heir, possibly a spare, and then you are free from your obligation."

"And what then?" Ewin asked as he sat down on his chair. "What happens to Lady Rebecca?"

"It matters not," George replied. "You can send her to live in the country while you reside with your mistress in Town."

Bringing the glass up to his lips, Ewin asked, "Is that what you intend to do with your new bride?"

George lowered the decanter back onto the drink cart. "Jane and I both willingly entered into an arranged marriage. I have no doubt that she understands what that entails. Besides, she will one day become a duchess. What more could she want?"

"It is my understanding that women generally want to be loved and appreciated by their husbands."

"Jane is not unfortunate to look at," George said, "and we tolerate each other. It wouldn't be inconceivable if we develop some type of affection towards each other."

Ewin placed his empty glass on the desk. "That sounds like the beginning of a happy union," he mocked.

"What is it exactly that you want in a marriage?" George asked.

Meeting his brother's gaze, Ewin replied, "I want to love my wife above all else."

George furrowed his brow. "Are you in earnest?"

"I am."

"Love doesn't exist in our circles," his brother asserted. "It is a wishful fantasy on your part. A young girl's desire."

Ewin leaned back in his chair, not deterred by his brother's cynical response. "I care not if you understand my reasonings. I will not marry Lady Rebecca."

A muscle twitched in his brother's jaw, and his eyes were shadowed with some dark emotion. "Do you not care that Father could be sued for breach of contract by Lord Frampton?"

"It doesn't bother me in the least," Ewin replied honestly. "It was foolhardy to enter into the contract with Lord Frampton without even speaking to me."

George walked over to an upholstered armchair and sat down. "Have you even bothered to meet Lady Rebecca?"

"I have, on multiple occasions," Ewin replied with a nod.

"She is beautiful."

"To some, perhaps."

George lifted his brow. "I daresay she is rather enchanting."

"Regardless, she is not very clever," Ewin said. "We struggled to carry on a conversation. She even mispronounced Napoleon."

George waved his hand dismissively. "Women don't have to be clever to bear our children. It is much more important for them to have a beautiful face and comely figure."

"I disagree completely."

"I am not surprised by that," his brother said with a huff.

"No matter how much you try to convince me, I won't change my mind," Ewin stated.

"Why?"

Ewin was growing tired of this conversation and sighed. "I have my reasons."

"Which are?"

"They are mine, and mine alone."

George gulped the rest of his drink before he rose. "Given time, you will squander your funds, and you will have no choice but to return home."

"Thank you for your faith in me," Ewin remarked dryly, "but I wouldn't get your hopes up."

His brother walked over to the drink cart and placed his empty glass on it. "Your high and mighty attitude is becoming irksome."

"That is not my intention."

"Then what is?"

Ewin met his gaze. "To control my own destiny."

George chuckled dryly. "You are the son of the Duke of Glossner," he stated, "and your destiny has already been predetermined."

"Then I shall have to change it," Ewin responded.

"I thought I could reason with you," his brother said with a shake of his head, "but I see that you will not be reasonable."

"I disagree," Ewin responded. "I can be very reasonable. I simply disagree with you on this matter."

George glanced over at the door. "Then I shall see myself out."

"Before you go," Ewin began, "how is Mother?"

His brother frowned. "She misses you."

"Would you pass along a message for me?" Ewin asked.

"I will."

Ewin leaned forward in his seat. "Tell her that I love her and miss her, too."

George bobbed his head. "I will, but I'm hoping you will come to your senses soon and return home."

"I would rather work than go home to Father," Ewin declared.

"That seems rather extreme, even for you, brother," George insisted as he stepped towards the door.

"Say hi to Jane for me," Ewin said.

George stopped at the door. "Being married isn't the worst thing, you know. It is surprisingly nice to have someone fussing over you."

"I can only imagine."

"Good night," George said, then departed.

Ewin leaned back in his chair and turned his head towards the window. He had been right to refuse being trapped in a love-less marriage, but his family couldn't see that. Besides, there was only one person that he would even consider marrying. But he knew it would take an inordinate amount of work to convince her that he was the one for her.

Luckily, he wasn't afraid of hard work.

Reaching into his jacket pocket, he removed Isabella's list and unfolded the piece of paper. He wasn't a fool. Most of these so-called requirements were ridiculous, but he knew some were real. Now he only needed to introduce her to just the right suitors.

Isabella decided that she had never been so bored in her life. She was sitting in the drawing room, watching Madalene embroider a blue baby blanket. Her sister-in-law hummed softly as she focused on her task.

Isabella's eyes drifted towards the window, and she debated about heading towards the stables at the rear of their townhouse. She could sneak off and enjoy an afternoon ride and no one would be the wiser.

Madalene's voice broke through her musings. "Everett would be furious if you went for a ride without him."

Isabella glanced over at her in surprise. "How did you know that I was entertaining that thought?"

"Because I know you," her sister-in-law replied. "You used to get the same look on your face at Miss Bell's Finishing School."

Pointing towards the needlework in Madalene's hands, Isabella asked, "How do you find joy in such tedious repetition?"

Madalene offered her an understanding smile. "I am making a blanket for my baby, and that brings me great joy." She lowered the needlework to her lap and announced, "I just felt the baby move."

"You did?" Isabella asked, her eyes widening.

Madalene nodded.

"What does it feel like?"

Placing a hand on her stomach, her sister-in-law revealed, "It feels like a fluttering in my stomach."

"That sounds awful."

Madalene grinned. "Oh, no. It is the most wonderful feeling in the world."

"Truly?"

Madalene nodded again. "I don't think I would ever tire of feeling my baby move."

She was about to respond when Howe stepped into the room and met her gaze. "Lord Ewin and Mr. Walter Gillingham are here to call on you, milady," he announced. "Are you available for callers?"

"I suppose I am," she said reluctantly.

Howe tipped his head. "Very good, milady. I will send them right in."

Madalene gave her a knowing look. "I am surprised you didn't turn Lord Ewin away."

"I have discovered that he might not be as infuriating as I once thought," she responded.

"May I ask what swayed your opinion?"

Isabella glanced over to the open door. "I said 'he might not be'," she clarified. "I haven't decided yet."

"Oh, my apologies," Madalene teased, her voice trailing off as Lord Ewin walked into the room.

Ewin was accompanied by a man she was sure she had never met before. He was short, with thinning black hair, and a pair of round spectacles sat on his long, thin nose.

"Lady Isabella," Ewin greeted with a slight bow. "Thank you for agreeing to see us." He gestured towards his companion. "Allow me to introduce Mr. Walter Gillingham. He is the grandson of the Duke of Somerset."

Isabella rose from her chair and dipped into a curtsey. "It is a pleasure to meet you, Mr. Gillingham."

Mr. Gillingham pushed his spectacles up higher on his nose. "You are a vision of perfection, Lady Isabella."

"Thank you," she replied graciously.

"You are more beautiful than a rose and less likely to draw blood when touched," Mr. Gillingham said with a slight chuckle.

"Pardon?"

Mr. Gillingham met her gaze and gave her an apologetic smile. "My apologies. It was just a little flower humor that I like to use."

Isabella glanced curiously at Lord Ewin. "I had not realized there was such a thing as 'flower humor'."

With a nod, Mr. Gillingham said, "Oh yes, quite a few. In fact, I had intended to organize all my dried flowers today, but I discovered I had more *pressing* issues."

Madalene started giggling and brought her hand up to cover her mouth.

Ewin spoke up. "Mr. Gillingham teaches botany at Oxford."

"Oh," Isabella replied, "this is starting to make sense now."

Gesturing towards Madalene, Ewin turned to face Mr. Gillingham. "I would also like to introduce Lady Northampton."

Mr. Gillingham tipped his head at the marchioness. "It is a pleasure to meet you, Lady Northampton."

"Likewise," Madalene said with a smile. "I must admit that I found your flower humor to be quite amusing."

"Thank you, my lady," Mr. Gillingham responded.

Ewin turned his attention towards Isabella. "I was hoping you would take us on a tour of your gardens on this fine day."

"I would be delighted to," she replied. "I have never had the privilege of speaking to an expert on botany before."

Mr. Gillingham puffed out his chest. "That is kind of you to say, Lady Isabella."

Ewin approached her and offered his arm. "May I escort you to the gardens?"

"You may," she replied, placing her hand on his arm.

As they exited the drawing room, Isabella led them towards the rear of the townhouse. A footman was standing at the rear entrance, and he opened the door.

When they stepped outside, Mr. Gillingham stopped and took in a deep breath. "Doesn't that smell wonderful?"

Unsure of how to respond, Isabella remained quiet.

Mr. Gillingham turned towards her. "To truly understand botany, one must be able to smell botany."

"Pardon?" she asked.

"You need to smell the flowers, the plants, and the grass," he explained. "Go ahead. Take a deep breath."

Isabella did his bidding and took a deep breath.

"What do you smell, Lady Isabella?"

She let out her breath. "I smell flowers," she attempted.

Mr. Gillingham bobbed his head approvingly. "But what kind of flowers?"

Her eyes landed on the red roses in front of them. "I smell roses."

"Incorrect," Mr. Gillingham declared. "What you are smelling is the irises by the pond."

Ewin tsked. "I was going to say irises, but Isabella spoke first."

"Very good, Lord Ewin," Mr. Gillingham praised. "The yellow iris is often used to purify the water. It is planted near the edge of a body of water, and the roots improve the water quality."

"I had no idea," Isabella commented.

Mr. Gillingham squinted his eyes as he glanced up at the sun. "The iris flower does best in bright, direct sun, and is ideal for gardens."

Isabella started walking down the footpath but was forced to stop when Mr. Gillingham leaned down to smell the red roses.

He glanced up at her. "Are you familiar with the history of the rose?"

She shook her head. "I am not."

"It is fascinating," Mr. Gillingham replied. "The red rose dates all the way back to Ancient Greece. In Greek mythology, roses were created by Aphrodite, the goddess of love." He reached out and caressed the rose petals. "Roses have been symbols of love, beauty, war, and politics. In fact, in the seventeenth century, they were even used as legal tender, and they were often used as barter and for payments."

Mr. Gillingham straightened to his full height. "Roses are one among the only three flowers mentioned in the bible." He looked at her curiously. "Can you name the other two?"

"No, I'm afraid I cannot," she said with a shake of her head.

Mr. Gillingham's eyes flashed with disappointment. "The others are lilies and camphire," he shared.

"Oh, I hadn't realized," she muttered.

Clasping his hands behind his back, Mr. Gillingham resumed walking down the gravel footpath. "May I ask what your favorite flower is, Lady Isabella?"

"Red roses," she replied quickly, "followed closely by daffodils."

"Ah, daffodils," he crooned, "which are botanically known as 'narcissi'." He smiled. "Both are a very good choice."

Ewin spoke up. "If I recall my Greek history correctly, wasn't Narcissus the classical Greek name in honor of a handsome youth who became so enamored with his own reflection that the gods turned him into a flower?"

"You are correct, Lord Ewin," Mr. Gillingham replied.

Even though she knew she might regret this question, she decided to ask it anyway. "May I ask what your favorite flower is?"

Mr. Gillingham let out a deep sigh as he looked up at the sky. "That is a difficult question," he remarked. "Very difficult, indeed, but I would have to say 'meadowsweets'." He paused. "I chose this particular flower because of its many white blooms and strong, sweet fragrance. Furthermore, it can be used for medicinal purposes and to sweeten the taste of food."

Ewin leaned closer to Isabella and asked in a soft voice, "Do you remember the meadowsweets that used to grow down by the river when we were little?"

She smiled fondly at that memory. "How could I forget?" she replied. "We used to spend countless hours down by that stream. Mother would get so mad at me when I arrived home and the bottom of my dress was soaked."

"But, if I recall correctly, your boots and stockings never got wet."

"That is because I was always smart enough to take them off first," she replied proudly.

He chuckled. "That you did."

Mr. Gillingham interjected, "May I ask what your favorite tree is?"

Glancing at the beech trees that lined the side of the garden, she answered, "I suppose the beech tree."

He frowned disapprovingly. "But you don't know for certain?"

Isabella glanced over at Ewin before admitting, "Frankly, I don't have a favorite tree."

"That is a shame. Everyone should have a favorite tree to be able to discuss freely," Mr. Gillingham said in a dejected tone. "I had just assumed you would have one, because Lord Ewin said that you shared my passion for botany."

"I do enjoy learning about botany," she defended, glancing over at Ewin with a frown, "and I was taught the finer points of botany while I was away at finishing school."

Mr. Gillingham stopped at a well-manicured shrub and ran his fingers along the green leaves. "Did you know that it can be very difficult to define the difference between a shrub and a tree?"

"I did not," she replied.

"That is one of the questions that I pose to my students at the beginning of my course," he shared. "Many botanists attempt to distinguish a shrub and a tree by height as the imperfect point of demarcation. Which, in my mind, is just rubbish."

Ewin nodded. "I concur," he agreed in a lighthearted tone. "That does sound like rubbish."

Isabella gently nudged Ewin with her elbow before asking, "How do you know the difference between a shrub and a tree?"

Mr. Gillingham smiled as they resumed their walk along the footpath. "I think it is more a matter of stem density, but that is just my humble opinion." He glanced over at her. "Have you recently read any books on botany?"

"No," she admitted. "I have not."

"If you would like, I could recommend a few for you," Mr. Gillingham remarked.

She smiled at him. "I would like that very much."

Mr. Gillingham gave her a timid smile before he started pointing out all the different flowers that were planted in the gardens.

And it was much, much later before they returned to her townhouse.

❧ 6 ❧

THE HACKNEY JERKED TO A STOP IN FRONT OF ISABELLA'S townhouse, and he reached over to collect the two small books lying next to him. Exiting the hackney, he walked up the few steps towards the main door. After he knocked, he stepped back and waited.

The door opened, revealing the butler. "Good morning, Lord Ewin," Howe greeted, stepping to the side to allow him entry.

"Good morning," he replied.

"If you wait here," Howe said as he closed the door, "I will announce you to Lady Isabella."

"Thank you."

As he watched the butler walk towards the drawing room, he saw Everett exit from a side room.

A bright smile came to Everett's face when his eyes landed on him. "Ewin. What a pleasant surprise," he greeted with his hands opened wide. "Are you here to call on Isabella?"

"I am," he replied.

Everett bobbed his head approvingly. "Very good. How is the matchmaking going?"

"It is going well," Ewin responded. "I introduced her to Mr.

Gillingham yesterday, and we had the most pleasant turn around the gardens."

"Ah, yes," Everett remarked. "Mr. Gillingham is a botany professor and the grandson of the Duke of Somerset."

"He is," he confirmed.

Everett smiled. "I must admit that our dinner conversation was most enjoyable with all of Isabella's newfound information on plants and shrubs. The history of the red rose was most enlightening."

"I am glad to hear that."

His friend took a step closer to him and lowered his voice. "Mr. Gillingham was an interesting choice for Isabella," he commented.

Ewin smiled. "One of the requirements that Isabella listed is that she wanted someone knowledgeable about botany."

Chuckling, Everett took a step back. "That he was."

The click of Howe's heels against the tile alerted them to his arrival. "Lady Isabella is expecting you in the drawing room, milord," the butler announced.

"Excellent," Ewin said, tightening his hold on the books in his hand.

"What do you have there?" Everett asked.

He held up the books. "They are botany books for Isabella."

"Botany books?"

Smiling, Ewin replied, "They come courtesy of Mr. Gillingham."

"Interesting tactic," Everett remarked, "attempting to woo a lady with books on botany."

"I daresay it won't work in this case."

"I agree with you," Everett responded with a smirk. "Would you care to go riding with us tomorrow morning?"

Ewin nodded. "I would."

"Excellent. I shall see you tomorrow," Everett replied, "and I wish you good luck with Isabella."

"I assure you that no luck is needed," Ewin said before heading towards the drawing room.

As he stepped inside, he saw Isabella had a deep look of concentration on her enchanting face as she appeared to be drawing on a piece of paper. She was dressed in a white gown with a periwinkle ribbon tied around her small waist. Her blonde hair was piled high atop her head, and two long curls framed her face.

"May I inquire what you are doing?" he asked, walking further into the room.

Isabella glanced up at him and shifted her body to hide the paper that she was working on. "I'm sketching."

"What are you sketching?"

She pointed towards a silver vase stuffed with red roses. "I'm sketching the vase and roses," she replied, "at least, I'm attempting to."

"Will you show me?"

A deep frown creased her beautiful forehead. "I would prefer not to."

"Why not?"

Isabella glanced down at the paper. "I enjoy sketching, but I am not very good at it."

He gave her a reassuring smile. "I can't imagine that to be true."

"Oh no, it is true," she said, blowing out a puff of air. "Miss Bell described my sketching abilities as 'adequate at best'."

Ewin chuckled. "There are many things that I pursue that I am not particularly good at."

"Such as?"

"Hunting," he replied decisively. "I am awful at hunting, but I keep participating in the sport. I have no idea why since I have never been able to kill anything."

"Not even pheasants?"

He shook his head. "I think pheasants and grouses take great pleasure in knowing that I will shoot at them but will inevitably miss."

Her eyes flickered with amusement. "Surely, you can't be that bad?"

"Sadly, it is all true." He came to sit down across from her. "And, for some unknown reason, I keep getting invited along on hunting parties. Perhaps I am invited because of my amusing personality." He smiled.

"No, that is definitely not it," Isabella rushed to say with a smile on her face.

Ewin held up the two books in his hand. "Mr. Gillingham asked me to deliver these books to you," he revealed. "He felt you would benefit by reading more books on botany, including *An Introduction to Botany, In a Series of Familiar Letters.*"

"Did he now?"

Leaning forward, Ewin placed the books on the table. "I, for one, think it would benefit you greatly if you became more knowledgeable about botany."

"And why is that?"

He shrugged. "It would make taking a turn around the gardens with you much more interesting," he replied. "Besides, I have often thought that your education in botany was lacking and that you should be reading more books on plants and flowers."

Isabella looked at him curiously. "Is that so?"

"After all, flowers aren't just 'pretty to look at'," he said, using her own words against her.

Isabella laughed a light, airy laugh that seemed to tug at the corners of his heart. "No, they definitely are not."

"You did manage to impress Mr. Gillingham, and he expressed interest in pursuing you further, if you are so interested," Ewin shared.

The humor didn't fully leave Isabella's eyes as she replied, "As much as I found Mr. Gillingham intriguing, I'm afraid I am not interested in him as a potential suitor."

Ewin pretended to feign disappointment. "That is too bad. I shall be forced to cross him off my list, then."

"Even though he did meet my requirement of being knowledgeable about botany, he didn't seem to know much about anything else."

"I see," he remarked. "Then I shall have to try harder on subsequent attempts. Which brings me to my next question, would you care to join me on a tour of the Royal Menagerie tomorrow with a potential suitor?"

"Yes," she responded quickly. "I do so love visiting the Royal Menagerie."

"I assumed as much, considering they have a bear there."

She nodded. "That is true, but it is also such a hodgepodge of animals."

Ewin smiled. "Good point. However, if you recall, your list specifically requested someone who had a pet bear," he reminded her.

"I remember."

"I couldn't find anyone with a pet bear, but I did find someone who is quite knowledgeable about bears."

"That is wonderful news," she replied.

"I thought you might be pleased."

Isabella glanced down at the piece of paper in her hand and asked, "If I do show you my drawing, you must promise that you won't laugh."

"I would never laugh at you."

She gave him a look that implied she didn't believe him. "We both know that isn't true," she argued. "You used to tease and torment me relentlessly."

He held up his hands in front of him. "I may have laughed at you when we were children, but not now. I wouldn't dare dream of it."

Reluctantly, Isabella extended the paper towards him.

As he accepted the paper, he saw a beautiful drawing of a

vase and roses. He took a moment to study it, admiring the great detail that presented itself on each individual rose.

"You are immensely talented, Bella. This is very good."

Her gaze turned downcast. "You are just saying that to be a gentleman," she murmured.

"You know me well enough that I would speak the truth around you," he stated. "I would never lie to you."

Bringing her gaze back up, she replied, "I suppose that is true." She paused. "Do you truly think it is good?"

"I do," he said. "I am pleasantly surprised, but my expectations were rather low. I was half expecting a drawing that a child would have done."

"Why would you have thought that?"

He shrugged. "I have never seen you draw before, and you did say that you weren't very good."

"It is not something that I am forthcoming about," she admitted.

"May I ask why?"

Isabella glanced over to the open door. "My family has these preconceived notions of who I am, but they are wrong. I can do so much more than they expect me to and be more than they think I am."

"What exactly are they wrong about?" he pressed.

Clasping her hands in her lap, she lowered her voice. "They seem to believe that I only care about riding my horse and that I'm living in some fantastical world."

"But you aren't?"

She shook her head. "No. I care about people, deeply, and I want to help the less fortunate. But I'm afraid I just don't know how or where to start. I have been so sheltered my whole life that the only time I can feel free is when I'm racing my horse. It is the one thing that I can control."

"I believe I can help you with that."

"You can?"

Ewin nodded. "I am a patron of an orphanage in the rookeries. Perhaps you would like to help there sometime."

Isabella's eyes grew wide before he saw disappointment creep in. "My family would never let me go near the rookeries."

"True, your family wouldn't," he agreed, "but, if you would allow me the privilege, I can escort you."

A line between her brow appeared as she asked, "You would do that for me?"

"I would," he replied. "I think it is admirable that you are looking past yourself to help others."

"Truly?"

Ewin moved so he sat at the edge of his chair. "I would do anything to ensure that you are happy, Bella. I hope you know that." He held up the drawing. "May I keep this sketch?"

"Why?"

"Because you drew it. It would mean more to me than any handkerchief with your initials embroidered on it."

A small, barely discernable blush came to Isabella's cheeks. "That is kind of you to say."

They continued to stare at each other until he cleared his throat and averted his gaze. "Um... I should be going," he said in a hoarse voice.

"Must you?" Isabella asked, then rushed to add, "After all, your company is much more tolerable than sitting alone in the drawing room."

He rose and tugged down on his dark blue waistcoat. "I'm afraid I must, but I will be joining you tomorrow for your morning ride with Everett."

Rising, Isabella said, "I shall look forward to it."

With a curt nod, Ewin spun on his heel and headed for the door, grateful that he had resisted the urge to reach out and pull Isabella into his arms.

Ewin sat at his desk in his study and reviewed his ledger. He needed to do something to procure funds, or he would run out of money in the foreseeable future. Buying a small estate and collecting rent from his tenants would be a solution to his problems. However, his solicitor had sent out inquiries, and so far, he had found nothing that he could afford.

It was rather disconcerting to be living on a fixed income, he decided. He never had to give money a thought until his father had cut him off. But he wouldn't change a thing. He'd made the right choice by refusing to marry Lady Rebecca.

A knock came at his door, interrupting his thoughts.

"Come in," he ordered.

The door opened, and his petite housekeeper, Mrs. Barr, stepped into the room. Her hair was pulled back tightly into a bun at the base of her neck and she wore a drab dress.

"You wanted to see me, milord?"

Ewin nodded. "Yes, I did." He pointed towards the chair that faced his desk. "Please have a seat. I have something I wish to discuss with you."

Mrs. Barr walked over and sat down with an expectant expression.

Ewin threaded his hands together and rested them on the desk. "I was hoping you might show me the finer points of needlework."

His housekeeper blinked. "Pardon?"

"I would like to learn how to embroider," he attempted again.

Mrs. Barr stared at him in disbelief. "But, why?" she asked. "I am more than happy to complete that menial task for you."

"I appreciate that, but I would like to learn how to embroider my initials on a handkerchief," he said, suddenly feeling very foolish about his peculiar request.

"Are you not satisfied with the way I embroider them, milord?" Mrs. Barr asked, wringing her hands together in her lap.

He unthreaded his hands and leaned back in his chair. This is not going well, he thought. He decided he should just be frank with his housekeeper and pray that she wouldn't laugh at his reasons.

Starting off slowly, he explained, "I am more than happy with the way you embroider my handkerchiefs, but I am attempting to woo a lady."

Mrs. Barr's brow lifted. "With needlework?"

He nodded.

"There are better ways to impress a lady," she argued. "Many, many ways, milord. In fact, I could spout off a dozen or so right now."

"True," he started, "but this particular lady has expressed an interest in a gentleman who knows how to wield a needle and thread."

Mrs. Barr's brow relaxed slightly. "I see," she replied. "Did she state why?"

"Lady Isabella has created an impossible list for a potential suitor to fulfill. I aim to prove to her that I could be the perfect suitor for her."

A smile came to his housekeeper's lips. "How romantic."

"It is only romantic if my gamble works," he responded honestly.

Mrs. Barr bobbed her head. "It will," she remarked. "I would be happy to show you how to embroider your initials on a hand-kerchief. Although, I should warn you, that it might take a considerable amount of time."

"I understand. Also, I would appreciate your discretion on the matter."

His housekeeper rose with a smile on her face. "For what it is worth, I think it is sweet that you are even making an effort to learn needlework for this young lady."

"You don't think it is foolhardy?"

"No," she said with a shake of her head. "Sometimes it is all right to act like a fool when you are in love."

"How did you know that I love the girl?"

Her face softened. "I can hear it in your voice, milord," she said. "Is there anything else I can help you with?"

"No. You have been most helpful."

"When would you like to start your needlework lessons?"

He glanced over at the longcase clock. "Would this evening work for you?"

"It would," she said. "I shall meet you in your study after supper."

"Splendid."

As he watched his housekeeper leave the room, he hoped that he was doing the right thing. If his friends ever heard that he was learning embroidery to impress a lady, he would never hear the end of it. They would tease him unmercifully.

Ewin closed the ledger in front of him and leaned back in his chair. He would do whatever it took to win Isabella's affections, even if his actions branded him a fool. Furthermore, he would need to contact the Colborne Orphanage in East London to set up an appointment to visit with Isabella. He had seen the eagerness in her eyes when he first brought it up.

"You want me to be an expert on bears?" his friend exclaimed from the doorway. "*Bears*?!"

"Is that a problem?" Ewin asked, watching Oliver storm into the room.

Oliver walked over to the drink cart and picked up the decanter. "Yes! I know nothing about bears."

"I sent along two books about bears with my note," he said. "Did you not receive them?"

Oliver turned back towards him, holding the decanter. "Oh, I received them, but I have no intention of actually reading them."

"Why not?"

"I have studied philosophy," his friend replied. "Why can't I be an expert in my own field?"

"By all means, you can be both," Ewin encouraged.

Oliver turned back around and poured himself a drink. He reached for the glass and took a sip before saying, "This is asinine, you know."

"In what way?"

With furrowed brows, Oliver answered, "Because no one in our circles is an expert on bears. We don't even have bears in England!"

"I'm certain that's why Isabella finds them so fascinating," Ewin attempted to explain, "which is why you need to have a basic knowledge of them."

Oliver sat down on the chair facing his desk. "The only two bears that I have ever seen were a dancing bear at a fair and the one at the Royal Menagerie. That hardly qualifies me as an expert."

"That is why you need to read the books," he pressed. "I must admit that it was nearly impossible to find two books on bears in all of London, and I believe one of those books was written specifically for children."

Oliver huffed. "You wasted your time."

"Please, Oliver," Ewin pleaded. "I need your help."

The fight seemed to drain out of his friend at his entreaty, and Oliver asked, "Pray tell, why is it so important to impress this girl?"

"Lord Northampton has offered me ten thousand pounds to find a suitor for his sister, Lady Isabella," Ewin revealed. "He will pay me once she has agreed to a courtship."

Oliver arched an eyebrow. "Lady Isabella is beautiful. Why does she need any help finding a suitor?"

"Because she has no intention of marrying this Season, or the next," Ewin shared. "Frankly, she is content to be a spinster, and her brother is worried about her."

"So, you are doing this for the money?"

Ewin shook his head. "No, I am doing this for Isabella."

"I'm afraid I don't understand," Oliver said with a puzzled look on his face.

Ewin grimaced before admitting, "I want to be the suitor."

Leaning his head back, Oliver laughed loudly, much to Ewin's annoyance. "You are smitten with the lovely Lady Isabella!"

Seeing no reason to deny it, Ewin remained silent.

Oliver leaned forward and placed his empty glass on the desk. "This is starting to make sense, but why the bears?"

"Isabella created a list of requirements that she wants in a potential suitor, and it includes someone who owns a pet bear."

"Who owns a pet bear?"

"No one, at least not anyone with a lick of sense," Ewin stated. "But Isabella is making impossible demands to try to prevent me from finding potential suitors."

"But you aren't *actually* finding suitors for her, are you?" Oliver asked.

Ewin shrugged. "I did introduce her to Mr. Gillingham yesterday. She said she wanted someone who had an extensive knowledge of botany."

Oliver laughed again. "That man can put a boisterous child to sleep just by talking."

"I won't disagree with you there," Ewin concurred, smiling.

His friend considered him for a moment, then said, "Fine. I will be an expert on bears, but I can't promise that all my facts will be accurate."

"Just make them believable, if at all possible."

Rising, Oliver remarked, "It is a good thing that I like you, Ewin. I wouldn't do this for just any friend of mine."

"I appreciate that."

Oliver adjusted his dark brown riding jacket and smirked. "Now, if you will excuse me, I have to study up before our trip to the Royal Menagerie tomorrow." He walked over to the door and stopped. "I hope this harebrained plan of yours works for you. I truly do."

As he watched his friend depart, Ewin sighed. He, too, hoped it would work.

❧ 7 ❧

Dressed in a dark green riding habit, Isabella knocked softly on the door of her mother's bedchamber, not wanting to disturb her if she was still sleeping.

"Come in," she heard her mother's muffled reply.

As Isabella opened the door, she was pleased to see her mother sitting up in bed, her back leaning up against the wall, sipping a cup of tea. Her skin didn't look quite as pale as it had the night before, and Isabella felt a great sense of relief.

"You are looking much better than you did last night," Isabella remarked.

Mary nodded. "I feel much better, as well. Never doubt the power of a good night's sleep."

"I couldn't agree with you more," Isabella responded as she walked closer to the bed. "I find sleeping is one of my favorite pastimes."

Perusing the length of her, her mother commented, "I see that you're dressed for riding."

"I am," Isabella replied as she sat down at the foot of the bed. "I'm riding out with Everett and Ewin, but I wanted to ensure you were being taken care of properly before we departed."

"That is kind of you, my dear," Mary said. "But you don't have to fuss over me. I am perfectly content right now."

"I know, but I will always worry about you, Mother."

Mary smiled kindly at her. "Do not fret. I am tougher than I look."

"I am glad to hear that," Isabella responded, returning her mother's smile.

Reaching over, her mother placed her empty teacup on the tray sitting on a side table. "I am pleased you are spending additional time with Ewin," she commented. "He is such a nice young man."

Isabella fought to keep the frown off her face. "He is tolerable, I suppose."

"Just tolerable?"

"It is better than being infuriating."

Mary laughed. "I must agree with you there, but when you were younger, there was no separating the two of you."

"I remember."

A reflective look came to her mother's eyes. "I recall that you two used to collect all the dry leaves and arrange them into a big pile on the lawn. Then, you would jump into that pile, and it would take days to remove all the tiny remnants of leaves from your hair."

Isabella smiled at the memory. "Ewin had to stop me from jumping out of my bedchamber window into the pile of leaves. I was adamant that the leaves would cushion my fall, but he convinced me I would just end up breaking something."

"He was always looking out for you, more so than your brothers."

Isabella huffed. "My brothers were no fun when I was younger," she declared. "They refused to play with me."

"But, if I recall, that didn't stop you from plaguing them with requests to play."

Isabella bobbed her head in agreement. "I think that is why I started riding as much as I did," she shared. "In a sense, my horse became my playmate."

"You have always shared a special bond with Maximus."

"That I have," Isabella murmured.

Her mother waved towards the door. "Now, off with you," she ordered. "Go enjoy your ride with Everett and Ewin, and I shall be here when you get back."

Isabella rose from the bed. "All right," she said, smoothing out her riding habit, "but I will be back shortly to check on you."

"Don't forget that the dressmaker is coming today to fit you for new gowns."

Isabella let out a groan. "Do I need more gowns?"

Her mother laughed. "Can a lady ever have too many gowns?" she asked. "Besides, you do need more ballgowns for this Season."

"As you wish, Mother."

After Isabella departed from the room, she headed towards the entry hall and saw her brother and Ewin waiting for her at the base of the stairs. She drew in a steadying breath at the sight of Ewin, dressed sharply in a dark blue riding jacket, buff trousers, and black Hessian boots. She frowned at her peculiar reaction to the sight of him.

"I'm sorry for keeping you waiting," she said as she stepped down onto the last step. "I was checking in on Mother."

"No apology needed, Bella," Ewin responded with a bow. "May I ask how your mother is faring?"

"She is better than she was last night," Isabella admitted.

"That is good."

Isabella nodded. "Seeing my mother like this makes me realize that growing old seems to have an inordinate number of difficulties."

Ewin chuckled. "Yes, it does," he replied, "but your mother has aged most gracefully."

"That she has," Isabella agreed.

Everett spoke up. "Our horses are saddled and waiting out front. Shall we?"

It wasn't long before they were racing their horses through Hyde Park, with Isabella's horse in the lead. Wisps of her blonde hair were flowing behind her as a bright smile graced her face. She glanced behind her and saw Everett and Ewin, both remaining low in the saddle, as they attempted to keep up with her.

She reined in her horse at the edge of the Serpentine River and waited for Everett and Ewin to do the same.

Ewin pulled back on his reins, and his horse came to a stop near hers. "You are an impressive rider, Bella."

"Thank you," she replied.

Everett dismounted and led his horse to drink. "Isabella has beaten me nearly every day since we started riding through Hyde Park."

Isabella gracefully slid off her horse and held the reins loosely in her hands. "This is true, but I can't take all the credit. Maximus is an exceptional gelding."

"How did you decide on the name Maximus for your horse?" Ewin asked as he dismounted.

With a smile on her face, she admitted, "In Latin, Maximus means 'greatest', and I thought it would be a good name for a horse."

"Ah," Ewin said. "That makes logical sense."

Isabella ran her hand down the length of Maximus's neck. "I was fortunate enough to take Maximus with me when I attended finishing school."

"I'm glad." Ewin's eyes scanned the river, and he didn't speak for a long moment. "It is lovely here."

She came to stand next to him. "It is," she agreed. "My father used to bring me here when I was younger."

"Were you close to your father?"

Isabella shook her head. "Not really," she replied. "But at

times, he made an effort with me, even if it was only for a short time."

"I'm sorry."

"Don't be," she said. "My father spent more time with me than with my brothers. Besides, my mother more than made up for my father's lack of caring."

"Mary is a good woman," Ewin commented.

"That she is," Isabella responded, her eyes downcast. "I don't know what I would do without her."

Ewin studied her, his eyes full of concern. "Is she truly that ill?"

Everett interjected, "The doctor says her heart is getting weaker. He is not sure how much longer she has left."

"That is horrible news," Ewin murmured.

Tears came to Isabella's eyes, and she had a hard time blinking them away.

"I can't imagine how different my life would be without my mother," she murmured. A stray tear rolled down her cheek, and she reached up to swipe it away. "I don't think I would be able to endure it."

"No, you are wrong," he replied. "You are stronger than you give yourself credit for."

Isabella gave him a timid smile as she brought her gaze back up to meet his. "Why are you so complimentary of me?" she questioned. "I scarcely deserve your praise."

"Because I know you, Bella," he replied, "and you *do* deserve my praise."

She shook her head. "No, you only think you know me," she argued. "But we haven't spent time together since our youth."

Ewin smiled. "You are the same girl that I used to chase through the fields surrounding our properties."

Isabella reached up and tucked a piece of her blonde hair behind her ear. "Then why do I feel so different?"

"I'm afraid I can't answer that," he replied.

Everett pointed towards a two-level building with a thatched roof in the distance next to the river. "Should we enjoy a cheese-cake at The Cake-house before we head back?"

Isabella smiled. "I do so love cheesecake."

"As do I," Ewin said. "May I assist you as you mount your horse?"

"I would appreciate that," she replied with a nod.

Ewin stepped closer to her, intertwined his fingers, and leaned down. As she placed her foot into his hands, he lifted her up and onto her side saddle.

After she was situated, Ewin remained close and placed a hand on Maximus's neck. When their eyes met, a smile tilted the corners of his lips.

"May I ask what is so amusing?" she asked.

His smile grew. "Do you remember that low-hanging branch that we used to swing on down by the stream?"

"How could I forget?" she questioned. "We spent hours swinging back and forth until our arms grew tired."

"Or until we dropped down into the stream," he reminded her.

"That was only during the summer months."

Ewin patted Maximus's neck. "We used to have such fun, you and I."

"We did."

He opened his mouth to say something, but then he closed it just as quickly. Finally, he said, "Allow me to mount my horse, and then we can race to The Cake-house."

Isabella nodded her reply, still wondering what Ewin had intended to say. And why had he stopped himself?

Sitting in the back of a barouche, Ewin asked his friend, "Did you have enough time to read those books about bears that I sent over?"

"Do not fret," Oliver responded. "I skimmed the books this morning over breakfast, and I am confident that I can fool the lovely Lady Isabella."

Ewin frowned in disapproval. "I truly doubt that. Lady Isabella is rather clever."

"But I doubt she knows anything about bears. The books you lent me were rather boring. I can't imagine a lady wasting her time on anything like that."

"You would be surprised," Ewin replied. "May I ask why you only glanced at them?"

Appearing unconcerned, Oliver explained, "I'm afraid I got distracted last night at the gambling hall, but I did manage to win fifty pounds."

Ewin gave him an exasperated look. "Pray tell, did you learn anything about bears?"

Oliver nodded. "All bears are brown."

"You are wrong," Ewin stated. "Haven't you heard of the white maritime bear that lives in the Arctic or the black bears that reside in America?"

"No, I haven't," Oliver said, shrugging. "But that is of little consequence. I doubt that Lady Isabella would know those tedious facts."

"What else did you learn from 'skimming' those books?"

"That bears are slow, dumb animals."

Attempting to control his growing annoyance, Ewin looked away, watching as the vendors tried to hawk their goods to the men and women passing by on the pavement.

After a long moment, he turned his attention back towards Oliver. "Again, you are wrong. Bears are incredibly fast, but they do not possess the ability to maintain that speed for long distances," he corrected his friend. "Furthermore, those books indicated that bears are incredibly smart animals."

Oliver gave him a smug smile. "You are working yourself into a frenzy for no reason, my good friend," he shared. "I will impress Lady Isabella with my knowledge of bears."

"You are an idiot," Ewin replied. "So far, nothing you have told me has been accurate."

The barouche rolled to a stop in front of Lady Isabella's townhouse, and Oliver reached to open the door. "Just trust me," his friend said.

Ewin followed him, stepping out onto the pavement. "Please give me one fact about bears that is accurate to appease my mind."

"Bears are nocturnal," Oliver said over his shoulder as he approached the main door.

Ewin remained rooted to his spot. His friend was a fool if he thought Isabella was going to fall for his pathetic charade.

After Oliver knocked on the door, he turned back to face him with an expectant look. "What is wrong?"

"You should know that bears are not nocturnal," he said, closing the distance between them.

"Are you sure?" Oliver asked. "The bear at the Royal Menagerie is always sleeping when we visit."

"I'm beginning to think you didn't even read the books," Ewin muttered, shaking his head.

"One book that you lent me did have a diagram of the bear's anatomy, but I daresay that a lady would never be interested in that."

"For my sake, I hope you are right," Ewin responded.

Oliver placed his hand on his shoulder. "You worry too much. I took some theatre classes when I was at Cambridge."

"It is not your acting skills that I am calling into question," Ewin quipped.

The door was opened, and Howe met them with his usual stoic face. "How may I help you?"

"I believe Lady Isabella is expecting me," Ewin said, removing his top hat.

Howe nodded as he opened the door wide. "She is waiting for you in the drawing room, Lord Ewin. Would you care for me to announce you?"

"That won't be necessary," Ewin replied, stepping into the entry hall.

Howe accepted their top hats and gloves. "Very good, milord."

As they walked across the entry hall, Ewin mumbled, "Please try not to embarrass me, Oliver."

His friend chuckled. "I am willing to bet fifty pounds that Lady Isabella doesn't even know the first thing about bears. She probably just considers them cute because of all their fur."

"I will take that bet," Ewin responded as he stepped into the drawing room.

His eyes eagerly scanned the room until they landed on Isabella who was standing in front of the window. She was dressed in the most alluring pink gown with white trim along the neckline and the waist. Her hair was piled high on her head and small ringlets framed her face. She turned to face them and smiled, but he immediately noticed the smile didn't reach her eyes.

Isabella dipped into a curtsey. "It is a pleasure to see you again, Lord Ewin," she said, her voice devoid of any emotion.

Rather than provide the introductions, he closed the distance between them and asked in a hushed voice, "What is wrong?"

She looked up at him in surprise. "Why do you suppose something is wrong?"

"You don't appear happy."

Lowering her gaze to his lapels, she replied, "I'm afraid I am just worried about my mother's failing health."

"How is she faring?"

Isabella sighed. "Her coloring has returned, and she was well enough to leave her bedchamber this morning."

"That is good, isn't it?"

She pressed her lips together before saying, "I suppose so."

"What is it?" he asked, gently placing a hand on her sleeve. "What are you not telling me, Bella?"

Bringing her gaze up, her eyes were moist with unshed tears. "I'm afraid I am just feeling fearful of the future."

"You must be careful," he advised. "Being fearful of the future robs your happiness from the present."

"How can I not be fearful?" she asked, her eyes searching his.

He smiled encouragingly. "Would your mother want you to worry incessantly about her?"

She shook her head, causing her blonde curls to sway back and forth. "No, she would not."

"What advice would she give you, right now, if she were here?" he asked.

A small smile came to Isabella's lips. "She would tell me to stop my worrying and to enjoy myself."

"Do you think that is good advice?"

Her smile grew. "I do, but..."

"No buts," he said, cutting her off. "Focus on the present. Don't spend your time worrying about what could happen in the future. That is no way to live, Bella."

"That is easy for you to say," she murmured as the smile left her face.

"I would agree, but that doesn't change my advice to you," he stated, lowering his hand to his side.

Isabella glanced over her shoulder at Oliver before returning her gaze to his. "We are being unfathomably rude to your friend," she murmured.

"Don't worry about him," he replied. "I am much more concerned about you and your well-being."

"You are being extremely kind."

"Am I?" he asked. "Or am I being a good friend?"

A smile came back to her lips. "A little of both, I suppose."

His eyes ran over her lovely face before he decided that he had lingered long enough. He turned towards his friend and held his hand out. "Lady Isabella, please allow me the privilege of introducing you to my friend, Mr. Oliver Braggs."

Oliver bowed. "I am delighted to finally be introduced to you."

Isabella curtseyed, then said, "I understand you are knowledgeable about bears."

"I am," Oliver replied, puffing out his chest.

"What fun!" she exclaimed. "I have so many questions to ask you."

"You do?" Oliver asked with surprise on his features.

Isabella nodded enthusiastically. "Have you always had a passion for studying bears?"

He cleared his throat, his eyes nervously darting around the room. "I have since my early years."

"Do you have a favorite species of bear?"

Oliver smiled. "Yes, the brown bear, since I find them to be most entertaining when they start dancing at the fairs."

"Oh? I find those displays at the traveling menageries to be rather cruel to the animals," she shared with a frown. "Don't you agree?"

Oliver's smile dimmed. "I had not considered that before," he remarked, "but I suppose it is rather cruel to treat the animals in such a fashion."

Isabella smiled approvingly. "Have you ever been close enough to pet a bear? If so, is their fur coarse or soft?"

"I'm afraid I cannot answer that question, because I am smart enough to have never gotten that close to a bear," Oliver replied.

"Do all bears have nonretractable claws?"

Oliver shifted his gaze towards Ewin. "I believe all bears

share that trait," he stated. "May I be so bold as to ask if you have a favorite bear?"

Isabella clasped her hands in front of her as she took a moment to ponder her response. "I would have to say that I am most intrigued by the grizzly bear."

"Pardon?"

"Are you not familiar with the grizzly bear, Mr. Braggs?" she asked curiously. "It is also commonly known as the North American brown bear. It was discovered by Meriwether Lewis and William Clark when they went on an expedition in the American continent."

"Yes, I am familiar with the North American brown bear," Oliver attempted. "I just have never heard them referred to as the grizzly bear."

"Oh, my apologies," she said. "By chance, have you read Constantine John Phipps's account on when he first encountered a white maritime bear in the Arctic?"

Oliver shook his head. "I have not."

"It is fascinating," she replied. "He also went into great detail about the ivory gull."

"Ivory gull?" he asked. "Is that another species of bear?"

She frowned. "No. It is a type of bird."

"Of course. My mistake," Oliver said with a nervous chuckle. "I shall have to read his book when I have the chance."

"May I ask what books you have read about bears?" Isabella asked, eyeing him closely.

Oliver blinked, then said, "I have learned the most when I attend lectures on bears."

"There are entire lectures on bears?" she asked in disbelief.

"Yes… um… all the time at Cambridge," he stammered out. "I just attended one last week… at Cambridge. It was well attended. Lots of people are interested in bears."

"Truly?" Isabella asked.

"Yes," Oliver replied, his panicked eyes darting towards Ewin.

Ewin decided to take pity on his friend and spoke up. "Shall we continue this riveting conversation on our way to the Royal Menagerie?"

"Please allow me to retrieve my bonnet and shawl," Isabella requested, turning towards him. "I shall be right down."

After she had departed, Ewin turned his attention towards Oliver. "I believe you owe me fifty pounds."

Oliver sighed. "You were right," he responded. "I vastly underestimated her cleverness and her interest in bears."

"I tried to warn you."

"Perhaps she is finished inundating me with bear questions?" Oliver asked hopefully.

Ewin chuckled. "I highly doubt it, especially since you said you just attended a lecture on them at Cambridge."

"I was afraid you were going to say that," Oliver sighed.

❧ 8 ❧

"I THINK YOUR FRIEND MAY HAVE OVEREXAGGERATED HIS interest in bears," Isabella commented over the rim of her teacup.

Ewin leaned back on the settee as he sat across from her in the drawing room. "Why do you say that?"

Lowering the teacup to her lap, she replied, "Because when we were standing in front of the bear's cage at the Royal Menagerie, I asked him if all bears hibernated, and Mr. Braggs just stared at me, befuddled," she explained. "I was then forced to explain to him what hibernation meant."

"Oh, I see," he remarked, looking down at his teacup. "Do all bears hibernate?"

She shrugged one shoulder. "I don't believe so, which is why I posed the question," she replied. "After all, the brown bear at the Royal Menagerie doesn't hibernate, nor do the dancing bears at the traveling menageries. I think it might have to do with the climate and the ability to forage for food."

"That would make logical sense."

"It is just perplexing to me that a man who claims to have an immense knowledge of bears seems to know very little about them," she mused.

"Perhaps he simply became a little tongue-tied around you," Ewin suggested before he took a sip of his drink.

Isabella shook her head. "No, I don't believe that was it," she responded. "He kept trying to shift the conversation away from bears and towards philosophy while we were touring the Royal Menagerie."

"Did that trouble you?"

"Not particularly. He seemed to be well-versed on that subject, unlike the topic of bears." She smiled. "Come to think of it, he didn't appear to have any interest in the other animals, either."

Ewin reached forward and placed his empty cup and saucer on the table. "I am not sure if he mentioned it, but Mr. Braggs did study philosophy at Cambridge."

"He did not, but that makes sense," she remarked, bringing the teacup up to her lips. "I was pleasantly surprised that we had a frank conversation about philosophy. Most gentlemen of the *ton* try to sway the conversation away from such heavy topics when speaking to women."

"With good reason," Ewin teased.

She arched an eyebrow. "Why do you say that?"

"If we discussed every topic with the ladies that we associate with, then what would the men discuss while we were at White's?"

Isabella was amused by his response but hid her smile. "I shall grant you that."

With a curious glance, he asked, "Now, I must pose the question, are you interested in Mr. Braggs as a potential suitor?"

"He is agreeable enough," she replied, hesitating, "but I don't believe I am."

Ewin bobbed his head. "Then I shall strike his name from the list."

"Thank you." She placed her empty teacup onto the table.

"May I ask how many more potential suitors you intend for me to meet?"

"As many as it takes for you to find the ideal suitor."

Isabella frowned. "That could take a considerable amount of time."

"Then so be it," he said with a slight shrug. "After all, we have the entire Season, and I have no intention of giving up. Do you?"

Her frown intensified. "Perhaps if we took a break," she hesitated, "at least for a day or two."

"I suppose that could work. I heard back from the Colborne Orphanage."

Isabella perked up at this pleasant, unexpected news. "You did?"

He nodded. "I have arranged a visit for us tomorrow afternoon, assuming that is agreeable to you."

"Most definitely," she replied eagerly.

Glancing over at the open door, Ewin leaned forward and spoke quietly. "I will call upon you tomorrow with the excuse that we will be taking a carriage ride through Hyde Park."

"That would work most splendidly, I think."

Ewin smiled at her, drawing her attention to his perfectly formed lips. "I can be rather clever when the situation warrants it," he remarked.

"I am aware of that fact," she bantered back, enjoying this playful side of him.

"The next gentleman that I intend to introduce you to is quite knowledgeable about architecture," he announced while maintaining her gaze.

She smiled approvingly. "I do enjoy architecture."

"I'm glad to hear that since you mentioned architecture as one of your requirements," he said. "Lord Egerton has been training under the famed architect, John Nash, for many years now."

"That is an impressive feat, considering Mr. Nash takes very few commissions and works mostly for the Prince Regent."

"You are remarkably well informed."

"I do read the morning newspapers."

He gasped. "How scandalous of you," he joked. "I can't believe Everett would allow you to do such a thing."

She laughed. "I don't know why a lady reading a morning newspaper is so scandalous amongst the *ton*."

"Because, my dear, then you start thinking and getting your own ideas." He shuddered. "Good heavens, what a horrible thought."

She laughed, feeling lighter than she had in weeks. "*If* I marry," she started, "I would want a husband who would respect my opinions and would consider me his intellectual match."

"As well you should."

Hesitantly, she voiced one of her greatest fears, knowing she was making herself vulnerable. "Do you suppose that such a man exists?"

Ewin studied her for a moment, and his eyes were thoughtful as if he was remembering something. "I do, Bella," he replied, "most ardently."

"How can you be so sure?"

One side of his lip curled upwards. "You must trust me on this one."

"I do trust you," she found herself admitting.

He appeared pleased by her admission. "I am glad."

"Why?"

Sliding forward on the settee, he sat on the edge looking earnestly at her. "Because you used to trust me when we were younger."

"That was a long time ago," she murmured, finding herself transfixed by his greyish-hazel eyes.

"It was not so long ago," he countered, "and it was a time that I look back on with much fondness."

"As do I."

A line between Ewin's brow appeared as he asked, "Then what changed between us, Bella?" he asked. "Why do you hold such contempt for me now?"

"I don't hold contempt for you," she paused, "at least, not anymore."

His eyes searched hers. "That is good, but we used to be the best of friends."

Clasping her hands in her lap, she replied, "I suppose we stopped being friends after you left for Eton."

"Why?"

"Because you changed," she shared honestly, "and you stopped spending time with me."

"Did I?"

"Yes," she replied, "and when you did spend time at our estate, you would tease me incessantly."

Ewin gave her an understanding smile. "You should know that I only tease the people that I care about."

"Oh, I hadn't considered that," she said, glancing down at her lap. "I had just assumed that you had grown tired of me."

"You think I grew tired of you?" he repeated incredulously. "How could I tire of someone who brought such great joy to my life?"

Bringing her gaze back up, she asked, "Do you mean that?"

"I do," he replied, "and I'm hoping that we could be friends again."

Isabella bobbed her head. "I would like that very much."

"I'm glad to hear that, Bella," Ewin murmured softly, almost reverently.

As they smiled at each other, Everett walked into the drawing room with Nicholas by his side. "I apologize for the intrusion," he started, "but Nicholas only has a limited time before Penelope expects him back home."

"Is that so?" Isabella asked in an amused tone.

Nicholas nodded. "It is true," he replied, wincing. "Penelope has been a bit demanding since our baby arrived, but she has graciously granted me permission to go visit White's." He turned his gaze towards Ewin. "Would you care to join us?"

Ewin rose from his seat. "I would," he paused, glancing down at her, "assuming that is all right with you."

"Why would it not be?" she asked, secretly pleased that he asked her permission.

"Then I shall call upon you tomorrow for our carriage ride through Hyde Park," Ewin said with a charming smile on his lips.

"I look forward to it."

"Blasted needle," Ewin mumbled under his breath as he managed to prick himself... again.

Ignoring the throbbing in his finger, he used his other hand to grab the end of the needle and pull it through the fabric.

"Good," Mrs. Barr said encouragingly. "You are getting better."

"Am I?" he questioned in disbelief. "I feel as though I am getting worse."

Mrs. Barr smiled. "Not at all. The tiny blood spots on the handkerchief add a nice touch," she teased.

"No wonder Isabella complains about needlework," he grumbled. "It is quite a violent pastime."

His housekeeper laughed. "Once you get the hang of it, needlework is really quite simple. At least until you get to the more complex, fancy work."

"Fancy work?" Ewin asked. "There's something more complex than this?"

"Yes," Mrs. Barr smiled gently. "There's cross stitching, knotting, and netting, to name a few."

He lowered the handkerchief to his lap. "I can't believe that women find enjoyment in this menial task."

"Many don't," Mrs. Barr revealed, "but it is an essential skill for us to have. Clothes have to be made and mended, and most don't have the luxury of hiring a modiste."

Glancing down at the handkerchief, he took a moment to admire his crude attempt at placing his initials into the fabric.

"The more you practice, the better you will become at it," Mrs. Barr encouraged. "Don't give up hope yet."

He held the fabric up. "At least, my initials are starting to become more prominent on the handkerchief."

"I agree," Mrs. Barr praised. "You have come a long way in a short period of time. If you would like, we could get a printed pattern from the Ackermann's Repository for you to practice on."

He shook his head. "That won't be necessary," he replied. "This is not a pastime I will be pursuing after I win Lady Isabella's heart."

"I think what you are trying to do is commendable, milord."

Reaching for the needle, he pushed it through the fabric, then said, "As I stated before, it is only commendable if my gamble works."

"I have no doubt that you will woo Lady Isabella, especially since you are going to such great lengths to do so."

"I wish I had your confidence."

To his horror, Ewin heard his friend chuckle from the doorway, and he brought his gaze up to see Oliver leaning his shoulder against the door frame.

"You are embroidering now?" Oliver asked, amused. "What is next? Cooking?"

Mrs. Barr rose from her chair. "I think it is time for a break," she suggested. "I will get some refreshment for us, and we can try again later."

Ewin forced a smile to his face. "Thank you, Mrs. Barr."

Oliver waited until the housekeeper left the room before he crossed his arms over his chest. "What the devil is going on here?"

Ewin held up his handkerchief proudly. "I am learning how to embroider my initials onto a handkerchief."

"So I see, and quite poorly at that," Oliver remarked. "But I must pose my question, why?"

He shrugged. "I thought it would be fun."

Oliver arched an eyebrow. "I don't believe you."

"Fine," Ewin said, placing his handkerchief on the table. "If you must know, it was one of Lady Isabella's requirements for a potential suitor."

"One of her requirements was needlework?" Oliver repeated slowly.

Ewin nodded.

"But no gentleman of the *ton* would know that skill, much less any other man," Oliver remarked.

Rising, Ewin tugged down on his ivory-colored waistcoat and replied, "Don't you think I already know that?"

Oliver uncrossed his arms and laughed. "Lady Isabella may be exceptionally beautiful, but are you sure she is worth all this effort?"

"I assure you that she is," Ewin responded, walking over to the drink cart. "Would you care for a drink?"

"I would." Oliver walked further into the room. "Would you care to join me at the gambling hall, or are you too busy practicing your needlework?"

"You know I don't have the funds to waste at the moment."

"You did just win fifty pounds from me," Oliver pointed out.

Ewin nodded. "True, but I intend to keep that money."

"You are no fun," Oliver remarked.

After pouring two drinks, Ewin walked over and extended a glass to his friend. "You could stay here and keep me company while I practice my needlework."

"No, thank you," Oliver replied, bringing the glass up to his lips. "That sounds rather boring."

Ewin walked over to the chair and dropped down. "By the way, you were a terrible bear expert. Isabella saw right through you."

Oliver smiled. "If you recall, I did answer some of her questions."

"No," Ewin said with a shake of his head. "You made up random facts about bears and Isabella was polite enough not to correct you."

"I don't even think those two books that you lent me covered half of her questions," Oliver remarked. "I have never met someone with such a voracious appetite for knowledge."

Ewin took a sip of his drink. "I tried to warn you."

"But we did have a pleasant conversation on philosophy."

"That you did," he agreed. "Isabella commented that she enjoyed conversing with you on that subject and appreciated the fact that you spoke so openly to her."

Oliver came to sit down next to him and asked, "If you are not successful at wooing Isabella, can I give it a try?"

"No!" he exclaimed. "Why would you even ask that?"

Oliver shrugged. "Because Isabella is beautiful and clever, a wonderful combination. You don't see that very often in a debutante."

"Find another girl," Ewin growled. "Isabella is mine."

Oliver lifted his brow. "Is she?"

"She will be," Ewin insisted, frowning. "At least after I convince her that I am the ideal suitor for her."

"I hope you are right."

Ewin sighed. "I hope so, too."

They sat in silence for a few moments, sipping their drinks, until Oliver spoke up. "Have you heard from your solicitor yet about properties to purchase?"

"I have," he replied. "There are a few that I can afford, including one that was originally used as a stud farm."

Oliver brought the glass down to rest it on the side of the chair. "Are you going to purchase it?"

"I will need to tour it first," he responded, "but I asked my solicitor to schedule a meeting with the owner."

"That is exciting."

Ewin nodded. "I was warned that the manor does require some extensive repairs before it will be habitable."

"That is most unfortunate."

"I thought so, as well, but my solicitor informed me that the estate has the potential to be extremely profitable."

Oliver rose and walked over to the drink cart. He put the glass down and announced, "I'd better hurry. I want to arrive at the gambling hall before it gets much later."

"Why not stay here and save your money?" Ewin joked.

Laughing, Oliver replied, "Unlike you, I have not been cut off by my father, and I have the funds to spend at my discretion."

"Must be nice," he muttered.

"It is," Oliver remarked. "Now, if you will excuse me, I also wouldn't want to disappoint the ladies who will no doubt have turned out to see me."

Ewin watched as his friend departed from the room, and he found himself grateful that he changed directions with his life. Night after night, going to the gambling halls had become exhausting, and it left him with a void in his life. A void that was now filled with Isabella.

Mrs. Barr walked in with a tray in her hands. "I have brought you some tea and biscuits. After a cup of tea, will you be ready to practice your embroidery again?"

He groaned. "I suppose we must."

9

With a rigid back, Isabella sat in the dirty, rickety hackney with her gloved hands clasped in her lap, grateful that she had worn one of her sturdier gowns. They were traveling to the Colborne Orphanage in the rookeries, and she wasn't sure if the inside or outside of the coach smelled worse. Regardless, the putrid odor was intensifying, and it was becoming much more difficult to keep the grimace off her face.

Ewin kept glancing over at her with a worried expression. "I know the hackney is not what you are used to riding in, and I'm sorry..." he started.

Isabella spoke over him. "You don't have to keep apologizing. I am perfectly content to ride in a hackney," she lied.

He gave her a knowing look. "Are you?"

"Well, I'm attempting to be," she replied honestly as she relaxed her shoulders slightly. "I do keep wondering why the floor is so incredibly sticky, and I have yet to discover where that foul odor is originating from."

"Ah," he began, "those are the many joys of riding in a hackney."

"May I ask what the other joys are?"

Ewin smiled. "The list is too great to count, but I believe a broken window is a thrill you have never encountered before." He pointed at the window as they passed by a series of blackened buildings. "Sadly, the rookeries are not known for their delightful aromas, either."

"That is a good point."

Ewin grew serious. "I am truly sorry that you were forced to ride in a hackney, but I assure you that it will attract far less attention here."

"I can imagine that would be the case."

"Normally, I would have borrowed one of my father's crested coaches to visit the orphanage, but those are not available to me at the moment."

Isabella heard the sadness in his voice, and she knew the estrangement was taking a bigger toll on him than he was willing to admit.

"May I ask why you and your father had a falling out?"

He waved his hand dismissively in front of him. "It was over a trifling little detail."

"Which was?" she pressed.

Ewin turned his attention back towards the broken window. "It matters not," he replied. "I do not wish to burden you with my problems."

"I would never consider you or your problems a burden," she stated with compassion in her tone.

"Regardless, I think it would be best—"

She cut him off. "That is rubbish!"

"I beg your pardon?"

"We are friends, are we not?" she questioned.

He nodded. "We are."

"And friends confide in each other, do they not?"

"They do, but…"

Speaking over him, she asserted, "Just tell me the blasted reason, Ewin."

Ewin's brow shot up. "I should consider your language offensive, but I must admit I find it oddly charming."

"Thank you," she said, smiling. "Now, out with the reason, and I want the truth."

He sighed as he admitted, "My father is trying to force me into an arranged marriage."

Isabella sat in stunned silence before finding her voice. "May I ask with whom?"

"He wants me to marry Lady Rebecca Galpin."

Isabella's eyes grew wide. "You can't marry her!" she declared. "Lady Rebecca is just awful. I have never met such a mean, spiteful person."

"I am well aware of this fact, that's why I refused to marry her."

"Why would your father want you to marry her?"

He winced. "Apparently, her father is willing to settle some debts for my father and still provide a dowry for Lady Rebecca."

"I see," she murmured.

Ewin leaned forward in his seat and revealed, "My father was foolish enough to enter into a wedding contract with Lady Rebecca's father, Lord Frampton. If I don't marry her, then Lord Frampton intends to sue him for breach of contract."

"How awful."

"But it matters not," he stated. "*If* I marry, it will only be to the woman that I love."

"Bravo," she cheered. "I feel the same way, but many members of the *ton* don't share our views. They cite duty is more important than love."

"That is why they are such an unhappy lot," he said with a nod. "Marrying the wrong person inevitably brings heartache and sorrow to the union."

"I agree."

He smiled as if he knew a secret that she was not privy to. "I am glad that we are in agreement, then."

"As am I."

Ewin shifted his gaze towards the window and didn't speak for a long moment. "I see all these filthy street urchins skirting the coaches in the street, and it makes me wish that I could help every one of them."

"I feel bad for them, as well."

"Our orphanage does help quite a number of children, but I wish we could do more," he said, his voice resigned. "My grandmother set up this orphanage before she died, and those funds are still supporting the operational costs to this day."

"That was most gracious of her," Isabella commented. "Does your father also support the orphanage?"

Ewin huffed before he continued. "No. If my father had his way, he would have already gambled away the money intended for the orphanage."

"I'm sorry," she murmured, not knowing what else to say.

He brought his gaze back to meet hers. "My patronage is really important to me," he admitted. "I come by the orphanage on a regular basis to ensure all their needs are met."

"That is admirable of you."

"There is nothing admirable about it," he disagreed with a shake of his head. "Helping people that are less fortunate than me is my privilege. It gives me something to hold on to, even when I feel lost or alone."

Isabella's eyes searched his face. "Frankly, I had not expected this side of you."

"I am not surprised," he said with a grin. "These past few months, I have been in a drunken blur. After gambling and enjoying every pleasurable pursuit that the Season offered, I realized that I wasn't happy."

"Why not?"

"Life is meaningless unless you find a purpose. A reason to get out of bed every morning."

"And you have found that purpose in the orphanage?"

Ewin's eyes grew reflective as he stared back at her. "Among other things," he replied softly.

Feeling bold, she prodded, "Such as?"

Smirking, he asked, "Have you always been such a busybody?"

"I have," she answered proudly, seeing no reason to deny it.

He chuckled before inquiring, "Have you found a purpose in your life yet, Bella?"

"I have not," she answered, shaking her head. "How do you suppose I should go about finding one?"

Ewin brought his hand up and rubbed his chin thoughtfully. "What are your favorite pastimes?" he asked. "We could start there."

"I love riding my horse, Maximus."

"That is fairly obvious," he replied. "Anything else?"

Isabella bit her lower lip. "I love reading, and I do want to find a way to help people that are less fortunate than me."

"Perhaps you could read to the children at the orphanage," he proposed.

A genuine smile came to her lips. "I would like that very much," she said. "I could even donate a few books to the orphanage's library."

"It isn't much of a library," he informed her.

"Then we shall have to change that, won't we?"

He nodded. "Yes, *we* will."

The hackney came to a jerking stop, and she fell forward. Immediately, Ewin put his hands out and caught her.

"Are you all right?" he asked.

She leaned back and straightened the straw bonnet pinned to her hair. "Is that one of the many joys of a hackney?"

Ewin laughed loudly. "The driver did stop a little abruptly, didn't he?"

"I should say so."

The door to the hackney was opened, and the driver stuck his gloved hand in. "May I help you out, ma'am?"

"No need. I shall assist her." Ewin exited the coach and extended his hand towards her.

She slipped her gloved hand into his and allowed him to assist her out of the coach. Once her feet were on the dirty pavement, she didn't remove her hand from his. Rather, she stepped closer to him as her eyes scanned the decaying buildings. She couldn't help but notice the bleak expressions on many of the people's faces as they brushed past her.

Ewin leaned closer. "The first time visiting the rookeries can be overwhelming," he said softly.

"I had no idea it was this bad for them," she murmured. "Even the skies seem blackened."

"Come, let's get you off the street," he encouraged as he slipped his arm over her shoulder and tucked her up against him, making her feel oddly safe. "I believe you will be pleasantly surprised by the condition of the orphanage."

They took a few steps towards a brown building. A freshly painted sign hung above the blue door, identifying it as the Colborne Orphanage.

Ewin pounded his fist on the door. A few moments later, the door opened, and a dark-haired, portly woman greeted them.

"Lord Ewin," she exclaimed, opening the door wide and ushering them into a modest entry hall with yellow papered walls. "Please come in. We have been expecting you."

Once the door was closed, the woman smiled at her. "Welcome to Colborne Orphanage," she said in a kind voice. "I am Mrs. Finch. I am the proprietress of this fine institution."

Rather than have Ewin introduce her, Isabella spoke up first. "Thank you for allowing me to visit, Mrs. Finch," she greeted. "My name is Lady Isabella Beauchamp."

Mrs. Finch smiled approvingly. "Would you care for a tour, Lady Isabella?"

"I would, very much."

"Follow me, then," the proprietress invited, spinning on her heel.

Ewin stepped closer and offered his arm. "Are you ready for an adventure, Bella?"

"With you," she replied, accepting his arm, "always."

With Isabella's hand securely tucked into the crook of his arm, Ewin kept glancing over at her, hoping she was enjoying the tour of the orphanage. For some reason, her approval meant a great deal to him. He wanted to share this part of his life with her.

Frankly, he wanted to share his entire life with her, but he mustn't rush her. Not yet, anyway. He could tell that she wasn't ready for him to declare his intentions, so he needed to continue to proceed with his plan.

Mrs. Finch's voice broke through his musings as she started walking up the narrow stairs. "That was the first level, but now I want to show you where the children primarily congregate."

Isabella spoke up. "Are orphanages generally this quiet?"

"All twenty of the children are in their assigned classes," Mrs. Finch replied, glancing over her shoulder. "We take learning very seriously here."

"What sorts of things do you teach them?"

Mrs. Finch stopped at the top of the stairs and turned to face her. "We teach the girls the skills they will need to find employment once they are old enough to leave the orphanage. Furthermore, the Colborne family has been generous enough that we can also hire tutors to educate them."

The proprietress smiled proudly and announced, "I'm happy

to share that the last girl who left us found employment as a lady's maid."

"That is an impressive feat!" Isabella praised.

Mrs. Finch gestured towards a closed door. "This is one of the instructional rooms," she said. "Would you care to observe?"

"I would like that, very much."

With an approving nod, Mrs. Finch walked over and opened the door. They stepped inside and saw six girls of varying ages sitting around in a circle practicing their needlework. A lanky young woman was crouching down next to one of the chairs, providing instructions.

The girls glanced up when they saw them enter, and a blonde-haired, freckle-faced girl shouted, "Lord Ewin!"

Ewin smiled fondly at her. "It is good to see you again, Maria."

Maria jumped up, spun back around, and placed her fabric back onto the chair. She then ran over and threw her arms around Lord Ewin's waist. "Are you here to play with us?"

"Not this time," he replied, returning her embrace, "but I shall return shortly to play some games with you."

Maria took a step back and brought her hand up to her mouth as if she intended to tell him a secret. "You should know that Hannah cheats at card games."

"I do not!" a brown-haired girl exclaimed. "You just don't know how to play whist."

The lanky young woman clapped her hands. "Girls!" she said. "Remember to mind your manners and apologize to Lord Ewin."

Maria lowered her gaze to the floor. "I'm sorry, Lord Ewin."

"No harm done," Ewin graciously stated. "What are you working on?"

With an overly dramatized huff, Maria replied, "We are stitching our initials in a piece of fabric, and I'm not very good at it."

"You're not?" Ewin questioned.

Maria shook her head. "No. Miss Diana says that my needlework is awful and looks rushed."

"Perhaps I can help?"

"You?" Maria asked with wide eyes. "But you are a man."

Ewin gave her an amused smile. "I'm glad that you noticed," he joked, "but I recently discovered that I have a knack for embroidery."

Isabella withdrew her hand and turned towards him with a surprised expression on her face. "Truly?"

"Truly," he repeated, relishing the moment. "I am not sure why it is so unfathomable that I know how to embroider."

Maria rushed over to pick up her fabric and brought it back to him. "Can you help me, then?"

Ewin glanced down at the scrap of white fabric and saw the uneven letters. "I might have to agree with Miss Diana," he replied. "You need to take more pride in your work."

"But I hate needlework," Maria declared. "Why can't I find a job that doesn't require me to know how to embroider?"

"Embroidery is an important skill for any woman to have," he counseled as he removed the needle from the fabric. "If you truly master the skill, you might even be able to become a dressmaker one day."

"That is much too grand for me," Maria murmured.

Ewin started to undo some of the stitching. "Never stop dreaming, Maria," he counseled, "because you never know what the future holds for you."

"But I'm only an orphan," she said in a resigned voice.

Crouching down to her level, he replied, "No, you are so much more than that. Don't ever let that reason hold you back. Promise me, Maria."

Maria bobbed her head. "I promise, Lord Ewin."

"Good," he said, rising. "Now, back to your needlework."

As he pulled the needle through the fabric, he asked, "Have you learned feather stitching or buttonhole stitching?"

The girl shook her head. "I know of them, but I have not learned them yet."

"My housekeeper demonstrated those stitches for me," he shared as he continued working on the embroidery, "and they looked nearly impossible to accomplish."

Maria pointed at a dark-haired girl that had her head bent over as she worked on her fabric. "Sarah can do all kinds of stitching," she shared.

Ewin pushed the needle back into the fabric and extended it towards Maria. "I undid some of your stitching and worked on your initials for a few moments."

With an amazed look, Maria stared up at him. "You are talented, milord."

"No," he said. "I am adequate, at best."

The lanky woman clapped her hands, drawing everyone's attention. "Class is now over, girls. Take your fabric up to your room so you can practice later this evening."

A bright smile came to Maria's face. "In my next class, we are learning about botany."

"I take it that pleases you," Ewin commented.

Maria nodded enthusiastically. "Mrs. Danvers just taught us about all the plants that are poisonous if we eat them."

Ewin lifted his brow. "I would be remiss if I didn't remind you that we don't use that knowledge to poison anyone."

Maria giggled. "You're funny, Lord Ewin!" she exclaimed as she ran out of the room.

With a chuckle, he turned back towards Mrs. Finch. "It is a good thing that I consider Maria harmless."

Mrs. Finch grinned. "That she is, milord."

Isabella was watching him with a bemused look on her face.

"What is it?" he asked as he stepped closer to her.

The twinkle in her blue eyes spoke of her amazement. "I can't believe you know how to embroider."

He shrugged, attempting to downplay its significance. "It is a skill that every gentleman should master."

"But I have never met a man who knew how to embroider."

Ewin winked. "You have now."

Isabella smiled, and her whole face lit up. "You continually amaze me, Ewin."

"That is good," he paused, "I think."

"I assure you that it is a very good thing," she replied, her voice soft.

As much as he wanted to stay in this moment, he knew that Mrs. Finch was waiting to continue their tour. "Shall we tour the rest of the orphanage now?"

"I think that is a grand idea," she replied. "I think botany class sounds fascinating."

"You aren't thinking about poisoning anyone, are you, Bella?" he teased.

She laughed as he hoped she would. "Not today."

He extended his arm towards her. "I am glad to hear that."

10

WITH THE AFTERNOON SUN STREAMING INTO HER BEDCHAMBER, Isabella closed her eyes, leaned back against her chaise lounge, and listened to the comforting sounds of birds warbling outside of her window.

She heard a knock at her door and reluctantly opened her eyes.

"Come in," she called.

The door opened, and her lady's maid entered the room. While she was closing the door behind her, she announced, "Lord Ewin is here to call upon you, milady."

"Just Ewin?" she asked hopefully.

Leah shook her head. "No, he brought a companion with him, but I did not catch the name." She paused. "If you give me a moment, I could go ask Howe."

"That won't be necessary," Isabella said, rising from the chaise lounge. "It's probably another suitor that he would like me to meet."

"You sound disappointed, milady," Leah observed as she walked over to the dressing table.

Isabella took a moment to adjust the blue sash tied around her waist.

"I know I should be elated to have gentlemen vying for my attention," she said, "but I must admit that I only feel dread."

"Why is that?"

"Because Ewin keeps bringing over suitors that meet the criteria from that list I made, but they are nowhere near my ideal suitor."

Leah patted the back of the chair. "Well, before you entertain anyone, I will need to fix your hair."

Without another word, Isabella crossed the room and sat down in the chair.

Her lady's maid removed the pins from her hair and placed them on the dressing table. As Leah began to brush out her blonde tresses, she suggested, "Why not just tell Lord Ewin that you want to modify the list that you gave him?"

"I suppose that could work."

"If you don't mind me asking, what kind of qualities are you looking for in a suitor?"

The image of Ewin came into her mind, but she quickly banished that thought. He was the last person that she would ever consider as a suitor, despite the fact that he was more than qualified.

"I don't know," she replied. "Some of the requirements that I had thought were so important before, don't seem as important to me now. Furthermore, I regret placing some of the more outlandish requirements on the list."

Leah placed the brush down and began to twist her hair into a tight chignon. "I believe the best course of action is for you to create a new list for Lord Ewin. One that is sincere and forthright."

"If I did that, then I would be forced to admit that I am interested in the possibility of being courted."

"Aren't you?"

She shook her head. "I don't have any intention of selecting a suitor this Season," she replied. "I never have."

"Then, why keep up this charade?" Leah asked, placing the pins in her hair.

"Because my brother and I have a deal," she reminded her.

Leah stepped back and commented, "I can't help but notice that you appear to enjoy spending time with Lord Ewin."

"We are friends," she asserted. "That is all."

Leah lifted her brow. "You are friends now?"

"Yes," she replied. "I find that he isn't as intolerable as I once thought he was."

"I see," Leah murmured. "That is interesting."

Isabella met her lady's maid's gaze in the mirror. "Why do you say that?"

"Do you suppose you are keeping up this charade because you want to spend additional time with Lord Ewin?"

She pursed her lips before replying. "No, that is most definitely not it."

Her lady's maid shrugged her shoulders innocently. "It just appears that you might have developed some feelings for Lord Ewin, milady."

"Well, I'm afraid you are wrong," she asserted.

"I apologize for bringing it up, then," Leah said. However, her words sounded anything but apologetic.

Isabella rose from the chair. "I'd better not keep Lord Ewin waiting for much longer," she murmured, ignoring Leah's knowing smile.

As she headed towards the drawing room, Isabella let out a disbelieving huff. Her lady's maid was wrong. She may enjoy Lord Ewin's company, but that didn't mean she had any feelings for him. They were just friends.

She stepped into the drawing room and saw Ewin standing

next to a tall, handsome gentleman with a long face, sharp nose, and blond hair that was slicked down.

"I apologize for keeping you waiting," she said, walking further into the room.

Ewin turned to face her with a dashing smile on his face. "You are always worth the wait, Bella."

Her breath unexpectedly hitched at his words, but she quickly recovered. "It is most kind of you to say so, Ewin."

He held his hand out towards his companion. "Lady Isabella, may I introduce you to Lord Egerton."

Isabella turned her gaze towards Lord Egerton and dipped into a curtsey. "It is a pleasure to meet you."

Lord Egerton stared incredulously at her. "You... um... are even more beautiful than I was expecting," he stammered out. "I had heard rumors of your beauty, but they pale in comparison."

"Thank you," she replied.

He cleared his throat, loudly. "Where are my manners?" he asked before performing an exaggerated bow. "It is an honor to meet you, Lady Isabella. A true, true honor."

She smiled politely. "Likewise, Lord Egerton."

"Why would it be an honor to meet me?" Lord Egerton questioned, looking confused.

Her eyes darted towards Ewin while answering, "Because I understand you have been training under the famed architect, John Nash, for many years now."

"I have," he confirmed, straightening his shoulders.

"That is an impressive feat since Mr. Nash works so closely with the Prince Regent," she said, hoping to engage him in further conversation.

Lord Egerton bobbed his head. "That is true, as well."

Isabella waited for him to expand on his answer, but when he didn't, she asked another question. "How did you become interested in architecture?"

"I have always been interested in architecture."

She offered him a polite smile. "I believe we both share that trait, then."

His eyes grew wide. "You are interested in architecture?" he asked, his voice full of surprise.

"I am."

"I have never met a woman interested in architecture before."

"You have now," she said. "In fact, I have read many books on architecture. I am most fascinated by Palladian architecture. Andrea Palladio's work holds true to the formal classical temple architecture of the ancient Greeks and Romans. Furthermore, his symmetry and perspective are most intriguing, wouldn't you agree?"

Lord Egerton ran his hand through his slicked hair, messing it up. "Will you marry me, Lady Isabella?" he blurted out.

"Pardon?" she asked, stunned, taking a step back.

Lord Egerton's face grew bright red, and he brought his hand up to his mouth. "Did I just say that out loud?"

Ewin spoke up. "I'm afraid you did, mate."

"Forgive me, Lady Isabella," Lord Egerton rushed out. "I spoke in haste. But… I have never met a woman like you before. Most of the time when I speak of architecture, I see the bored looks on the women's faces. So, I find it utterly remarkable that a beautiful lady, such as yourself, would be interested in the subject."

Thankfully, before she could respond, a young serving girl entered the room, carrying a tray of refreshment. She placed it on the table and asked, "Would you like me to pour, milady?"

"That won't be necessary," Isabella replied.

After the servant left the room, Isabella sat on a chair in front of the table. "Please have a seat," she encouraged as she reached for the teapot. "May I pour you some tea, Lord Egerton?"

"Yes… um… I would love some," he stammered as he came

to sit across from her. "Again, I must apologize for blurting out a marriage proposal. That was poorly done on my part."

Isabella extended him a teacup. "Consider it forgotten."

"Thank you, Lady Isabella," he said, accepting the cup. "You are much kinder and more gracious than I thought you would be."

"And why is that?"

"Because you are so beautiful," he responded. "I had half expected you to be a shrew."

Isabella stilled. "Is that so?"

"But you aren't," he clarified. "You are anything but a shrew."

Reaching for the teapot, she replied, "I appreciate your candor, Lord Egerton."

He frowned. "Forgive me, Lady Isabella," he said dejectedly. "I'm afraid I am just nervous around you."

"You have no reason to be," she assured him. "We are all friends here."

Lord Egerton smiled, but it looked more like a grimace. "I appreciate your understanding."

Isabella extended a teacup towards Ewin and asked, "May I ask how you two became acquainted?"

"We were mates at Eton," Ewin revealed before taking a sip of his drink, "and we both frequent White's."

"Yes, White's is quite enjoyable," Lord Egerton declared, "but only gentlemen may enter its walls."

"I'm well aware of that fact," she said, picking up her teacup and taking a long sip.

A silence descended over them, and before it became awkward, Isabella asked, "Will either of you be attending Lady Humphries's ball tomorrow evening?"

Ewin nodded. "I plan to attend."

"As do I," Lord Egerton said.

Isabella took another sip of her tea. "What fun, then."

Lord Egerton shifted his gaze towards the pianoforte and the other musical instruments. "I can play the guitar," he announced suddenly.

"Can you now?" she replied, following his gaze to the guitar resting against the wall in the corner.

He put his empty cup back onto the tray. "I would play for you, but I get sweaty palms when I am nervous."

"I see," she said, wishing he hadn't revealed that detail about himself. "Would you like me to play?"

Lord Egerton's mouth dropped. "You can play the guitar, too?"

"Yes," she responded. "It is becoming increasingly more common for ladies to learn the guitar."

"I have heard that, but I have yet to meet a woman who could play," Lord Egerton remarked.

Isabella nodded. "I was fortunate enough to attend a finishing school that allowed us to learn how to play the guitar, assuming we were already proficient in playing the pianoforte and the harp."

"That sounds like rather a progressive finishing school," Lord Egerton commented.

"I suppose it was, and I will always look back to my days at Miss Bell's Finishing School with much fondness," she stated. "Not only did I receive an impressive education, but I forged many deep, long-lasting friendships. It helped me to become the lady that I am today."

Lord Egerton's eyes studied her as he asked, "Do you enjoy shuttlecock?"

She furrowed her brow at his abrupt change of topics. "I do."

"You are the perfect woman," Lord Egerton muttered under his breath.

Ewin placed his teacup onto the tray and rose. "And with that," he paused, "it is time for us to depart."

"Must you?" she asked, rising.

"I'm afraid so," Ewin replied. "But I intend to call on you tomorrow for our carriage ride through Hyde Park."

She smiled. "I am looking forward to it."

"As am I," he said, offering her a private smile.

Lord Egerton rose from his seat and asked, "Would you be kind enough to save me a dance tomorrow at Lady Humphries's ball?"

Isabella turned her smile towards Lord Egerton. "I would be honored."

"Thank you, Lady Isabella," he replied. "It will be a true honor to dance with you."

She watched as the men departed from the room, but Ewin stopped at the open door and smiled at her.

"You are looking especially lovely today, Bella," he said, smiling. "But then again, you are always the vision of perfection."

Isabella arched an eyebrow. "You are resorting to flattery now?"

He chuckled. "I will see you tomorrow, my dear."

As Ewin left the room, she found herself staring at the door. What did he mean by that term of endearment? Was it a slip of the tongue or did he mean something by it?

Regardless, she found she rather enjoyed it.

"At least this hackney doesn't smell as bad as the last one," Isabella commented with a smile on her face.

Ewin chuckled. "That is because I turned two other hackneys away before I hired this one. I wanted you to have a much more pleasant experience."

"Well, I appreciate it. My half-boots are not sticking to the floor in this one," she said as she lifted her right foot off the ground to prove her point.

"That is a relief," he joked, "because I specifically requested an unsticky floor."

"I'm glad," Isabella said, her smile still intact as she maintained his gaze.

His eyes were drawn to her lips, and before he could stop himself, he remarked, "You have a lovely smile, Bella."

A slight blush came to her cheeks as she murmured, "Thank you."

Isabella shifted her gaze towards the window, giving him time to admire her beautiful features and comely figure. She was dressed in a yellow gown with white embroidered flowers along the round neckline, and a straw hat sat slightly askew on her head.

He adjusted the top hat on his head before broaching on an uncomfortable subject. "I would like to apologize for Lord Egerton's behavior yesterday," he said. "I hadn't realized he would act like such a bumbling buffoon around you."

"There is no need to apologize," she responded. "I found his behavior oddly endearing."

His brow lifted in surprise. "You did?"

"I did."

"Well, then I must agree with Lord Egerton."

"In what way?"

Smirking, he replied, "You aren't very shrewish at all."

Isabella giggled, and her gloved hand flew up to cover her mouth. "That poor man," she said. "He must not spend a lot of time around ladies."

"I think his problem is that he doesn't spend a lot of time around '*beautiful*' ladies," Ewin corrected, "or around women who enjoy architecture."

"Apparently not," she said, "but he was the first to offer for me. So, he shall not be easily forgotten."

Ewin gave her a pointed look. "If I recall correctly, that was your second marriage proposal."

With a baffled look on her face, she asked, "It was?"

He nodded. "Don't you remember that I offered for you down by the stream when we were children?"

"That does not count."

His hand came up to his chest, feigning outrage. "You wound me, fair maiden."

Isabella laughed her light, airy laugh that caused his heart to soar. "Somehow, I think not," she teased.

Lowering his hand, he said, "After I proposed to you, I marched right home and told my mother that I was going to marry you one day."

"And what did your mother say?"

He leaned forward in his seat. "She said that you were a brilliant choice."

"Did she now?"

"She did," he confirmed. "But my father was not as supportive of my choice."

A line appeared between Isabella's brow. "May I ask why?"

"He told me that I was much too young to make a decision of that nature," he shared, "and encouraged me never to fall in love."

Isabella cocked her head. "He did? Why?"

" 'Because only fools fall in love'," Ewin said, quoting his father. "He informed me that love in marriages does not exist in our circles, and it is more than acceptable to seek it outside of the bonds of matrimony."

She reared back slightly. "He encouraged you to have a mistress?"

He huffed. "No, he encouraged me to have many," he replied dryly. "After all, why should I limit myself to just one?"

"What an awful thing to say to your child."

"My father has claimed to have loved many women over the

years, but I am a firm believer that the only person he has ever loved was himself."

"I'm sorry, Ewin."

He winced before sharing, "Right before I had left for Eton, I had happened upon a conversation between the upstairs maids. They were discussing how they were all fearful of my father, and they only felt relief when he was away on business."

"Did they state why?"

Ewin smiled weakly. "At the time, I naively thought they were afraid of my father because of his nasty temper." He hung his head. "However, when I came home from a holiday at Eton, I learned that two of our maids had been dismissed because they were increasing."

"I'm sorry, Ewin."

"When I confronted my father, he just smirked proudly and said those maids had been compensated fairly. He ruined those women's lives, and he felt no remorse for it."

She leaned forward and placed her hand on his sleeve, providing him with much needed comfort. "What your father did was a terrible thing, Ewin."

"Do you know what my greatest fear is?" he asked, bringing his gaze back up.

"What?"

Blinking back tears, he revealed, "That I will become like him."

Isabella didn't speak for a moment, but when she did, her words were soft but firm. "I know one thing for certain," she began, "and that is you will never be like your father."

"How can you be so sure?" he asked hopefully.

"Because," she hesitated, her eyes searching his, "you have, and always will be, an honorable gentleman."

"Do you truly mean that?"

"I do."

Ewin gave her a timid smile as he placed his hand over hers.

"Thank you for your kind words," he said. "They mean more than you will ever know."

The hackney came to a jerking stop in front of the orphanage, and Isabella withdrew her hand from his sleeve. He opened the door, exited and turned back to assist her.

She slipped her gloved hand into his and stepped out of the coach. Once her feet were on the pavement, he took her hand and placed it into the crook of his arm. As he led her towards the main door of the orphanage, she stopped and turned her attention towards a filthy street urchin who was tugging on her yellow skirt.

The young, thin girl was dressed in a brown, shapeless frock and her face was smudged with dirt.

Rather than swat the girl's hand away, Isabella crouched down to the girl's eye level. "Hello," she greeted softly. "What is your name?"

"My name is Nancy," came a soft reply.

Isabella smiled. "It is nice to meet you, Nancy," she said. "My name is Isabella."

The girl returned her smile. "Are you a lady?"

"I am."

Nancy placed a hand on her stomach and revealed, "I'm hungry."

"Are you now?" Isabella asked, placing a hand on the girl's shoulder. "When was the last time you ate?"

"Three days ago," Nancy revealed.

Isabella's brow lifted. "Good heavens, why so long ago?"

Nancy lowered her gaze towards the ground. "My momma just had a baby, and I ain't got no father. She told me to leave and not to come back until I found some work."

"Your mother told you to find some work?" Isabella repeated back in disbelief. "May I ask how old you are?"

"I'm six," she said, holding up her fingers. "But no one will hire me, and I'm awfully hungry."

"Well, we will just have to fix that, won't we?" she asked, looking up at Ewin.

Ewin nodded. "Why don't you come with us into the orphanage, and we will get you something to eat?"

Nancy's eyes grew wide. "You promise?"

"I do," he replied.

The girl clapped her hands together as Isabella rose from her crouched position. Then, Nancy slipped her dirty hand into Isabella's and looked up at her with excitement in her eyes.

Together, they walked towards the main door of the orphanage, and Ewin knocked. It was opened, and Mrs. Finch greeted them politely.

"Good afternoon, Lord Ewin and Lady Isabella." Her eyes shifted towards Nancy. "And what do we have here?"

Ewin put his hand out towards the girl and announced, "I have hired this young woman to help you around the orphanage. Her name is Nancy."

An approving smile came to Isabella's lips as she continued to hold Nancy's hand.

Mrs. Finch did not appear as pleased by his announcement, but she was gracious enough not to say anything in front of Nancy. She opened the door wide and encouraged, "Please come in."

After they were in the entry hall, Mrs. Finch perused the length of the child before saying, "I think it might be best if we feed Nancy before we put her to work."

"I agree, Mrs. Finch," Ewin replied.

Mrs. Finch held out her hand to the young girl. "Come on, now," she said. "I will escort you to the kitchen for something to eat and drink."

Nancy eagerly reached out and took her hand.

With a kind smile, Mrs. Finch started leading her towards a narrow passageway that led towards the kitchen.

Isabella turned to face him. "I would like to sponsor Nancy to be a student here at the orphanage."

He smiled. "An orphanage is not a boarding school," he reminded her, "but I will ensure that Nancy not only has a job but that she is taught some additional skills to help her find future employment."

"Thank you, Ewin," Isabella said with a bright smile on her face.

Grinning, he took a step closer to her. "I must admit that it is rather easy to please you, my dear."

"I suppose it is," she bantered back.

He eyed her for a moment. "You are a remarkable person, Bella," he said.

"In what way?"

"Sadly, I know of no other woman of your station that would have taken the time to stop and help Nancy," he replied honestly, "but you stopped and even conversed with the child. Why was that?"

"I did nothing that deserves praise," she remarked. "She clearly needed some help."

"I disagree," he said. "What you did was praiseworthy."

Isabella shook her head good-naturedly. "Why am I not surprised that you are disagreeing with me?"

He chuckled. "My apologies," he said, "I only intended to compliment you."

"Well, stop it."

"Stop complimenting you?"

The right side of her mouth curved upward. "Yes."

"As you wish, my lady."

Mrs. Finch walked back into the entry hall and revealed, "Nancy is eating some bread by the fireplace. After she is done, I will need to give her a bath."

"Thank you, Mrs. Finch," Isabella said.

The proprietress waved her hand dismissively in front of her.

"It is such a trifling thing, and we were fortunate enough to have extra bread left over from breakfast this morning," she replied. "Now, are you ready to read to the younger girls?"

"I am," Isabella replied.

Mrs. Finch smiled approvingly. "Follow me, then. The girls have been eager for your arrival. After all, it is not every day that a lady reads to them."

11

"We need to open an orphanage," Isabella declared as they rode in their coach to Lady Humphries's ball.

Everett lifted his brow as he sat across from her. "Pardon?" he asked. "Did you just say 'we need to open an orphanage'?"

She nodded decisively. "I did."

Everett frowned. "I was afraid of that," he stated. "May I ask why?"

"Because there are many children in the rookeries who could use our help."

"That may be true, but…"

Speaking over him, she pressed, "Ewin's family has an orphanage in East London."

"I am well aware of that fact," her brother said, "but orphanages take a lot of work. Who would even run it?"

"I would," she announced.

His brows drew together in a frown. "You?"

Not deterred by his response, she lifted her chin defiantly. "Yes, me. And I would do so splendidly."

"Until you got bored with it," Everett muttered.

"I beg your pardon?"

132

Everett met her gaze, challenging her. "The only thing you seem to care about is riding Maximus."

"That is not true!"

"Isn't it?" he asked. "Besides riding your horse multiple times a day, what other things occupy your time?"

"I read, draw, and practice the pianoforte, harp, and guitar," she said.

With a pointed look, he asked, "And how does that make you qualified to run an orphanage?"

She pursed her lips together, knowing that her brother had made a valid point.

"You are right," she conceded. "I'm not qualified. But I have an overwhelming desire to help. Isn't that enough?"

"No, it is not," he said. "Good intentions are not sufficient to solve these social injustices."

Isabella slumped back in her seat. "So, what you are saying is that I am powerless to help those poor children in the rookeries."

Everett's voice softened. "Instead of opening an orphanage, perhaps we could find other ways to assist them?" he suggested. "We could donate clothing, food, and other essentials to help the street urchins in need."

She perked up. "What a wonderful idea!" she exclaimed. "Then I could deliver those items to them."

"No, we would send along footmen to complete the task. It is not safe for a lady to go anywhere near the rookeries," Everett warned. "There are dangerous men in East London, and they would hurt you without hesitation."

"I can protect myself," she contended.

"No, you can't," he replied, "and for you to assume that you can is laughable."

Isabella held up the white reticule around her wrist. "I could start by carrying an overcoat pistol in my reticule," she suggested.

"Absolutely not."

Madalene spoke up from next to Everett. "It is not uncommon for ladies to carry small pistols in their reticules."

"It matters not," Everett said. "No sister of mine will carry a gun in her reticule."

"Why?" Isabella asked.

Everett gave her a frustrated look. "Because it is my duty to keep you safe."

"Is it also your duty to stifle me?"

"I am doing no such thing," he argued. "I am attempting to keep you protected from the harshness of the world."

"What if I don't want to be protected anymore?" she asked, crossing her arms over her chest.

"Until you are married, it is my right to take care of you," her brother explained, his voice rising. "And I intend to protect you, even from yourself."

She arched an eyebrow. "When will you see that I am not a little girl anymore?"

"It is not about that," he said with a shake of his head.

"Then what is this about?"

"You live in a privileged world, Isabella. Very little vexes you or annoys you," he stated. "You can't possibly understand the plight of the children who live in the rookeries."

"But shouldn't we help them?"

Everett adjusted his white cravat. "Even your responses are naïve," he said. "What could one person do to help all those children?"

"If I can only help one child, it would be worth the effort," she replied firmly. "But I can do more than what society expects from me; than what *you* expect from me."

He stared at her for a long moment before he let out a deep sigh.

"Fine," he conceded. "Perhaps later, we could discuss setting up a foundation to help some of those children." He held up his hand. "It wouldn't be very grand, mind you, but at least it would be something."

"Thank you, Everett," she responded.

"But I would expect you to oversee it."

Isabella bobbed her head. "Gladly."

Everett smiled indulgently at her. "You will discover that I am not a complete tyrant."

"I never thought you were."

He chuckled. "Liar."

The coach came to a stop outside of a three-level, white townhouse with columns framing the front door. The coach door opened, and Everett exited first.

After he assisted the ladies as they stepped out, he extended an arm towards each of them and led them inside the townhouse. They had just stepped into the ballroom when they were greeted by Lord and Lady Humphries.

The short earl with thinning hair smiled kindly at them. "It is a pleasure to see you this evening, Lord Northampton."

Everett bowed. "The pleasure is all mine, Lord Humphries," he replied, gesturing towards them. "Please allow me to introduce you to my lovely wife, Lady Northampton, and my sister, Lady Isabella."

Lady Humphries's eyes perused her white silk gown with its green sash tied around her waist. "You are a remarkably beautiful young woman, Lady Isabella," she remarked. "I can see why you are so popular this Season."

"That is kind of you to say, my lady," she replied, dropping into a curtsey.

Lady Humphries nodded in approval. "I hope you have an enjoyable evening," she said before turning towards her next guest in line.

As they stepped further into the rectangular-shaped ballroom, Isabella's eyes landed on the two large ornate chandeliers hanging from the ceiling mural. The ivory papered walls had golden leaf accents running the length of them, and the dance floor had been chalked with Lord Humphries crest.

"This ballroom is exquisite," she acknowledged.

Everett nodded. "I agree," he replied as he led them towards one of the far corners of the ballroom, where the crowds had thinned out.

"This is a *crush*," Madalene commented.

Isabella nodded her agreement. "Mother informed me that Lady Humphries's balls are immensely popular, and invitations are highly coveted amongst the *ton*."

The room grew silent as the first dance was announced, and she watched as the men in the room moved to secure their dance partners. Lord Egerton emerged from the crowd, his eyes scanning the room. She all but expected to be asked to dance by him, but his eyes didn't land on her. Instead, his gaze became fixed on the dark-haired beauty, Lady Rebecca Galpin, who was standing next to three finely dressed young women. They all had their heads down, fans out, and they were conversing with one another.

Isabella watched as Lord Egerton approached Lady Rebecca with a determined stride. He stopped to the side of her and opened his mouth to speak. But before he was even able to utter a word, Lady Rebecca shifted her back towards him.

Madalene stepped closer to her and asked, "Did Lady Rebecca just give that gentleman the cut direct?"

"She did," Isabella murmured. "What an awful thing to do to such a nice man."

Lord Egerton's face turned bright red, and he quickly turned away from Lady Rebecca. All eyes were on Lord Egerton as he walked away, his shoulders slumped. Feeling compelled to act, and not caring about the repercussions of her actions, she swiftly closed the distance between her and Lord Egerton.

"I have come to collect the dance that you promised," she said boldly.

A look of great relief flashed on Lord Egerton's face. "Gladly," he responded swiftly. "But I must ask, is this because you saw what just transpired between me and Lady Rebecca?"

"It is, and I wanted you to know that it was wrong of Lady Rebecca to treat you so unjustly," she replied as she noticed their conversation was starting to garner some attention. "Perhaps it would be best if we just danced a set and continued this conversation later."

Lord Egerton nodded. "I would agree, Lady Isabella." He extended his arm towards her. "And thank you." His words were spoken with sincere gratitude.

"You are welcome," she said, smiling over at him.

As they lined up to dance the cotillion, Isabella couldn't help but notice Ewin was standing near the doorway, watching her intently. Their eyes met across the crowded room, and it felt like time stood still. With a hint of a smile on his lips, he tipped his head at her, and it was evident to her what he was trying to convey. *He was proud of her.*

And that made her feel oddly content.

Ewin found his heart was bursting with pride at the way Isabella handled the situation with Lord Egerton. He had witnessed Lady Rebecca giving Lord Egerton the cut direct, and he wasn't entirely surprised by her behavior. Lady Rebecca had just confirmed what he already knew that she was petty and cruel.

He couldn't seem to take his eyes off Isabella as she danced with Lord Egerton. It was true that she was an incomparable beauty, but she also had a kind and loving heart, which was an anomaly amongst the *ton*. She was a beautiful person, inside and out. That was just one of the many things he loved about her.

Now, he just had to convince her to allow him to court her, which was proving to be much more difficult than he had anticipated. She almost seemed immune to his charms.

His friend's voice broke through his musings. "You may want to stop staring so intently at Lady Isabella, or everyone in the room will see right through you," Oliver advised, coming to stand next to him.

Ewin turned to face him. "Is it that obvious?"

"I'm afraid so, mate," Oliver replied, taking a sip of his drink. "Perhaps you should shift your attention towards another girl this evening."

"Not interested," he said firmly.

Oliver chuckled. "Why am I not surprised?"

Glancing over at the open door, he asked, "Why are you not playing games in the card room?"

"I was on my way to the card room, but I got distracted by the enchanting face of Miss Phoebe," Oliver revealed, smirking. "But do not fret, I intend to spend most of the night gambling."

"What a relief," Ewin joked. "I was worried that you might have changed your ways for the better."

"No, I am happy with my life." Oliver's eyes shifted towards Isabella. "She looks especially lovely tonight."

"That she does."

Bringing his gaze back, Oliver asked, "When are you going to offer for her?"

Ewin winced slightly. "She isn't ready yet."

"No?"

"She still considers me just a friend," he replied.

Oliver took a sip of his drink before saying, "Has she shown any interest in the suitors you have introduced her to?"

He shook his head. "None."

"That is a good sign for you."

"Perhaps."

Oliver placed his hand on his shoulder. "Just don't take too long to make your move, or you risk losing her."

"That is what I am afraid of."

Dropping his hand, Oliver said, "Don't give up hope yet. From what I have witnessed, I suspect that she has feelings for you."

Hope filled his heart. "Do you truly mean it?"

"I do," Oliver replied. "I have observed that her eyes always light up when they land on you."

"That bodes well for me."

Oliver tossed back the rest of his drink and placed the glass on the tray of a passing servant. "Now, if you will excuse me, I am needed in the card room," he announced before he turned and left the ballroom.

After the orchestra played the last note of the cotillion, Ewin watched as Lord Egerton escorted Isabella off the dance floor. He moved to intercept them when his brother, George, stepped in front of him, blocking his path.

"Hello, brother," George said snidely.

He lifted his brow. "What do you want?"

"Nothing, but the pleasure of talking to my brother."

Ewin huffed. "I truly doubt that."

"I see that Lady Rebecca is here," George commented. "Have you spoken to your betrothed yet?"

"No, I have not, nor do I intend to."

"That is a shame."

"Is it?" he asked. "Because, as I have informed you and Father on multiple occasions, I have no intention of pursuing Lady Rebecca."

George smacked his lips together. "Lady Rebecca is beautiful, is she not?" he questioned. "Almost as beautiful as Lady Isabella."

Ewin knew his brother was baiting him, so he didn't bother responding to his comment. "If you will excuse me..."

George put his hand up, stilling his excuse. "Before you go, I have a message from Mother."

Now his brother had his attention. "What did she say?"

A sad look came into George's eyes as he reached into his jacket pocket and pulled out a folded piece of paper. "She wrote you a letter," he said, holding it up.

Ewin accepted the paper. "Thank you," he acknowledged, placing it into the pocket of his waistcoat.

George stood there for a moment before saying, "I just don't understand why you won't marry the chit."

"I believe I sufficiently explained my reasons before," he replied as he watched Isabella being reunited with her brother, Everett.

His brother followed his gaze and asked, "It is because of Lady Isabella, isn't it?"

"That is none of your concern."

George's words grew condescending. "You may fancy yourself in love now, but will she return your affection when you can't afford to give her the lifestyle that she deserves?"

Ewin's eyes snapped towards his brother. "My life does not concern you."

"But it does," George retorted. "If you marry Lady Rebecca, then some of Father's debts would be wiped clean, which affects me greatly as the heir."

"I'm truly sorry, but that does not alter my decision."

George narrowed his eyes. "You would conscientiously subject Mother to slanderous gossip about Father?"

"You are the heir, not me," he stated dryly. "I am merely the second son, the spare, and it is not my duty to save our family from Father's mistakes."

Taking a step closer to him, George said, "You are just as stubborn as Father is."

"And that is where our similarities end," Ewin contended as

he brushed past him, eager to be finished with this infuriating conversation.

As he approached Isabella, he forced a smile, hoping it was somewhat convincing. He saw the moment that she saw him, because her eyes lit up and a smile came to her face.

"Lord Ewin," she greeted. "I am so pleased to see you this evening."

He stopped in front of her, his smile turning genuine. Just being near her made him immensely happy.

"Not that I am complaining, but may I ask why?" he asked.

"Everett and I are going to set up a foundation to help the children in the rookeries," she announced proudly.

"Is that so?" he asked, glancing over at Everett.

Everett nodded. "It is true," he replied, "and Isabella will oversee it."

"But she is a woman," he jested.

Isabella placed her hands on her hips. "That was a rather offensive thing for you to say."

"My apologies. I was just teasing you," he assured her. "You are the most clever woman I know."

Lowering her hands to her sides, Isabella offered him a private smile. "As apologies go, that wasn't the worst one that I have heard."

Ewin chuckled. "That is a relief," he said as he heard the waltz being announced.

Holding out his gloved hand, he asked, "Would you care to dance, Bella?"

She looked at his proffered hand before saying, "But this is the waltz."

"I am well aware of that fact," he said, amused by her response.

Looking entirely unsure of herself, she replied, "I have never danced the waltz before, at least not with a man."

"Then I must assume you learned how to dance the waltz at finishing school."

She nodded, still staring at his hand.

He wiggled his fingers. "Trust me, Bella," he murmured. "I promise it will be enjoyable."

Hesitantly, she brought her hand up and accepted his hand. "What if I step on your feet and hurt you terribly?"

"I will take my chances," he said before he started leading her to the dance floor.

They stopped and turned to face one another. Ewin took her hand, gently encompassing it and held it up as he slipped his left hand onto her waist. When he heard her inhale sharply at his touch, he realized that she might not be as impenetrable to his charms as he'd led himself to believe.

As they began dancing, he couldn't help but notice that she remained stiff in his arms. He pulled her closer and whispered, "Is my touch so repulsive to you?"

"Why would you think that?" she asked in a hushed voice, keeping her gaze lowered.

"Because I can't help but notice you are incredibly tense."

A line appeared between her brows as she said, "That is because I am trying to concentrate on the dance."

"You don't need to worry about that," he assured her.

She brought her gaze up. "And why is that?"

"Because I am a superb dancer."

"I just don't want to step on your feet."

"Do not fret about that," he remarked. "Just relax in my arms and allow me to lead you."

Ewin felt the moment that Isabella surrendered to his touch, and he quickly tightened his hold around her. Together, they danced the waltz in graceful harmony, and he recognized how perfectly Isabella fit in his arms.

As the orchestra wound down, Isabella met his gaze and smiled. "That was quite pleasurable."

"I knew you would enjoy it."

"You are much more fun to dance with than Charlotte," she joked.

He grinned. "I am glad to hear that."

Isabella's eyes twinkled with merriment. "Perhaps next time, you will let me lead," she teased. "I was quite proficient at it when we waltzed at school."

He chuckled. "I dare say that would cause quite the scandal."

The music came to an end, and he reluctantly dropped his arms and stepped back with a little bow. "Thank you for dancing with me."

She curtsied. "You are most kindly welcome."

"I'd better return you to your brother so you can secure your next dance partner," he said, offering his arm to her.

A slight pout came to her lips. "I would rather retain you as my dance partner all evening."

At her bold admission, Ewin turned to look at her in surprise and saw a deep blush forming on her cheeks.

"What I meant was… uh… that I enjoyed dancing with you," she stammered out. "I never meant to imply…" She closed her eyes.

Taking pity on her, he placed his hand over hers and said, "I know what you meant, Bella."

"Do you?" she asked, opening her eyes.

He gave her a reassuring smile. "I do, and I feel the same way."

"Thank you, Ewin," she breathed out, the relief evident in her tone. "You are a good friend."

Friend.

No, he didn't want to be her friend! He wanted Isabella as his wife. Blast it. His plan wasn't working, and he was running out of time.

❧ 12 ❧

DRESSED IN HER RIDING HABIT, ISABELLA GRACEFULLY descended the stairs and headed towards the dining room. She had just stepped into the room when she spotted her mother sitting at the table.

"Mother!" she exclaimed. "What a pleasant surprise!"

Mary shifted in her chair to face her. "I was tired of eating alone in my bedchamber, so I decided I would take my breakfast in the dining room this morning."

Everett spoke up from the head of the table, looking over the top of a morning newspaper in his hands. "And we are most thankful for that."

Isabella kissed her mother on her cheek. "I know that I am," she said. "I love nothing more than seeing you out of bed."

"How was the ball last night?" her mother asked.

"It was uneventful," Isabella replied vaguely as she stepped over to the buffet table.

"Is that so?" Mary questioned.

Isabella started filling her plate with food and opened her mouth to reply, but Everett answered first.

"Our Isabella was the belle of the ball last night. Men were practically lined up to speak to her."

Her mother smiled. "That does not surprise me in the least."

"I was hardly the belle of the ball, and Everett's account is grossly exaggerated," she contested as she sat down next to her mother. "But I was fortunate enough to secure dance partners for every set."

Mary clapped her hands together. "What wonderful news," she declared. "Did you happen to favor one of your dance partners?"

Ewin.

She shook her head. "No, I did not," she lied.

Her mother eyed her for a long moment before asking, "Who was your dance partner for the waltz?"

"Ewin," she replied, reaching for her white linen napkin.

"Interesting," Mary muttered.

"There is nothing interesting about it," she said as she placed her napkin on her lap. "He was gracious enough to ask me to dance, and I accepted. We danced the waltz, and then we went our separate ways."

"The waltz is the most romantic of all the dances," her mother commented.

"Ewin and I are friends, nothing more," Isabella insisted, reaching for her fork.

"If you say so," Mary responded.

"I do."

Everett folded the newspaper and placed it on the table. "Isabella does have some exciting news to share."

Mary turned towards her with an expectant look on her face. "Is that so?"

Isabella smiled, set her fork down and straightened her shoulders. "Everett and I are starting a foundation to help the children in the rookeries," she announced.

"You are?" Mary asked, shifting her gaze between them. "That seems like quite the undertaking."

Everett nodded. "Isabella and I discussed it at great length this morning on our ride, and we are working on a plan that will execute Isabella's vision."

Mary brought her gaze to meet Isabella's. "Your vision?"

"Yes, my heart aches for the little children in the rookeries who are going without so much," she replied. "I want to help them, in any way that I can."

"That is most gracious of you," her mother remarked.

"It is the least I can do," Isabella said. "After all, I have been so blessed. It is time for me to start helping other people."

Her mother reached her hand out and tenderly placed it over hers. "I have never been more proud of you than I am right now, my dear."

"Thank you, Mother, but I haven't done anything yet," Isabella insisted.

"But you will accomplish great things," Mary said.

She was about to return to eating her breakfast when Howe stepped into the room, holding a bouquet of red roses in his hand. His gaze landed on her.

"Five bouquets of flowers have been delivered for you, milady," he informed her.

"Did you say five?" she asked in disbelief.

He nodded as two footmen walked into the room. Both were holding a bouquet in each hand. "Would you care to read the cards?" the butler asked.

"I would."

Howe approached her and extended her a card. "This card was attached to the red roses, milady."

"Thank you." She unfolded the note and was pleasantly surprised to see that the card was from Ewin. She read, " '*Your beauty outshines even the most perfect rose. Thank you for making the waltz so memorable*'."

A FOOLISH GAME: A REGENCY ROMANCE

"Who were the roses from?" her mother asked.

She folded the note and slipped it into the pocket of her riding habit. "They were from Ewin," she remarked nonchalantly.

"Ewin?" her mother repeated. "That was kind of him."

"It was, wasn't it?"

Howe extended her the other cards. "Here are the other cards, milady."

Isabella took a moment to read each card before placing them onto the table and picking up her fork.

Everett looked at her curiously. "May I ask who else sent flowers?"

"Lord Egerton, Lord Harold, Mr. Fernside, and Mr. Gibbons," she shared.

"Were those the men that you danced with last night?" her mother inquired.

She nodded. "They were."

Her mother smiled in approval. "It is considered good manners to send flowers to a young woman whom you have danced with the night before," she shared. "Most likely, all those gentlemen will call on you today, in hopes of securing your affections."

Isabella stifled a groan. "That sounds dreadful," she complained.

"I thought you said you enjoyed the ball last night?" Mary asked.

"I did," she replied, "but that doesn't mean I want to entertain them today."

Everett chuckled. "My poor sister," he joked. "What a hard plight you must endure. To be loved by all."

Ignoring her brother, she started eating her breakfast when Howe stepped back into the room. "Lord Harold is here to call upon you, milady," he declared. "Are you available for callers?"

"No," she rushed to answer.

Her mother laughed. "Of course, she is," she said. "Will you show Lord Harold to the drawing room and inform him that she will be along shortly?"

Howe bowed. "Yes, milady."

Turning to face her, Mary instructed, "You need to run along and change into a more appropriate gown to entertain your guest."

"Do I?" she asked, placing her fork down. "But I have barely eaten."

Mary smiled encouragingly at her. "You must not keep your suitor waiting."

"But I don't want Lord Harold as a suitor."

Everett spoke up. "Why ever not?" he asked. "He is rich, handsome, the second son of a marquess, and the catch of the Season."

Removing the napkin from her lap, she placed it on the table. "He is also rather arrogant," she shared. "When we did speak, he only spoke of himself."

"Have patience with the poor man," Everett encouraged. "He may have just been nervous around you."

"I doubt that." Isabella rose from her chair. "I assure you that it would have been much simpler if I had sent him away."

Isabella exited the dining room and hurried up the stairs. She arrived at her bedchamber and flung open the door, startling her lady's maid.

"Good heavens," Leah exclaimed, bringing a hand to her chest. "You scared me."

"My apologies," she said, closing the door behind her. "I need to change into a gown."

"Are you going into Town?"

She shook her head. "No, Lord Harold is here to call upon me."

Leah walked over to the armoire, pulled out a pale green

afternoon gown, and held it up for her inspection. "Would this suffice?"

"It would," she replied.

A short time later, she was dressed appropriately with her hair elaborately coiffed. She walked down the steps and stopped at the bouquet of red roses sitting on a table in the entry hall. She leaned in and took a deep breath, inhaling the sweet scent.

The image of Ewin came to her mind, bringing a smile to her face. It had been so thoughtful of him to send red roses. Hopefully, he would come to call today so she could properly thank him.

Isabella had just taken a step back from the roses when Howe approached her, informing her, "Besides Lord Harold, Lord Egerton, Mr. Fernside, and Mr. Gibbons are all waiting for you in the drawing room."

"There are four gentlemen in the drawing room?" she asked, her voice squeaking a little. "To see me?"

Howe nodded. "Yes, milady, and I have already ordered some refreshment to be sent up."

"Wonderful," she muttered.

Her usual stoic butler cracked a smile. "I wish you luck, milady."

"Thank you," she replied. "I am going to need it."

As she stepped into the room, she saw the four gentlemen standing around, staring intently at one another.

"Gentlemen," she started, drawing their attention, "what a pleasant surprise."

Lord Harold met her gaze, and she took only a moment to admire his dark hair and square jaw. "I hope we did not call upon you too early," he said.

"Not at all," she replied. "I have been up for hours."

"You have?" Lord Harold asked in surprise.

She nodded, coming to a stop in the center of the room. "My

brother, Everett, and I enjoy riding through Hyde Park in the early morning hours."

Lord Harold nodded his approval. "I must agree with you. I also enjoy riding in the mornings," he shared. "Perhaps I could join you one day soon."

"You are more than welcome to," she responded, "but you will need to speak to my brother concerning it."

A smile came to Lord Harold's lips. "I look forward to it."

Mr. Fernside ran his hand through his blond hair. "I enjoy riding, as well," he exclaimed in an overeager tone.

Isabella smiled graciously at him. "Then you shall have to join us, too," she invited, pretending not to notice that Lord Harold was staring daggers at Mr. Fernside.

Lord Egerton approached her. "Would you be interested in going on a carriage ride with me this afternoon?" he asked, his tone hopeful.

She could see the line of sweat forming on his forehead.

Poor Lord Egerton, she thought. At least he didn't blurt out a marriage proposal again.

Clasping her hands in front of her, she replied, "I suppose I could make time for that, Lord Egerton."

Before the short, heavyset Mr. Gibbons could open his mouth, a maid walked into the room with a serving tray in her hands. She placed the tray down on the table and moved to sit in the corner of the room.

Isabella sat in front of the table and poured five cups of tea. As she held them out, each gentleman accepted one and blissful silence descended over the room. She slowly sipped her tea, attempting to think of a way to rid herself of these gentlemen without appearing to be rude.

Mr. Gibbons lowered his cup and said, "It is a fine day that we are having, is it not?"

"I agree with you," she replied with a bob of her head. "Most fine, indeed."

Lord Harold leaned forward and placed his empty teacup onto the tray. "Would it be too presumptuous to ask you to play the pianoforte for us?"

Lord Egerton interjected, "What if you play the guitar, instead?"

"Perhaps I could play both?" She placed her teacup on the table and walked over to the pianoforte. "I believe I shall start with Mozart."

As she reached for the sheets of music, Isabella wished, and not for the first time, that Ewin had come to call. How did he have the uncanny ability to make everything seem so much more enjoyable?

<hr />

"Four blasted suitors!" Ewin mumbled under his breath as he glanced into the drawing room. The four men were sitting around Isabella as she played the guitar, and they all had enamored expressions on their faces.

When he'd arrived, he had been eager to see Isabella, but Howe had informed him that four gentlemen had already come to call. *Four.* But, frankly, the only one that he perceived as a threat was Lord Harold. Women had started carrying around portrait miniatures of him, and it was rumored that he was looking for a wife this Season.

Well, it wouldn't be Isabella. He was sure of that.

Everett's amused voice came from behind him. "Do you intend to go into the drawing room and make your presence known, or are you going to continue hiding out in the entry hall?"

"I am not hiding," he contended.

"No?" Everett asked. "Dillydallying, perhaps?"

"I am not dillydallying, either."

Everett gave him a knowing look. "Then, pray tell, what is it exactly that you are doing out here?"

"I'm ensuring that Isabella is properly chaperoned," he attempted.

"Is that so?" his friend said in a tone that implied he didn't believe him.

He nodded, tugging down on his blue waistcoat. "It is."

Everett smirked. "Well, did you happen to notice that a maid is sitting inside of the drawing room, protecting her reputation?"

Wincing, he muttered, "I hadn't noticed."

Glancing into the drawing room, Everett commented, "I can see why. It is rather crowded in there."

"I agree," he remarked.

Everett brought his gaze back to his. "Perhaps it might be best if you come have a drink with Nicholas and me."

"Nicholas is here?"

"He arrived shortly before you did." Everett started walking backwards. "You can join us, or you can continue doing whatever it is that you are doing out here," he jested before spinning on his heel and heading towards his study.

Shifting his gaze towards Isabella, he watched her for a moment before he hurried and caught up to Everett.

As he stepped into Everett's study, he saw Nicholas sitting on a settee, staring absentmindedly out the window. A glass was in his right hand, but it was resting on his leg, apparently forgotten.

"Is Nicholas all right?" Ewin asked in concern.

Everett nodded as he crossed the room to the drink cart. "He is just exhausted from being up most of the night with their son."

"Why was it necessary for him to help with the baby?" he asked.

Picking up the decanter, Everett explained, "Apparently, he can't sleep when Penelope is tending to the baby in their bedchamber."

"Why not just employ a nursemaid?"

Nicholas finally joined in on their conversation. "Why, indeed?" he asked. "I have argued this point incessantly, but Penelope doesn't think we require a nursemaid."

"Why not just hire one yourself?" Ewin inquired.

Nicholas's brow shot up, drawing attention to the bags under his eyes. "And risk Penelope's wrath?" he asked. "No, thank you. I am much smarter than that."

"You could always sleep in a separate bedchamber," he suggested.

Nicholas humphed. "That wouldn't matter," he said. "Have you heard the wail of an infant?"

"I have not," he confirmed.

"It seems to penetrate every corner of our townhouse, and every fiber of your being," Nicholas shared. "You can't escape from it, no matter how hard you try."

"Surely, you jest?" Ewin questioned.

"The only time I get some peace is when Jacob is sleeping," Nicholas said, "but then I am worried he is being too quiet, and I wonder if he is still breathing. So, I am constantly getting up to check on him."

Everett poured two glasses of brandy and placed the stopper back into the decanter. "Because of Nicholas's plight, I have encouraged Madalene to hire a nursemaid before the baby comes."

Nicholas held his drink up. "Smart man," he declared. "I hadn't considered how much time was consumed with an infant at home." He took a sip of his drink. "But Penelope is adamant that we don't need any help raising our son, even though I contend that fighting a bloody war is less work than tending to a baby."

"I see that you are prone to exaggeration," Everett teased.

Nicholas shook his head slowly. "Sadly, I assure you that I am not," he said. "Just sleep now as much as you can before your baby arrives."

Everett chuckled as he extended a glass towards Ewin.

"Thank you," Ewin acknowledged.

With a nod, Everett sat down next to Nicholas on the settee. "Have you made any progress with Isabella?" he asked with a pointed look.

He stilled. Did Everett know that he was attempting to woo Isabella? Hesitantly, he asked, "Pardon?"

Everett took a sip of his drink before saying, "Has Isabella begun to show favor towards any of the potential suitors that you have paraded in front of her?"

"Not yet."

With a frown, Everett said, "That is disconcerting."

"These things take time," Ewin reassured him.

"Can you hurry it along?"

Ewin shook his head. "When you are dealing with matters of the heart, you have to let these things run their course. You can't rush them."

Everett looked at him with a hopeful expression. "But you still believe she will pick a suitor by the end of the Season?"

"I do."

"Good," Everett said with a bob of his head. "That pleases me immensely."

Ewin walked over and sat in an upholstered armchair across from his friends. "Did I mention that my solicitor has found an estate for me to purchase?"

"No, you failed to mention that fact," Everett said, glancing down at his drink.

"It is a modest estate in a hamlet near a coastal village in Kent," he shared.

"Have you had a chance to tour the property?" Nicholas asked, placing his nearly full glass onto a side table.

"No, I haven't," he admitted. "But I intend to."

Nicholas bobbed his head in approval. "Never buy a property sight unseen."

"I agree, which is why I intend to ride out tomorrow to visit the property," he said.

Isabella's stunned voice came from the doorway. "You are leaving?"

He quickly rose and turned to face her.

"I will only be gone for a few days," he assured her. "Then, I will be back to introduce you to more eligible suitors, if you so desire." He smiled his most charming smile.

A frown came to her lips. "Why didn't you tell me that you were leaving?"

"Frankly, I didn't think it would matter to you," he replied with a slight shrug of his shoulders.

Something flashed in Isabella's eyes, and it was that something that caused him pause. He couldn't seem to decipher it.

"You are right, of course," she said curtly. "I hope you have a safe journey."

Before he had the opportunity to reply, she spun around and departed, not sparing him another glance.

Ewin stared at the empty doorway, unsure of what he should do. Why was Isabella acting so irrationally?

Nicholas cleared his throat. "Aren't you going after her?"

"I don't think she wants me to," he replied, turning to face them.

Everett mumbled something under his breath before saying, "Trust me. All women want you to go after them."

"They do?"

Everett waved towards the door. "Just go after her, you imbecile. We can discuss this later."

Needing no further encouragement, he rushed out the door and into the entry hall. He saw Isabella as she was hurrying up the stairs towards the second level.

"Wait, Bella," he urged, his voice echoing through the entry hall.

She stopped on the stairs but kept her gaze straight ahead. "What do you want, Ewin?"

"May I speak to you?"

"You are speaking to me," she remarked dryly.

Ewin stepped closer to the stairs. "Alone, please?"

Isabella didn't speak for a few moments, and he feared that she was going to refuse his request. Fortunately, she turned back around and started to descend the stairs.

"We can speak freely in the drawing room," she said, brushing past him.

He followed her into the drawing room, and she turned to face him with an expectant look on her face. "What would you like to discuss with me?"

This is not starting well, he thought. "I wanted to apologize for not informing you earlier of my plans to leave London."

"You don't owe me an apology," she replied, crossing her arms over her chest.

"But..." His voice trailed off, attempting to formulate his next words carefully. "I thought you were upset with me for leaving."

She started tapping her foot on the carpet. "Why would you think that?"

Realization dawned. He now knew why she was acting so irrationally, and he worked hard to stifle his smile. But he failed miserably. "You are going to miss me, aren't you?"

"No," she said, shaking her head vehemently. "That is most definitely not it."

His smile grew. "If you say so."

"I do," she replied, jutting out her chin.

Ewin took a step closer to her, and she now had to tilt her head to look up at him. "It is all right to admit it, Bella."

"Could I ever truly miss a thorn in my side?" she asked, arching her eyebrow.

Leaning closer, he whispered next to her ear, "I will miss you, too."

He heard her swift intake of air, pleasing him immensely. He stepped back and clasped his hands behind his back, hoping to suppress the undying desire to pull her into his arms.

"I have been considering purchasing an estate, and my solicitor has found one that meets my specific criteria," he explained.

"Which is?"

He smiled. "Affordable."

"Oh," she murmured, her eyes still downcast.

"I shall depart tomorrow and be back in three days' time," he explained.

In a rushed voice, Isabella started, "You don't owe me an explanation..."

He spoke over her. "But I do," he asserted. "After all, friends are forthright and honest with each other. Wouldn't you agree?"

"I do," she muttered.

"I would have told you earlier, but I saw you entertaining four gentlemen. They seemed to enjoy listening to you play your guitar," he teased.

"You saw that?"

He nodded. "I did, and I must agree with Lord Harold." He paused before adding, "You play the guitar splendidly."

"Thank you."

Turning his gaze towards the window, he asked, "If you are not opposed, would you care to take a turn around your gardens with me?"

A twinkle came to her eyes, but her words came out hesitant. "I suppose I could make the time."

"That is most gracious of you," he responded, amused by her reluctant tone, "and not at all shrewish."

Isabella laughed as he'd hoped, and the sound warmed his heart. That was a sound he knew he would never tire of.

❧ 13 ❧

ISABELLA CLASPED HER HANDS IN FRONT OF HER AS THEY
walked towards the rear of the townhouse. She consciously
avoided looking over at Ewin. Quite frankly, she was embar-
rassed that she had acted so irrationally in front of him. What
had she been thinking? When she overheard him saying that he
was leaving, she had felt a surge of panic come over her, something she had never experienced before. And she wasn't sure
why. It wasn't as if they had an understanding between them.
They were just friends, nothing more. But if that was the case,
then why was she so afraid of him leaving?

Perhaps, just possibly, she did harbor some feelings for him,
she admitted reluctantly to herself. But that didn't mean she
should act upon them. She didn't dare sacrifice her friendship
with Ewin. He may flirt with her, but that didn't mean he
returned her affections. Nor did she want him to. She was happy
with the way things were with him, and she didn't want to
change it. She didn't want to go back to a time when Ewin
wasn't in her life.

"The weather is most agreeable today. Is it not?" Ewin asked
as they stepped onto the gravel footpath.

"It is."

Ewin glanced over at her. "Should we discuss the state of the gardens, as well?" he asked with mirth in his voice. "Or should I ask how your family is faring?"

She offered him a timid smile. "My apologies, I'm afraid I was woolgathering."

"Ah," he said, "that is a polite way of saying that you're bored with me."

She stopped and turned to face him. "That is not at all what I am saying, Ewin. Please do not take offense when none was intended."

"I know," he replied, his tone softening. "I was just teasing."

"Oh."

He watched her closely, and she couldn't help but admire his handsome face. She even had the strangest desire to reach out and run her fingers along his square jawline.

"Is everything all right, Bella?" he asked.

Realizing that she had been caught staring, she turned her attention towards the gardens and replied, "Yes, of course it is."

"You just don't seem to be yourself today."

Feeling his gaze still upon her, she rushed to assure him, "I'm perfectly fine."

"I shall take you at your word, then."

"As well you should."

Ewin's gaze shifted towards the red roses. "I wish I had an interesting joke or anecdote about roses like Mr. Gillingham did."

"Mr. Gillingham did have an extensive knowledge of flowers," she said as she walked over to the rose bushes.

"That he did."

Isabella ran her hand down the stem of a red rose, being mindful of the thorns. "Did you know that a thorn protects the rose from an unwanted predator?"

"I did," Ewin replied, coming to stand next to her.

Her fingers navigated towards the soft rose petals. "It is a shame that something so beautiful needs to keep itself protected from the world."

"I think that is wise."

"Do you?"

Instead of answering her question, Ewin replied, "Every rose has a thorn, but not every thorn bush has a rose."

"Well, it's not an anecdote, but you did have an interesting maxim, after all," she teased.

He chuckled. "I suppose I did."

Leaning closer, Isabella took a moment to smell the roses before saying, "I find that I can relate to the rose."

Eyeing her curiously, he asked, "In what way?"

She brought her hand up and gently touched a thorn. "Sometimes, the only way to protect yourself is by creating your own thorns," she admitted softly.

Ewin took a step closer to her. "Who hurt you, Bella?" he prodded gently, but she didn't miss the anger in his words.

Burning tears came to her eyes, but she furiously blinked them away. "No one hurt me, per se."

"Then who did they hurt?"

Withdrawing her hand, she brought it back down to her side. "My mother was the one who was hurt."

"Who hurt your mother?"

Bringing her gaze back up to meet his, she shared, "My father hurt her, destroyed her, really."

"In what way?" Ewin prodded.

"He took her spirit, and he slowly chipped away at it until she lost who she was," Isabella said. "You see, a thorn protects a rose, but there was nothing to protect my mother's heart from his harsh words."

"How do you know this?"

Isabella bit her lower lip. "When I was younger, I used to hear my mother crying in her bedchamber from down the hall, but she would always stop the moment I knocked on the door," she revealed. "She would never cry in front of me."

"Were your parents not a love match?"

"Heavens, no!" she exclaimed. "My parents' marriage was arranged at a young age, but neither one realized how ill-suited they were for each other until they were already wed. Then, it was too late."

Resuming her walk along the path, Isabella shared, "My mother told me that she was a lot like me when she was younger, but she was forced to change when she married my father."

"Change how?"

Isabella sighed. "My father was quite a demanding man, at least when he was around," she remarked. "He wasn't entirely sure what to do with me, but he did at least try to make an attempt with me, whereas he spent most of his time and energy on berating my mother and brothers."

Ewin glanced her way, his gaze mournful. "That sounds awful."

"It was," she responded. "I later learned that my father used to parade around Society with his mistress to taunt my mother. He had no shame or qualms about hurting her."

With a clenched jaw, Ewin remarked, "What a terrible thing to do."

"What's worse is that there was nothing my mother could do to alleviate the situation," she said. "She was forced to endure the pain and humiliation until my father died."

"What your father did was unfair to your entire family, not just your mother."

Stopping short, she turned to face him. "That is why I don't ever want to marry," she confessed. "It took years after my father's death before my mother even began to recover."

Ewin's face softened. "Not every marriage is like theirs."

"That may be true, but I won't take the risk that I will forever be trapped in a loveless marriage."

"Then don't be."

She huffed disbelievingly. "If only it were that easy."

Ewin reached out and placed a hand on her shoulder. "It can be," he asserted, his greyish-hazel eyes imploring hers.

"I believe everyone hides a part of themselves from other people, even from the ones that they love the most," she shared. "It protects you from becoming too vulnerable."

"The only way to fall in love is to allow yourself to become vulnerable," he pressed.

She shook her head. "Then it is not worth the risk," she murmured. "I won't take the chance of getting hurt."

"Oh, Bella," Ewin said, running his hand down her sleeve and encompassing her hand. "Love is always worth the risk."

"How can you be so sure?"

He brought her hand up to his lips and kissed her knuckles. "Because, my dear, you are worthy of being loved, wholly and unconditionally."

Her eyes pleaded with him to understand. "But what if I get it wrong?"

"You won't," he assured her, "not if you follow your heart."

"And if my heart leads me down the wrong path?"

"It won't."

"But what if it does?" she pressed.

He chuckled as he lowered her hand, but he didn't release it. "You are asking too many questions," he teased. "You must trust me on this."

"I do trust you."

"Then know this, Bella," he said, "love has a way of finding you when you least expect it, and it will consume you, heart and soul."

Isabella furrowed her brow. "That sounds terrifying."

"And wonderful."

"No, more terrifying," she half-joked.

He smiled, drawing her attention to his mouth. His very

lovely mouth. So distracted was she that she failed to notice that Everett was approaching them from the townhouse.

"I thought I would join you on your walk," Everett announced when he was only a short distance away.

Ewin dropped her hand and took a step to the side. "What wonderful news," he remarked in a hoarse voice. "Isn't it, Bella?"

"Yes, truly wonderful," she replied, hoping her words sounded somewhat convincing.

Everett came to stand next to them. "I was watching you both from my study window having such a lovely time that I thought a turn around the gardens sounded most invigorating."

"Where is Nicholas?" Ewin asked.

"He left a short time ago," Everett revealed, extending his arm towards her. "Shall we, sister?"

Isabella placed her hand on his. "We shall."

"This is the manor you intend to buy?" Oliver asked skeptically as they exited the coach.

Ewin stepped onto the round gravel courtyard, his boots grinding on the loose rocks, and looked up at the two-level stone manor. "It is," he confirmed. "It is known as Eathorne Manor."

"It is much less grand than I had envisioned," his friend muttered under his breath.

Ewin's eyes scanned the building with its four bay windows, a portico over the main door, and a slate roof. "It will do," he replied.

"Shall we go inside?" Oliver asked as he came to stand next to him.

Ewin nodded. As he opened the white-painted, main door, he was met with stale air, followed by the distinctive sounds of mice scurrying across the wood floor. A moment later, it turned eerily quiet.

Ewin stepped into the entry hall and was pleasantly surprised to see that the green papered walls and woodwork appeared to be in good condition. On the opposite wall, a narrow set of stairs led up to the second level.

"This will do nicely," he said approvingly before he headed towards a drawing room directly off the entry hall.

He stepped into the square room and noticed the furniture had white cloths draped over them.

"Does this manor come furnished?" Oliver asked, peering in from the doorway.

"It does," he confirmed as he stepped closer to the bay window, looking out onto the overgrown gardens.

"That is most fortunate."

He nodded. "It is."

Oliver walked further into the room and commented, "This room receives an abundance of light."

"That will be a good thing, especially when we entertain callers." He stepped away from the window. "Shall we continue the tour?"

For the next short while, they toured the ground floor, which held two receiving rooms, a kitchen, a study, a conservatory, and a dining room.

After they toured the five bedchambers on the second level, Ewin descended the stairs and headed towards the rear of the manor. He stepped outside and saw two granite cottages that were linked to the main house by a covered walkway.

"Those two cottages must be the servants' quarters," Ewin said.

Oliver walked over to the first granite cottage and opened the door, making its rusted hinges squeak in protest. He looked inside before saying, "This cottage will require some work before anyone can live here."

"Wonderful," Ewin replied dryly.

His eyes roamed the manor as he attempted to calculate how much it would cost to bring this dilapidated manor up to scratch. He knew he had enough funds for the work, but not much more than that. He hoped it would be worth the risk.

Oliver walked over as he wiped his hands off on his grey trousers. "This manor hardly befits a man of your station."

Ewin humphed. "You seem to forget that my father has cut me off."

"You are still the son of a duke," his friend said, giving him a pointed look.

"An impoverished son," he corrected.

Oliver sighed. "Does this mean you are going to purchase it and live the boring life of a landowner?"

"I intend to," he replied, "but don't judge it so harshly. We still haven't toured the stables. My solicitor said they were most impressive."

"Why not just purchase a townhouse in London?"

"Because I need a way to produce an income," he explained. "This estate doesn't look like much, but at least I would be able to collect rent from my tenants."

"Being a landowner sounds exhausting," Oliver stated.

Ewin smiled. "I am not afraid of hard work."

"You should be," Oliver quipped. "It is quite unbecoming of you to want to work."

The sound of the wind rustling through the trees caught his ear, and he closed his eyes in contentment. "I could be happy here," he muttered.

"But do you think Lady Isabella could?" Oliver asked knowingly.

His eyes opened. "I believe she would be, especially since I intend to breed horses."

Oliver frowned as his eyes roamed the manor, the displeasure clearly on his features. "I daresay that Lady Isabella might not care for Eathorne Manor."

"Why do you say that?"

Meeting his gaze, Oliver replied, "It is so different than the life she is accustomed to."

"I know that it is smaller—"

Oliver cut him off. "Smaller? This entire manor could fit inside of her family's ballroom in London," he declared, tossing up his hands.

It was Ewin's turn to frown. "It is not that small."

"I exaggerate, but only to prove my point."

Ewin crossed his arms over his chest and asked, "Which is?"

"My point is," Oliver said, taking a step closer to him, "Lady Isabella won't be accustomed to living so rustically. Eathorne Manor is situated in a small hamlet surrounded by countryside. The closest village is ten miles away."

"She will manage," he asserted.

"And if she doesn't?"

Dropping his arms, Ewin turned to face the manor, delaying his response. What if his friend was right? What if Isabella didn't enjoy living in the country?

Oliver came to stand next to him. "I'm sorry to be such a naysayer."

"You've made some excellent observations," he started, "but it could be a moot point anyway."

"In what way?"

Turning to face him, Ewin said, "Isabella hasn't agreed to become my wife."

"That is because you haven't asked her," Oliver pointed out.

Ewin huffed. "It is not that easy," he argued. "Besides, she is adamant about not marrying anyone."

"Did she say why?"

"She is afraid of matrimony."

Oliver gave him a baffled look. "What woman is not interested in marriage?"

"Isabella."

Shifting his gaze towards the granite cottages, Oliver asked, "What do you intend to do about it?"

"I plan to break down her defenses, one by one, until I convince her to take a chance on me," he replied. "Then, I intend to marry her."

"How long do you think that may take?"

Ewin shrugged. "I am unsure, but I don't plan to give up."

"Good," Oliver stated. "I think you are right to fight for her affections."

"Thank you."

"Besides, with her dowry, you can fix this place up, and perhaps even add on a wing to the existing structure," Oliver suggested.

Ewin shook his head. "No. I don't want to use her dowry to fix up Eathorne Manor."

"Why ever not?"

"Because I don't want her to ever think that I only married her for her dowry," he explained.

Oliver lifted his brow. "I think your reasoning is foolhardy. Once you get married, the dowry belongs to you, and you can spend it at your discretion."

"I am well aware of that fact," Ewin said, "but I want Isabella to know that I married her because I love her, not because of her dowry. I don't ever want her to doubt my love for her."

Oliver humphed. "You are a man of foolish principles."

"That I am," he agreed. "But I would have it no other way."

"Nor should you."

"Shall we tour the stables?" Ewin asked. "According to the map my solicitor gave me, the stables are just on the other side of the gardens."

"Lead the way," Oliver said.

❧ 14 ❧

SITTING IN THE DRAWING ROOM, ISABELLA DRUMMED HER fingers on the writing desk as she stared out the window. She was dreadfully bored, and frankly, she missed Ewin. For the past three days, she had attempted to entertain herself, even resorting to practicing her needlework, but nothing seemed to help her melancholy. All she could think about was how much she missed him.

Glancing down at her drawing paper, she couldn't help but admire the sketch she'd created of Ewin's face. His handsome face. And she couldn't help but wonder if he missed her, as well.

She stifled a groan at her own simpering behavior. What had become of her? Impulsively, she took the paper and crumpled it in her hands. She had spent entirely too much time dwelling on Ewin, and it ended now. She wouldn't let *him* have that control over her.

The longcase clock chimed, alerting her to the time, and she knew that Lord Harold would be arriving shortly to take her on a carriage ride through Hyde Park. Why she had agreed to another carriage ride with him was beyond her.

Her mother stepped into the room with a smile on her face.

"What a lovely day it is," Mary remarked cheerfully. Obnoxiously cheerful.

"I suppose it is," she replied in a small, sad voice.

Not deterred by her lukewarm response, Mary suggested, "Perhaps we could go shopping after your carriage ride with Lord Harold."

Isabella placed the crumpled paper on the writing desk. "Are you sure you are feeling up to it?"

"I am."

"That is wonderful news," Isabella responded with a small smile.

Mary walked over to the writing desk and pointed at the crumpled paper. "Were you displeased with your drawing?"

"Not particularly."

Her mother eyed her thoughtfully. "May I see it?"

"If you would like," she agreed reluctantly, retrieving the paper.

As her mother unfolded the paper, she let out a little gasp. "I had no idea you had become so skilled at drawing."

"Thank you, but I fear that you are biased."

"That is true. A mother is always biased when it comes to her child." Turning the paper towards her, Mary said, "However, this is an uncanny likeness of him. Why did you crumple it up?"

"I'm afraid I was tired of looking at it."

Mary placed the paper on the writing desk and asked, "You miss Ewin, don't you?"

"No," Isabella lied. "That is the furthest from my mind."

Her mother smiled knowingly at her. "It is all right to admit that you miss him."

"He may have mentioned something similar before he left," she remarked.

"I see," Mary replied. "Did you admit it to him, then?"

"Absolutely not!" she exclaimed. "What a mortifying thing to say aloud."

Her mother walked over to the settee and sat down. "May I ask why?"

"Because I refuse to give a gentleman any control over me," she admitted, straightening her shoulders.

"Even if that gentleman is Ewin?" her mother questioned.

"Yes, especially Ewin."

"Why?"

Isabella let out a small huff. "If he discovered that I held any affection towards him, then he would tease me unmercifully."

"Do you truly believe that?"

"Yes!"

Her mother leaned back on the settee, appearing amused. "Oh, my dear child," Mary said, "you know nothing about the ways of men."

"Regardless, I do not wish to sacrifice my friendship with Ewin, for any reason," she remarked firmly.

"Sometimes, we must sacrifice something to obtain something far greater in the end," her mother counseled. "What are you willing to give up for a chance at happiness?"

"Nothing," she replied. "I am content with the way things are."

"Are you?"

She nodded decisively. "I am."

Smiling, her mother said, "Ewin is a good man with an even better heart. You could do much worse."

"Mother, please," she started, "I do not wish to discuss this any further."

Mary was studying her curiously, and her eyes were remarkably steady. "You are scared, aren't you?"

"Of what?"

"Of losing Ewin."

Isabella shifted her gaze away from her mother's knowing gaze. "I suppose I am," she replied honestly.

"That is a good thing, Isabella."

Her lips parted in disbelief. "In what way?"

"You are opening up your heart to another."

She shook her head vehemently. "I am doing no such thing," she asserted, "and this has nothing to do with matters of the heart."

"I disagree," her mother replied. "This has *everything* to do with the heart."

"You are wrong, Mother."

Mary opened her mouth to reply when Howe stepped into the room and met her gaze. "Lord Harold is here to call upon you, milady."

"Please send him in," Isabella responded, rising from her chair.

A moment later, Lord Harold entered with a bouquet of flowers in his hand. His eyes landed on hers and a broad smile came to his face.

He bowed. "Lady Isabella," he began, "somehow you grow more enchanting every time I see you." He turned his gaze towards her mother. "Lady Northampton, it is always a pleasure to see you."

"Likewise, Lord Harold," Mary said. "How is your mother faring?"

"She is well, and she inquired about you, as well," Harold shared.

Her mother rose and smoothed out her maroon gown. "Please inform your mother that I shall call on her next week."

"I will," Lord Harold replied, turning his gaze back towards Isabella. "I was hoping we could take a turn in the gardens before our carriage ride."

She smiled begrudgingly. "That sounds lovely."

"Excellent." He walked closer and extended the flowers towards her. "I brought these for you."

Reaching out, she accepted them. "That was most gracious of you," she acknowledged. "Please excuse me for a moment while I place these in a vase."

She quickly left the room and nearly collided with Howe just outside of the door. "I'm sorry," she muttered.

"No harm done," Howe said. "May I take those flowers from you, milady?"

"You may," she replied, extending them towards him.

As Howe started walking away, she turned back towards the drawing room, feeling only trepidation. Lord Harold wasn't an awful person. He was actually quite personable and even likeable. But she held no affection towards him. Furthermore, he met a lot of her requirements, but she still found him lacking. Why was that?

She stepped back into the drawing room and asked, "Are you ready for a tour of the gardens?"

Lord Harold closed the distance in a few strides, appearing entirely too eager. "Nothing would make me happier."

"Nothing?" she questioned.

He gave her a puzzled look. "What do you mean?"

She shrugged one shoulder and joked, "I daresay that a jam tartlet would make me happier, on any given occasion."

A slow smile came to his face. "You are rather witty, Lady Isabella."

Oh bother, she thought. He was trying entirely too hard to win her affection.

"Come, allow me to show you to the gardens," she said, spinning on her heel.

They didn't speak as they walked towards the rear of the estate. A footman opened the door, discreetly following them into the courtyard. It wasn't until they stepped onto the footpath that Lord Harold spoke up.

"I was hoping to speak to you about an important matter."

"Oh?" she asked, secretly hoping he would regale her with information about plants.

He clasped his hands behind his back. "As you know, I have been searching for a wife this Season."

Dread now filled her heart at his words. "No, I wasn't aware of that fact."

Lord Harold glanced over at her. "You weren't?"

"I wasn't."

He cleared his throat. "I just assumed that you had heard."

"I tend to avoid the gossipmongers," she replied honestly.

Stopping on the footpath, Lord Harold turned to face her. "I have enjoyed spending time with you these past few days, and I am even more convinced that we would suit." He smiled as if giving her a long-awaited treat.

"Suit in what way?" she asked. "As friends? If so, I must agree, Lord Harold. We most definitely suit as friends."

He furrowed his brow. "No, you misunderstood me. I meant we would suit as husband and wife."

She closed her eyes, wishing she were anywhere but here. After a moment, she opened her eyes, knowing that he was still waiting for her response. "Are you offering for me?"

He reached for her hand and brought it up to his lips. "I am. At least, I am trying to." Again, he smiled.

Pursing her lips together, she fixed her gaze on a bee landing on a rose and attempted to free her hand from his firm grip.

"My answer is no."

"Excellent! We will be wed…" His voice trailed off as his eyes grew wide. "I beg your pardon? Did you just refuse my offer?"

"I did," she replied, tugging her hand out of his.

"May I ask why?"

Smoothing out her pale blue gown, she replied, "We hardly know one another."

"Does that matter?"

Isabella blinked. "Yes, it matters," she contended.

"We will have our whole lives to become more acquainted with one another," he pressed, waggling his eyebrows.

"I am sorry, Lord Harold," she said with a shake of her head. "I am flattered by your offer, but I must decline."

He waved his hand dismissively in front of him, but she could tell by the stiff stance of his body that she had hurt him.

"I must admit that I am surprised by your rejection," he remarked. "After all, I was willing to overlook many of your flaws—"

She spoke over him. "My flaws?"

"It is widely rumored amongst the *ton* that you ride astride and are a bluestocking." He lowered his voice, but she could hear the disapproval in his voice.

She brought a smile to her face. "I'm afraid that both of those things are true. Furthermore, I have been known to ride in trousers, as well."

Lord Harold lifted his brow and spoke with plaintive seriousness. "Perhaps I was wrong to assume that we would suit. I would expect my wife to behave with the grace and decorum befitting her station."

"Then I daresay that we would not suit, because I rarely behave, my lord," she replied cheekily. "I wish you luck in your search for a bride. Good day to you."

She dropped into a curtsey and started walking back towards the townhouse, not bothering to look back.

Exhausted from his travels, Ewin walked down the narrow hallway towards his Albany apartment. He would rather be calling on Isabella, but it was much too late. He would have to wait until tomorrow to visit her, much to his disappointment. He opened the door to his apartment and was immediately greeted by his butler.

"Welcome home, milord," Cluett said. "Did you have an eventful trip?"

"I did," he replied, extending his gloves and top hat towards him. "Will you inform Mrs. Barr that I will not require supper? I will be joining Mr. Braggs at White's this evening."

"I shall inform her at once." Cluett stepped closer to him and lowered his voice. "Your brother is waiting for you in your study."

Ewin swore under his breath and proceeded to walk towards his study. What did his blasted brother want? Their discussions never seemed to end well.

As he walked into the room, he saw his brother sitting on an upholstered armchair with a drink in his hand.

"What do you want, brother?" he asked as he walked over to the drink cart.

George chuckled. "No salutations for me?"

"No," he replied. "I would prefer it if you would say what needed to be said and be done with it."

Leaning back in his chair, George considered him for a moment before saying, "May I ask why you are considering purchasing a property in a hamlet in Kent?"

"How exactly did you know about that?" he asked, eyeing his brother with suspicion.

George tsked. "Come now, did you truly believe Father wouldn't hire someone to follow you?"

"Yes, I did," Ewin replied.

"Then you don't know Father well enough," George affirmed.

"How long exactly has Father been spying on me?"

"Since you moved out of Stanwich House," his brother revealed.

Ewin poured himself a drink and set the decanter down. "Will you kindly inform Father that I am no longer his concern?"

"I won't do that."

"And why not?"

George frowned with displeasure. "Because it is time for the prodigal son to come home and do your duty. This tantrum of yours needs to end now."

"You keep calling it a 'tantrum,' but I consider it freedom from Father's oppressive rule," Ewin responded, picking up his glass.

"You are embarrassing the family—"

Ewin cut him off. "I must contest that Father has done a rather splendid job of embarrassing the family himself."

"Be that as it may," George began, "you cannot possibly be serious about becoming a landowner. You don't know the first thing about taking care of an estate."

"I will learn," Ewin replied, bringing the glass up to his lips.

"If you marry Lady Rebecca, you will be financially secure for the remainder of your days," George pressed. "You would want for nothing, and you wouldn't have to settle for a dilapidated manor in a hamlet."

"I would be miserable," he maintained.

"But you would be rich."

"Frankly, I would rather be poor than marry Lady Rebecca," he admitted. "Besides, I do not consider that I am 'settling' for Eathorne Manor."

George leaned forward and placed his glass onto the table. "You should know that no marriage is not fraught with strife."

"You are mistaken," he said. "I believe happiness is entirely possible in a marriage."

"Just marry the blasted chit, Ewin," his brother growled, his voice rising.

Ewin chuckled dryly as he sat across from his brother. "I will not and nothing you say will change my mind."

"Father posted the banns today," George revealed slowly.

Jumping out of his chair, Ewin exclaimed, *"He did what?!"*

George nodded. "It is true," he responded. "Father also placed an announcement in the morning newspapers."

Ewin slammed his glass down, causing the liquid to spill onto his hand. "How could he do that to me? To Lady Rebecca?"

"He wanted to force your hand," his brother said.

He could feel the anger welling up inside of him as he started pacing. "Well, it won't work."

"What are you saying?"

"I am not marrying Lady Rebecca."

George shot up from his chair. "You have to!" he shouted. "If you don't, then her reputation will be in tatters. As will yours."

"I don't care," he proclaimed. "This is Father's fault, not mine."

"But Lady Rebecca is an innocent in all of this," George argued. "You would punish her for Father's misdeeds?"

Ewin stopped pacing and stared at his brother. "I'm sorry, but my mind is already made up. As I have already stated multiple times, I will not marry Lady Rebecca."

George narrowed his eyes. "This is about Lady Isabella, isn't it?"

"Leave her out of this," he growled. "I'm warning you."

"It is about her." George scoffed. "It always has been, hasn't it?"

Ewin remained silent, not wanting to dignify his question with a response.

"Do you truly believe that Lady Isabella will be impressed with that run-down structure in the countryside?" George asked.

"I will admit that some work will be required—"

George spoke over him. "Some work?" He chuckled. "The Bow Street Runner said it was barely habitable."

"That is not true," Ewin contended.

"Regardless, the daughter of a marquess will never be happy living miles away from the nearest village."

Ewin crossed his arms over his chest. "It won't change anything," he declared. "I already purchased the property."

George reared back. "You did what?!"

"I purchased Eathorne Manor," he repeated slowly, taking great pleasure in unnerving his brother.

"You are a bigger fool than I gave you credit for," George exclaimed. "You squandered your inheritance on a worthless estate."

Ewin uncrossed his arms and walked over to his desk. "I hope you can see your way out," he remarked, dismissing his brother.

"How do you suppose Lady Isabella will react when she reads the morning newspaper tomorrow and discovers that you are engaged to Lady Rebecca?"

"I don't know," he replied, picking up a piece of paper off a pile on his desk.

George walked closer to him with a smug smile. "She will think you played her for a fool, and she will resent you."

"Then I shall have to explain the situation to her."

Rocking back on the edge of his heels, George asked, "Pray tell, what woman would want a man who would jilt his own betrothed?"

Ewin glanced down at the paper in his hand, appearing to be uninterested in what his brother was saying. "Thank you for your candor, brother," he remarked dryly, "but it is unwarranted."

"In three weeks, you are set to be married."

"Frankly, I am worried about you, George. Your mind seems to be rather sluggish," Ewin mocked. "As I have repeatedly informed you, I will not be marrying Lady Rebecca."

"If you don't, it will cause a scandal."

"Then so be it," he replied. "I intend to leave London anyway."

His brother's ruddy face spewed hatred and madness as he stared at him. "I will leave it to you to tell Father then."

"I shall."

"Good."

Ewin sat down on the chair. "Good evening to you, George."

His brother stepped closer to the desk and tapped on it. "Lady Isabella may be beautiful now but looks fade."

"Not her kind of beauty," he contested. "She is beautiful inside and out.

George huffed. "I wonder how she would feel to know that you are only marrying her for her dowry."

He stiffened. "That is not even remotely true."

"Isn't it?" George asked with an uplifted brow.

Ewin glared at his brother. "Stay away from Lady Isabella," he warned.

A smile came to George's face as he started backing up towards the door. "It might be time that Isabella and I caught up. After all, it has been years since we last spoke."

"Don't you dare!"

His brother's smile grew sinister. "I guess we shall see how understanding Isabella is, now won't we?" George asked before exiting the room.

Ewin stared at the doorway, half debating about going after his brother and knocking some sense into him. But that would resolve nothing.

Blazes!

What had his father been thinking? Sadly, he already knew the answer. His father was only thinking about himself. But his father's ruse wouldn't work. He had no intention of marrying Lady Rebecca.

He would marry Isabella or none at all.

❧ 15 ❧

LATER THAT EVENING, EWIN STOOD ON THE PAVEMENT STARING up at Stanwich House, a three-level, red brick structure that backed up to Hyde Park. Three months ago, when he had stormed out of the townhouse, he had vowed he would never set foot in it again. But here he was, and he was dreading the upcoming confrontation with his father.

He climbed up the familiar ten steps to the main door and knocked. He didn't have to wait for long for the door to be opened.

"Welcome home, Lord Ewin," the white-haired, aged butler said, stepping to the side to allow him entry. "You do realize that this is your home, and you aren't required to knock."

"It's not my home, Dunn," he replied, "not anymore."

Dunn offered a sad smile at Ewin's admission as he closed the door. "What has brought you by this evening?"

Working hard to keep the terseness out of his voice, he asked, "Is my father home?"

"He is, milord," the butler confirmed. "He is in his study."

His eyes scanned the entry hall, including the high, domed ceiling with its painted mural. "Is my mother home, as well?"

"She is out in the portico."

With a sigh, he said, "I suppose I shall start with the unpleasantries and meet with my father first."

"Would you care for me to announce you?" Dunn asked.

He shook his head. "That won't be necessary," he replied. "I have no doubt that he is expecting me."

"Very good, milord."

Ewin crossed the tiled entry hall and headed towards the rear of the townhouse where his father's study was tucked away. He stopped outside the door and saw his father sitting at his desk, his head bent over a ledger.

His father wasn't large in stature, but he made up for it with his commanding presence. His black hair was starting to turn grey along the temples, and the lines around his mouth had grown deeper, more pronounced since the last time Ewin had seen him.

Taking a deep breath, he stepped into the room and said, "Father."

The duke's hand stilled above the ledger, but he didn't look up. "It is about time you came home," he remarked in a clipped tone. "Did you run out of funds?"

"I did not."

His father placed the quill down next to the inkpot and looked up at him. "Then I must assume that you came home because I finally posted the banns."

"I did," he said, walking further into the room. "That was a foolhardy thing to do."

"I disagree," his father replied, "it was well past due."

"For whom?"

The duke frowned. "The contract clearly indicates that you are to wed Lady Rebecca by the end of the Season, and I saw no reason to dawdle any longer."

"My position still has not changed," he asserted. "I will not marry Lady Rebecca."

"But you must!" his father exclaimed, pounding his fist onto the desk.

He shook his head. "I will not."

"If you don't, it could mean ruination for this family."

Ewin walked over to the black mantle that sat above the fireplace and picked up a small red floral vase. "No, Father," he began, "you led our family to ruination with all of your gambling debts. You did this to yourself."

His father rose from his chair. "If you don't marry Lady Rebecca, then I could be thrown into debtor's prison," he stated in a steely tone.

"Then so be it," he remarked. "It is no less than you deserve."

"Why, you pompous, arrogant jackanapes!" his father shouted. "You have no idea the sacrifices I have had to make for this family. *For you!*"

"You need to calm down, Father," Ewin remarked dryly. "No one is going to throw a duke into debtor's prison. You could remedy this problem yourself by selling one of your many manors." Ewin put the vase down. "On another note, perhaps you should have showered your mistresses with less expensive gifts."

Placing his hands on the desk, the duke leaned forward. "If you marry Lady Rebecca, you would be a very rich man. What more are you looking for in a spouse?"

"That is the problem," Ewin contended, turning to face his father. "You don't listen to me; you never have. I don't care about being rich."

"Ah, that is right," the duke mocked. "You wish to marry for *love.*"

"I do."

Straightening to his full height, his father said, "Only fools marry for love. The smart ones marry for security."

Ewin had enough. He was tired of having the same argument

with his father, time and time again. Neither of their positions had changed.

"I would appreciate it if you would inform Lady Rebecca that I won't be marrying her."

"You will ruin Lady Rebecca if you don't marry her."

Ewin winced slightly, knowing his father was speaking the truth. "You should have never posted the banns," he argued. "This is your fault, and yours alone."

"Your reputation won't go unscathed, you know," the duke pressed. "What woman would want to marry someone who has jilted another?"

"That is a chance that I am willing to take." He performed an exaggerated bow. "If that will be all, I shall see my way out."

As he turned to leave, his father's next words caused his steps to falter. "I know about your intimate relationship with Lady Isabella."

He spun back around. "I beg your pardon?"

A smirk came to his father's lips. "The Bow Street Runner that followed you reported that you two shared a hackney to go into the rookeries."

"You will leave Isabella out of this!" he exclaimed.

His father put his hands up. "I will," he hesitated before adding, "assuming you marry Lady Rebecca."

"Are you mad?" he asked.

The duke came around his desk. "If you don't marry Lady Rebecca, then I will inform the gossipmongers that you are having a tryst with Lady Isabella."

"You wouldn't dare!"

"I would," his father replied in a hardened tone. "I would do anything to save this family."

"You mean, save yourself," Ewin scoffed.

His father shrugged. "That is not the way I see it."

Ewin jabbed his hand through his hair as he felt the anger build inside of him. His own father was trying to force his hand, and he refused to be a pawn in his game. Not anymore. But how was he going to protect Isabella from his father's threats?

He watched as his father walked over to the desk and pulled out a drawer. He retrieved a handful of gold coins and began to stack them onto the desk. "Are you in need of funds?"

"No, I am not."

"Pity."

Ewin huffed. "You always have believed that any problem in this world could be solved by throwing money at it. But you are wrong," he declared. "You can't buy my affection."

"I don't want your affection," his father drawled. "I want you to do your duty."

"No, you just want me to do your bidding, and I won't do it. Not anymore." He turned and started walking towards the door.

"Then *you* have ruined Lady Isabella," his father exclaimed.

He stopped and said over his shoulder, "No, Father, this is entirely your doing."

"I thought you cared about Isabella?"

Slowly, he turned around, his gaze firmly set on his father. "Make no mistake about that, but I don't just care about Isabella," he asserted. "I love Isabella, and I will do everything in my power to keep her protected from *you*."

His father's eyes narrowed. "And what of your mother? Do you not care for her?"

"I do," he said, "and she will always have a home with me."

Pointing at the door, his father warned, "If you walk out of that door, then I shall disown you, and you will never be welcomed at Stanwich House again."

A smile came to his lips. "Thank you for making this the easiest decision I have ever had to make."

His father's face grew red. "Then go! I never want to see you again!"

Needing no further encouragement, Ewin turned and exited

his father's study, feeling a tremendous relief lift off his shoulders.

As he walked towards the portico room, he saw his mother step out into the hall. Her eyes were filled with tears as she put her arms out. He quickly rushed over to embrace her.

"Oh, my dear son," Esther whispered against his hair. "How I have missed you."

"I have missed you, as well," he replied, tightening his hold around her.

His mother stepped back but remained close. "I heard you and your father fighting," she said in a worried tone.

"I'm sorry you had to hear that."

"Don't be," she admonished. "Do you really love Lady Isabella?"

He nodded. "With all my heart."

"I am so pleased to hear that," she said. "She was always such a lovely girl."

In a hushed voice, he revealed, "I bought an estate in Kent. You are always welcome to come live with me." He smiled. "With us, assuming Isabella agrees to my courtship."

"That is sweet of you to offer, but I will stay with my husband for now."

"But if you change your mind..." He let his voice intentionally trail off.

Esther reached up and cupped his cheek. "Do not concern yourself with me," she said, "and I shall speak to your father about you."

"Don't bother," he insisted, "he intends to disown me."

"I heard that, as well." Her voice was resigned.

He brought his hand up and placed it over hers. "I will continue to write to you."

"Please do," she murmured. "I always look forward to your letters."

"I love you."

"And I love you," she replied as she lowered her hand.

Ewin smiled tenderly at her. "This isn't a goodbye. I promise."

"I shall take you at your word, then."

"Please do, Mother," he replied. "Please do.

The sun was shining, the birds were chirping, and Isabella was in an extraordinarily fine mood. She exited her bedchamber, dressed in a jonquil muslin gown, eager for the day to unfold. She did not doubt that Ewin would call on her today. And she couldn't seem to make the time go any faster.

She hurried down the stairs and headed towards the dining room. As she stepped into the room, she saw Everett sitting at the head of the table with a morning newspaper in his hands.

Lowering the newspaper, her brother commented, "Good morning, sister."

"Good morning, brother," she replied, walking over to the buffet table. "Would you care to go riding after breakfast?"

"I would."

She filled her plate with food before she sat to the right of Everett. "Anything interesting in the morning newspaper?"

"Just the usual articles, I'm afraid," he responded, his eyes scanning the paper. "Would you care to read it after I am done?"

"I would, very much." Isabella reached for her napkin as she shared, "I stopped by mother's bedchamber on the way down, and she intends to join us for dinner this evening."

"That is splendid news."

"I thought so, as well."

Everett brought the paper back up as she started eating her breakfast. She had just finished her Bath bun when she heard her brother shout, "What in the *blazes*?!"

"Whatever is the matter?" she asked, wiping the crumbs off her fingers.

He lowered the paper and announced, "Ewin is engaged."

She stared at her brother, dumbfounded. After a long moment, she finally found her voice. "But that is impossible."

"I'm afraid it is not," her brother informed her, folding the paper and extending it towards her. "His engagement is listed in the Society page."

Isabella reached for the newspaper, and her eyes scanned the paper until they landed on the announcement, scarcely believing what she was reading.

"Ewin is engaged to Lady Rebecca?" she muttered under her breath.

"Apparently so."

"But he dislikes her," she argued, her brows drawn together in confusion. "I know, because he told me as much."

Everett stared at her with concern on his face. "I don't know what to say, Isabella."

Dropping the paper onto the table, Isabella attempted to control her raging emotions. Why did it feel like Ewin had betrayed her? It was ludicrous. They didn't have an understanding between them, and Ewin was free to marry whomever he wanted.

If that was the case, then why did her heart ache so uncontrollably?

"I'm sorry," Everett said, breaking into her musings. "I truly am."

She waved her hand dismissively. "It matters not who Ewin marries. We are just friends."

"I think we both know that isn't true," Everett prodded with sympathy in his voice.

Squaring her shoulders, Isabella met Everett's gaze. "Regardless, the banns have been posted, and Ewin will be marrying Lady Rebecca."

Howe stepped into the room and met her gaze. "Lord Ewin is here to call upon you, milady."

She pressed her lips together, delaying her response. The last person she wanted to see right now was Ewin.

"Please inform Lord Ewin that I am unavailable for callers," she ordered.

"As you wish," the butler said, turning to depart.

Everett lifted his brow. "You are turning him away?"

"It is not appropriate for an engaged man to call on an unattached lady," she attempted.

"It is when they are a family friend," Everett corrected.

Isabella placed her napkin onto her plate and rose. "If you give me but a moment, I shall go change into my riding habit," she said, attempting to sound cheerful.

"We don't have to go riding."

"I know, but I would like to."

Howe stepped back into the room and announced, "Lord Ewin informed me that he will remain until he has had a chance to speak to Lady Isabella."

"Oh, botheration," she breathed. "I should have known he wouldn't leave so easily. That man is a maddening pest."

Everett pushed back his chair. "Would you like me to speak to him?"

She shook her head. "That won't be necessary." She turned her gaze towards Howe. "Will you inform him that I will speak to him in the drawing room?"

The butler tipped his head and departed from the room.

"Aren't you at all curious about what he wants to speak to you about?" Everett asked.

With a wave at the newspaper, she replied, "I am sure he just wants to inform me about his engagement to Lady Rebecca."

Everett nodded, but she could still see the pity in his eyes. But she didn't want his pity. She *may* have developed some feelings for Ewin, but that didn't mean he returned her feelings.

Which clearly he didn't, since he was betrothed to Lady Rebecca. This was exactly why she hadn't wanted to form an attachment to him. Besides, feelings made you vulnerable, and she refused to be vulnerable around Ewin.

Isabella headed towards the drawing room with a purposeful stride. As she stepped into the room, she saw Ewin was standing next to the window, staring out towards the gardens. His brows were knitted together, and he appeared deep in thought.

"Lord Ewin," she greeted, forcing a smile to her lips. "I see that you are back to making a nuisance of yourself." Her words were spoken lightly as she worked hard to keep the curtness out of her voice.

Ewin turned back to face her. "And you are back to using my title again."

"I am," she said, "since circumstances have changed between us."

"I am too late, then," he sighed. "You have already read the morning newspaper."

She saw no reason to deny it, so she replied, "I have."

"Bella… you must know that…" He hesitated, before adding, "I had nothing to do with that announcement," he stammered out.

Clasping her hands in front of her, she asked, "Are you not engaged to Lady Rebecca?"

"Yes…" he paused, "and no."

She arched an eyebrow. "Thank you for clearing that up."

He took a step towards her, and she took a step back, gently bumping up against the settee behind her.

"My father posted the banns," he explained, frowning. "He felt it was time that I stopped shirking my responsibilities."

"I see."

"No, you don't see," he asserted with a shake of his head. "I have no intention of marrying Lady Rebecca."

"But the banns are already posted," she insisted, "and the announcement has already been made in the morning papers."

"I don't care," he remarked firmly.

Unclasping her hands, she stated, "If you don't marry Lady Rebecca, then her reputation will be shattered. She may never marry."

Ewin ran a hand through his hair, visibly frustrated. "I understand that, but I have no desire to tie myself to such a woman for the remainder of my days."

"Then why did you let your father post the banns?"

"I didn't!" he shouted, tossing up his hands. "That is what I am trying to tell you! He did it all on his own, without my knowledge or consent."

Isabella felt relief wash over her at that news. "Oh," she muttered.

"You didn't think I..." His voice stopped.

"Think what?"

Ewin was studying her with a crestfallen look on his face. "You didn't think I would become engaged to someone else, did you?"

Feeling his intense gaze on her, she lowered her gaze, feeling a blush creep up onto her cheeks. "I didn't know what to think," she admitted softly.

"Oh, Bella," he said, closing the distance between them. "I meant what I said that I will only marry for love. Don't you believe me?"

"I do, but it isn't uncommon for gentlemen to marry for security over love." She paused, bringing her gaze up. "And when I saw the announcement..." Her voice trailed off.

"It is my fault," he said. "I should have arrived earlier."

"It is not your fault."

Ewin's eyes searched hers. "I don't care what happens to my reputation as a result of refusing to marry Lady Rebecca, but I do care about what happens to yours."

She furrowed her brow in confusion. "Why would your broken engagement affect my reputation?"

He frowned deeply. "If I don't marry Lady Rebecca, my father threatened to tell members of the *ton* that we are having a tryst."

Isabella reared back, stunned. "What?" she exclaimed. "We are having no such thing."

"I know," he assured her. "But my father had someone following us and saw us traveling to the orphanage together."

"But we are friends," she asserted.

"Yes, but my father is trying to force me into marriage with Lady Rebecca, by any means necessary. He is not above making up lies to achieve his horrendous purpose."

"He is blackmailing you," she breathed. "What a horrible thing for a father to do to a son."

"I agree, but I have come to expect that behavior from my father."

She bit her lower lip before asking, "Do you think he will make good on his promise?"

"I do, without a doubt," he replied. "But I have a plan."

"Is it a good plan?" she joked, attempting to lighten the mood.

He didn't smile like she hoped he would, but rather he appeared more solemn. "You may not like this plan, but it is for the best."

"What does the plan entail?" she said, eyeing him in concern.

Ewin stepped closer to her. "We marry first."

"Pardon?" she asked, fearing she misheard him.

"I have a coach waiting out front," he said, "we can travel to Gretna Green and marry."

She stepped away from him, not daring to believe what she was hearing. "You want to elope?" She lowered her voice. "Are you mad?" she asked, studying his face.

He appeared sane as he replied, "It is the only way to ensure you are safe from my father's lies."

"No, it is not," she asserted. "Besides, if I eloped with you, an *engaged* man, then my reputation would be in tatters regardless."

"But we would be married," he pressed, "and I would be able to protect you."

Isabella put up her hand. "My answer is no," she said. "There has to be another way; there *must* be."

"But, Bella," he began, "there is no other way. If you would just listen—"

She spoke over him. "No," she declared. "I would not force you into an unwanted marriage. After all, isn't that what you are trying to avoid with Lady Rebecca?"

"That is the thing," he said, placing a hand on her shoulder, "it is not unwanted."

Looking up at him in surprise, she asked, "What are you saying, Ewin?"

"I care for you," he started, swallowing slowly, "I always have. In fact, I lov—"

Brushing his hand off her shoulder, she cut him off. "Please don't say it. Some words are better unheard, better unsaid."

"Not these words."

She shook her head as she created distance between them. "I want you to leave, Ewin."

He looked unsure. "Now?"

With a nod, she replied, "You have presumed too much, and I think it would be best if you would go."

"Do you want to know what I think?" he asked, his eyes imploring hers.

"No, frankly, I do not."

Taking a step closer to her, he said, "I think you feel the same, but you are too scared to admit it."

She put her hand up, stopping him. "Do not come any closer."

"You must understand that I am only trying to protect you."

"No, you are trying to trap me," she contended.

His face fell. "Is that what you truly think?"

"I don't know what to think," she replied honestly, edging her way towards the open door, "but I will not be forced into marriage, for any reason."

"But my father…"

She interjected, "Has no power over me."

"He intends to ruin you… ruin *us*," Ewin expressed.

"So be it," she replied, tilting her chin defiantly.

"Bella…" he said, tossing his arms up, "you are being infuriatingly stubborn right now. Do you understand what is at stake?"

Standing next to the door, she replied, "I do. And I thank you for your offer, but my mind is made up."

Ewin pressed his lips together in disapproval. "This conversation isn't over, Bella."

"It is for me."

He walked closer until he stopped in front of her. "I shall give you time to dwell on what we just discussed, and I will call upon you tomorrow."

"I'm afraid my position won't change."

She stiffened as Ewin leaned close and whispered in her ear, "I will do whatever it takes to keep you protected, my dear."

Her traitorous heart leapt at his nearness, but she refused to show that she was affected by him. "And I intend to protect myself," she countered, stepping back.

"Until tomorrow, then."

"You are wasting your time."

A smile came to his lips, though it didn't reach his eyes. "It is my time to waste," he said before he exited the room.

When he was gone, Isabella dropped down onto the settee in the most unladylike fashion. Good heavens, Ewin wanted her to elope with him! What was he thinking? She refused to trap him into a marriage of convenience, no matter how hard he tried to convince her otherwise.

If his father did ruin her reputation, then she would be content spending her days as a glorified spinster. After all, isn't that what she'd wanted all along?

So why did the thought of living without Ewin suddenly seem so torturous?

🎍 16 🎍

EWIN STRODE ACROSS THE COURTYARD OF HIS ALBANY apartment in a foul mood. He couldn't seem to wrap his brain around Isabella's refusal. Didn't she realize what was at stake? His father would ensure that her reputation was ruined, causing her to be shunned by Society. Marrying him was her best option. Yet, she still refused him.

Why? He knew that she held him in some regard. What was holding her back? What was she afraid of?

He opened his apartment door, wondering why he happened to love the most infuriating woman in all of England.

His butler stepped out from a room and greeted him.

"Morning, milord," Cluett said, approaching him with a solemn look on his face. "I regret to inform you that a young woman is in your study. She has been waiting for nearly an hour."

"How did she get into Albany?" he asked, knowing women and children were strictly forbidden at the Albany apartments.

"She is disguised as a pageboy," Cluett clarified.

He gave his butler a baffled look. "Does this 'pageboy' have a name?"

"She did not give one."

Ewin sighed. "Then I suppose I should go discover who has come to call and her reasons behind it."

"Would you like me to fetch Mrs. Barr?"

"No," he said with a shake of his head. "I shall handle this myself."

Cluett bowed. "As you wish, milord."

As he started walking towards his study, Ewin found himself curious about what young woman would be brazen enough to dress as a pageboy to come to call on him. Fortunately, he didn't have to wait long to discover her identity.

He stepped into the room, and to his surprise, he saw Lady Rebecca Galpin sitting rigidly on the upholstered settee, her lips firmly set together. She was dressed as a lad, but it did little to hide her feminine features. Her dark hair was tucked under a brown wool ivy cap that was sitting low on top of her head.

"Your disguise isn't very convincing," he commented as he walked over to his desk and sat down. "Do I need to remind you that women are not allowed in the Albany?"

With a smug smile, she replied, "My disguise worked well enough that the porter let me in."

"I daresay that the porter needs spectacles," he contended.

Lady Rebecca rose from the settee. "I won't say that you are wrong," she responded, walking over to a chair in front of his desk.

"Why are you here, Lady Rebecca?" he asked, not bothering to begin with the usual pleasantries. "I'm afraid I don't have time for your games at the moment."

Lowering herself gracefully onto the chair, she didn't respond right away. Instead, she gave him a polite smile. "I thought we should discuss a few things, privately, of course, now that we are engaged."

"About that," he started, "my father was the one who posted the banns. And I have no intention of…"

She spoke over him, waving her hand dismissively. "I am well aware of your reluctance to marry me," she said, "and you should know that I feel the same."

"You do?"

She nodded. "I, too, had no intention of marrying you, a mere second son," she revealed. "I was led to believe that I was going to marry your eldest brother, George, but my father arranged this marriage without my consideration or regard." Her smile turned strained. "Perhaps, if we are so fortunate, your brother will have an untimely death and you will become the next Duke of Glossner."

His jaw clenched at Lady Rebecca's callous remark. "I have no desire to be a duke," he said, "especially not at the expense of my brother."

"Who wouldn't wish to be a duke?" she asked. "I daresay that no one is content with being second best."

Tired of this ridiculous conversation, he decided to say what needed to be said, hoping his unwanted guest would leave. "I apologize, but as I have previously notified my father, on multiple occasions, I will not be marrying you."

Lady Rebecca gasped, bringing her ungloved hand up to cover her mouth. "But you must!" she exclaimed. "The banns have been posted and announcements went out in the morning newspapers. We have no choice but to marry."

"I respectfully disagree," he explained. "My father was the one who entered into a contract with your father, without my consent, mind you, and I have no intention of honoring it."

Moving to sit on the edge of her seat, Lady Rebecca attempted, "If this is because of your affection towards Lady Isabella…"

"What affection?" he asked, speaking over her.

Lady Rebecca huffed. "It was fairly obvious that you were smitten with her at Lady Humphries's ball," she said. "The only time I saw you smiling that evening was when you were in her presence."

"I may hold Lady Isabella in high regard, but—"

"Then make her your mistress!" she exclaimed, cutting him off.

He stared at her in disbelief. "I beg your pardon?"

"I said, 'make her your mistress'," Lady Rebecca repeated slowly as if he was a simpleton. "I care not what you do with your time as long as you are discreet about it."

Recovering from his shock, he replied, "I will not make Lady Isabella my mistress."

"Then cast her aside after you have had a dalliance with her," Lady Rebecca remarked, "and move on to another woman. I care not what you do with her."

Ewin leaned back in his chair. "You astound me, Lady Rebecca," he said, bringing his hand up to rub his chin.

"Thank you."

"That wasn't meant as a compliment."

"It sounded like one."

"Then I must have said it wrong."

Lady Rebecca's eyes narrowed. "That is bold speech coming from a man whose father gambled away their fortune and will soon be relying on my dowry to support himself."

"You are wrong about one thing," he said. "I will not need your dowry to support myself."

"No?"

"I purchased a modest estate in a hamlet in Kent," he informed her. "It isn't much, but it is mine."

Rearing back, Lady Rebecca proclaimed, "I don't want to live in a hamlet."

"That is good, because I have no intention of marrying you," he said dryly.

The hard line of her lips pressed together in a disapproving scowl. "I shall just reside in your London townhouse, then."

Ewin shook his head. "I'm afraid you are not listening to me," he began, "we are not going to marry. Furthermore, I do not own a London townhouse, nor do I have any plans to purchase one in the future."

"Then where shall we reside when we come into Town for the Season?" she asked. "I refuse to rent a townhouse like an impoverished person."

Leaning forward in his chair, he rested his arms on his desk. "Clearly, we do not suit, Lady Rebecca," he said. "If we wed, our union would be rife with contention."

"It doesn't matter if we suit," she replied. "We are not going into this marriage as a love match, nor would it ever be. At best, we can hope for mutual toleration."

"That may be what you desire, but I want more in a marriage."

She laughed condescendingly. "Come now," she mocked. "You want love, do you?"

"I do," he admitted freely.

"You need to be realistic, Ewin. There is no such thing as a happy union in our circles, and there never will be."

"I disagree. I believe it is possible."

"Then you are a fool."

He rose and tugged down on his black waistcoat. "If that will be all…" His voice trailed off as he pointed towards the door.

"We are not finished yet," Lady Rebecca remarked. "We have much to discuss about our upcoming wedding."

"I will not now, *nor ever*, marry you, Lady Rebecca," he said deliberately. "It was our fathers who were fools to enter into a betrothal contract for us."

Lady Rebecca squared her shoulders and spoke haughtily. "If you don't marry me, then my father won't pay off your father's gambling debts. He could be thrown into debtor's prison."

"Then so be it."

Her lips parted in surprise. "You wouldn't be so cold and unfeeling as to let your father rot in debtor's prison?"

"I would," he replied, "without a second glance."

Rising, Lady Rebecca adjusted the ivy cap on her head. "If you do not marry me, then both of our reputations will be ruined."

"I am well aware of that fact, and I apologize for it."

"I don't want your apology," she spat out. "This is all your doing, and you have the power to remedy the situation."

He shook his head. "No, this is my father's doing," he corrected.

Lady Rebecca stepped closer to the desk and declared, "If you don't marry me, then you will regret it."

"Frankly, I think I would regret it *more* if I did marry you."

She narrowed her eyes at him. "No man jilts me," she stated. "I assure you that you will rue this day."

"I have enjoyed our little chat, but I'm afraid it is time for you to leave," he said. His tone brooked no argument.

"This is not over," she replied before spinning on her heel to depart.

After Lady Rebecca had exited the room, he waited a moment, then heard the main door slam shut.

Mrs. Barr stepped into the room, and the concern was evident in her features. "Are you all right, milord?"

"I am," he assured her.

"I couldn't help but overhear that your betrothed paid you a visit."

"She did," he confirmed, "but she isn't truly my betrothed."

Mrs. Barr let out a relieved sigh. "I'm glad to hear that," she said. "I think I much prefer this Lady Isabella that you have spoken of."

"As do I," he replied with a bob of his head.

Isabella stared down at the ivory keys of the pianoforte, lost in her own thoughts. She still couldn't believe that Ewin had wanted her to elope with him. What had he been thinking of proposing such an outlandish offer? The idea was almost laughable. Wasn't it? After all, she and Ewin would never suit. Ewin may be devilishly handsome, but he was also infuriatingly obnoxious. They would drive each other to distraction. The last thing she wanted to do was enter a marriage of convenience with him.

Then why did she keep dwelling on the thought that she had made the wrong decision by turning down his offer? Her heart had soared when he admitted that he had feelings for her, but she had stopped him before he said something that he would regret; something that they would both regret.

Ewin couldn't possibly love her. Most likely, he was only saying that to convince her to marry him, to protect her from his father. Although, he had appeared rather convincing. Drat! Why did Ewin have to go and complicate their friendship? That wasn't fair of him. She was happy with the way things were. Why couldn't he be content, as well?

Everett's amused voice broke through her musings. "Should we be concerned about Isabella?" he asked. "Perhaps we should fetch a doctor."

"She has been staring at those keys for a considerable amount of time," Madalene replied with mirth in her voice.

Her mother spoke up. "Leave her be," she said lightly.

Isabella brought her gaze up and met their expectant faces. "My apologies. I'm afraid I was woolgathering."

"May I ask what has you so preoccupied?" her mother inquired as she lowered her teacup to her lap.

"Nothing of importance," she replied.

Everett huffed, clearly not believing her. "You have been acting strangely since Ewin left this morning."

"Have I?"

He nodded. "You have," he commented. "Which makes me wonder why."

"You think too much, brother," she remarked, attempting to sway the conversation away from her.

Everett considered her for a moment before asking, "Is Ewin truly engaged to Lady Rebecca?"

She shook her head. "No, he assured me that he would not be marrying Lady Rebecca," she informed them. "His father posted the banns and had the announcement printed in the morning newspapers without his consent. His Grace is trying to force Ewin into an arranged marriage."

Madalene placed a hand on her protruding belly. "I am so relieved that he is not marrying that horrid Lady Rebecca. She is just awful."

"I'm relieved, too," Isabella agreed.

"If that is the case, then why have you been so out of sorts all day?" Everett asked.

"I haven't been," she defended.

Everett gave her a knowing look. "You let me win today when we were racing our horses through Hyde Park, you keep retreating into your own thoughts, and I even saw you practicing your embroidery in the drawing room."

"I thought you wanted me to practice my embroidery?" she challenged.

"Make no mistake about that, my dear," her mother chimed in, "especially since I fear that you are actually getting worse at needlework as time goes on."

"That is not true."

Mary smiled. "I was just teasing you."

The memory of Ewin teaching that little girl embroidery

came to her mind, and her next words slipped out before she could stop them. "Did you know that Ewin can embroider?"

"Can he now?" Everett asked, smiling.

She nodded. "I was surprised, as well, but it is true."

"What else can Ewin do?" Madalene asked innocently.

Rising, Isabella moved to sit next to her mother on the settee. "I just found it unusual that a gentleman knows how to embroider, especially the son of a duke."

"I would agree," Everett replied. "That is an odd pastime for a gentleman of his station."

"How did you discover that Ewin could embroider?" her mother asked.

Moving to sit on the edge of her seat, Isabella reached for the teapot on the tray and poured herself a cup of tea.

"I saw him demonstrating it to a young girl at his family's orphanage," she revealed, preparing herself for her brother's wrath.

Everett's next words were slow and precise. "You accompanied Ewin to East London to visit an orphanage?"

"I did," she said before taking a sip of her tea. "Twice."

"Do you have any regard for your reputation or safety?" Everett asked in a steely voice.

Lowering the teacup to her lap, she replied, "I was perfectly safe with Ewin escorting me."

"Do you know what could have happened to you in the rookeries?" Everett questioned, his voice rising.

Tilting her chin up, she declared, "I am not a child anymore, Everett."

Everett humphed. "You are still naïve to the ways of the world, the ways of men," he scoffed. "Did Ewin at least take along any footmen?"

"No," she responded. "We took a hackney."

Everett's eyes widened. "You *what*?!" he exclaimed, jumping up from his seat.

Knowing that she had said too much, Isabella decided to bite her tongue and wait for the inevitable tongue lashing from her brother.

He started pacing. "Let me see if I understand this correctly," he said. "My sister took a hackney to the heart of East London to visit an orphanage. Not once, but *twice*."

Isabella brought the teacup up to her lips. "That is correct."

Everett stopped pacing and stared at her in disbelief. "The rookeries are lawless," he bellowed. "Do you even understand how lucky you are to be alive?"

"I do," she murmured.

"Promise me that you will never go into the rookeries again," Everett said.

With a shake of her head, she replied, "I'm afraid I can't promise that."

Everett's brow lifted. "And why not?"

"Because I loved helping those girls in the orphanage," she explained, her voice taking on a determined edge. "And I will do it again the next time Ewin invites me to go along."

Everett opened his mouth to argue, but her mother spoke first. "What Everett is trying to convey is that the rookeries are hardly a place for a lady."

"I know," she agreed, "but I enjoy feeling like I am making a difference."

Everett came to sit down across from her. "And you shall," he insisted, "as soon as we start up your foundation."

"I can do both."

"Please be rational, Isabella," Everett argued, "there are dangers lurking around every corner in the rookeries."

"I am well aware of that fact."

"And yet, you would still go?" Madalene asked.

Isabella nodded. "I am tired of being coddled when I can be so much more," she explained. "Ewin is the only one who can see that, and he trusts me. Why can't everyone else?"

The room grew silent, and she could see Everett and Madalene exchanging worried glances. Finally, after what seemed like
hours, but was probably only moments, Everett spoke.

"It is not a matter of trust as much as safety."

Placing her empty teacup onto the table, she remarked,
"Then next time, I will take our coach and bring along two
footmen."

"Four footmen," Everett demanded. "And I will go with
you."

"All right," she conceded. "I can agree to your terms."

"When is the next time you are heading to the orphanage
with Ewin?" Mary asked.

Isabella started wringing her hands in her lap. "I don't know,
but I hope soon."

"Why do you not know?" Madalene prodded.

With great reluctance, she found herself sharing, "Ewin and I
had a falling out this morning."

"Finally," Everett muttered, shifting in his chair. "Will you
tell us what happened?"

She held her breath before admitting, "He wanted me to
elope with him."

Everyone grew silent, but to her surprise, they all stared back
at her with wide smiles on their faces.

"What is so amusing?" she asked incredulously.

Everett spoke up first. "You are," he said. "What did you say
to Ewin's offer?"

"I said 'no', of course," she stated.

"Why?" Madalene asked. "It was evident to everyone that
Ewin cares for you."

She was taken aback by this news. "It was?"

Her mother smiled at her. "Just as we all know that you
return his feelings."

"I may care for him," she admitted slowly, "but I refuse to
sacrifice our friendship over such a trifle thing as feelings."

"Why not?" her mother pressed.

"Because I have no desire for matrimony at this time," she said firmly.

"Oh, dear," her mother murmured. "This will be much harder than we thought."

Everett and Madalene both nodded in unison.

Unsure of what they were talking about, Isabella asked, "What will be harder?"

Mary shifted on the settee to face her. "We all wanted you to work this out on your own, but we now realize that we must intercede on your behalf." She paused, maintaining her gaze. "You are in love with Ewin."

"What?" she asked, rearing back. "Impossible."

"Is it?" Madalene asked.

Rising, she exclaimed, "I couldn't possibly be in love with Ewin!"

"Why not?" her mother pressed.

"For so many reasons," she rushed to reply.

Everett leaned back in his chair. "Please share the reasons so we can understand the errors of our ways."

"Well, first...." Her voice trailed off as she attempted to think of something that would help them understand her reasoning. *Anything.* But inexplicably, she was unable to think of one justification for not loving Ewin.

He was infuriating, but he had a smile that caused her to lose all rational thought. He treated her as his intellectual equal and could always make her laugh, even at the most inopportune times. She cared for him immensely, but that didn't mean she loved him.

Was it even possible to fall in love so fast? And why was her heart pounding at the mere thought of him? The realization hit her with such force that she felt her knees grow weak, and she lowered herself onto the settee.

She brought her gaze up. "I love Ewin," she murmured.

"We know," Mary said, smiling.

Tears came to her eyes as she reluctantly shared, "But I still can't marry him."

Her mother's smile dimmed. "Why ever not?"

"I can't risk having a marriage like yours," she admitted weakly. "I don't want to lose a part of who I am."

With love in her eyes, Mary reached out and cupped her cheek. "Your father and I had a horrid marriage, but it will be nothing like the one that you and Ewin will experience."

"How can you be so sure?" she asked, daring to hope.

"Because you are marrying someone who loves you, cherishes you," Mary said, lowering her hand. "That is something I have never experienced."

Everett placed his hand over his wife's and smiled. "If you marry the right person, not only do you not lose a part of yourself, but they will help you become a better version of yourself."

Isabella closed her eyes, dreading her next question. "What if you are wrong?" she asked. "What if I will be trapped in a loveless marriage for the remainder of my days?"

"Listen to your heart, it will know what to do," Madalene encouraged.

Her eyes opened, and a disbelieving puff of air left her lips. "If only it was that simple."

"It can be," Madalene replied right before a yawn escaped her lips. She brought her hand up to her mouth. "Excuse me. I must be more tired than I realized."

Everett jumped up and extended his hand towards her. "Let's get you to bed, my dear."

"Thank you," Madalene said, slipping her hand into his.

As Isabella watched them leave the room, her mother counseled, "If you are lucky enough to marry your best friend, then every day will be like an adventure."

Her mother rose and smiled down at her. "Now, if you will excuse me, I believe I shall retire for the evening."

Rising, Isabella walked over to the darkened window, staring out into the cloudless sky full of stars and the bright, round moon. What was she going to do? Should she throw caution to the wind and marry Ewin, or should she protect her heart from being broken?

She wrapped her arms around her waist. How did she manage to do something so intolerably stupid like go and fall in love with her best friend? Apparently, she wasn't as clever as she thought she was.

❧ 17 ❦

EWIN EXITED HIS ALBANY APARTMENT AND WALKED SWIFTLY across the cobblestone courtyard. He had spent all night reliving his last conversation with Isabella, and he was even more determined to make her his. He could see in her eyes that she loved him, but she was afraid. She had erected barriers around her heart that he needed to patiently dismantle until she finally recognized that they were meant to be together.

"Looking for a hackney, sir?" a tall, husky man asked as he leaned up against the fence surrounding the Albany.

"I am, actually," he replied, pleasantly surprised at the ease of securing a hackney this morning.

"Very good." The man straightened and approached a black hackney in the street. As he opened the door, he asked, "Where to?"

"The Marquess of Northampton's townhouse," he replied as he approached the vehicle. "Are you familiar with it?"

"I am."

Ewin bobbed his head in approval as he stepped into the darkened carriage.

The driver stuck his head in. "I should warn you that the

windows don't open," he shared. "That is why the drapes are closed."

"That won't be an issue," he replied, adjusting his white cravat. "It isn't too far to Lord Northampton's townhouse."

"The streets are rather congested around this time of day," the man said. "It might take longer than normal to arrive at your destination."

"Understood."

The man closed the door. A moment later, he felt the coach dipped to the side as the driver sat on the driver's box.

Ewin felt the coach jerk forward, and he leaned his head back until it rested against the wall. He decided it was the perfect opportunity to rest his eyes. He felt exhausted. He had tossed and turned all night thinking about Isabella and what he could say to change her mind about matrimony.

He loved her, and he would fight to win her affections. Because without Isabella in his life, it would be undeniably bleak and dreary. He wanted Isabella to be by his side. She was his match, in every sense of the word. Now he just had to convince her. That was going to take considerable work, but it would be worth it in the end.

The next thing he knew, he awoke with a crick in his neck. He thought he must have dozed off as he took his hand and rubbed it along the back of his neck.

He could feel the coach moving at a clipped pace, and he was surprised by its speed. Generally, coaches' movements were more sluggardly because of the number of coaches on the streets of London.

Pulling back the curtain, he was astonished to see the rolling green hills of the countryside. What was he doing out of the city? And where was the driver taking him?

He reached for the handle and attempted to open it, but it was locked. *Blazes*! Why had the man abducted him? Perhaps this was a robbery attempt.

Ewin could feel the coach begin to slow down, and he braced himself for the inevitable. He wasn't about to sit back and do nothing as the driver attempted to rob him... or worse. He looked for anything in the hackney that could be used as a weapon, but his search yielded nothing.

The coach jerked to a stop, and he felt the coach dip to the side as the driver stepped down. Ewin clenched his hands into tight fists and waited for the door to be opened. A long moment passed before the door was wrenched open, and he found himself staring into the barrel of a pistol.

"Get out of the coach or you are a dead man," the man ordered before he took a step back.

Realizing the precariousness of the situation, Ewin kept his hands in front of him as he started to exit the coach. He stepped down onto the ground and saw two additional men pointing pistols at him, as well. Up ahead, another coach was stopped along the side of the road.

"What is the meaning of this?" he asked.

The driver chuckled dryly. "We don't have to answer that since you ain't in charge."

"I demand to know who is!"

"You will find out soon enough," the driver drawled as he lowered his pistol and walked over to the other coach. He placed his hand on the handle, pulled down, and opened the door.

To his utter astonishment, he watched as Lady Rebecca gracefully exited. She took a moment to smooth out her blue traveling habit before she brought her gaze up. When their eyes met, she smiled at him and waved.

"Ewin," she said cheerfully. "I am so glad that you made the trip unscathed. I was worried that you would try to fight the inevitable, and these ruffians would have no choice but hurt you."

"*You* abducted me?" He furrowed his brow in confusion. "For what purpose?"

Her smile grew. "So we can elope to Gretna Green."

"As I have stated previously, I am not going to marry you," he remarked firmly.

She pouted, drawing attention to her full lips. "It is so adorable that you think you have a choice in the matter."

Her words caused him to pause. "And why do you say that?"

"Look around you," she said, putting her hands up, "I have hired these men to ensure you marry me. I have been assured that they are very good at their jobs."

He shook his head. "I will fight you every step of the way."

"Then you will die," she stated, stepping closer to him, "and I don't want that. Then I would have to try to find a new betrothed."

"You are mad."

Her eyes narrowed to slits. "No, you are mad for thinking you could jilt me."

Perusing the rough-looking men, he noticed their dirty clothing. "How did you even know where to hire these men?"

"My father is in trade, and he frequently attracts the attention of unscrupulous men," she explained. "He helped me arrange all of this."

"Your father is an earl," he commented in disbelief.

She huffed. "Your father is a worthless duke who is relying on my father to pay his debts," she spat out.

"If you hold such disdain for my father, why do you want to marry me?"

With a shrug of her shoulders, she replied, "You are not terrible to look at, and, if I play my cards right, I could be the next duchess."

"You don't intend to kill my brother, do you?" he asked, eyeing her suspiciously.

She let out a cold laugh. "Good heavens, you must think me a monster," she replied, but it hadn't escaped his attention that she hadn't actually answered his question.

"Frankly, I don't know what to think, Lady Rebecca," he remarked honestly.

"Well, I have no desire to kill your brother, considering we are after the same thing," she shared.

He frowned. "Which is?"

"For you and I to be married, then my father will pay off an enormous amount of *your* father's debt," Lady Rebecca said. "Then your father will tragically have an accident, thus preventing him from spending any more of his money."

"You intend to kill my father?" he asked with an uplifted brow.

She shook her head. "I don't," she replied, "but George will."

He humphed. "George isn't capable of killing anyone, much less his own father."

"Greed is a powerful motivator," she proclaimed. "Your brother is tired of watching your father squandering away the family fortune, and I want to be a duchess."

"Then why didn't you marry my brother?"

She visibly stiffened. "George and I were to be wed, but your father married him off to Jane. He ruined everything, forcing me to formulate a new plan. A better one."

"Which is?"

She laughed. "I'm afraid I'm not at liberty to say. Although, I'm sad to admit that you won't like my plan very much."

"You won't get away with this," he said, taking a step towards her.

He froze when he heard the sound of cocking pistols. Slowly, he put his hands up in front of him.

Lady Rebecca smirked. "Trust me, I will," she said. "Your father is a joke amongst Society. No one will miss him. Not even *you*."

"That doesn't mean I would want my father dead."

"Even after everything that he has done to you?" she asked, watching him intently.

He bobbed his head. "Even then."

She let out a sigh. "George was right."

"What about?"

"He told me that you wouldn't go along with our plan, but I was adamant that I could sway you," she shared. "I'm afraid I underestimated how stubborn you are."

"I am sorry to disappoint you."

Lady Rebecca clasped her hands in front of her. "I thought I could convince you to come willingly, but I see that I will need to resort to more barbaric tactics."

"What do you mean by that?" he asked, not liking the sound of that.

"You shall see."

He barely discerned the sound of someone coming up from behind him before everything went black.

With the guitar in her lap, Isabella strummed her fingers along the strings as the morning sun streamed into the drawing room. She was working hard to keep herself engaged with tasks to avoid thinking about Ewin.

Ewin.

Her thoughts repeatedly kept returning to him, but she didn't want to dwell on the fact that she loved him. She couldn't. She wanted things to remain as they were.

"Good morning, Isabella," a familiar voice said from the doorway.

She looked up and saw Nicholas. "Good morning," she replied. "How is Penelope?"

A smile came to his face. "She is well. Our son was gracious enough to sleep through the night, giving us both a much-needed respite from our sleepless nights."

"What wonderful news!"

"It is," he agreed.

"I can't wait to meet baby Jacob."

The duke puffed out his chest in pride. "You will meet him at the christening."

"I shall look forward to it."

Nicholas stepped further into the room and asked, "Is everything all right?"

"Yes," she replied. "Why do you ask?"

"I couldn't help but notice that you seem distracted."

"In what way?"

He gave her a knowing look. "I was standing in the doorway for nearly ten minutes before you finally acknowledged me."

"Oh," she replied as she moved the guitar off her lap and rested it against the settee. "I must have been woolgathering."

Everett's voice spoke up from behind Nicholas. "She was most likely thinking about Ewin," he said in an amused voice.

"I should have assumed as much," the duke remarked.

Her brother stepped into the room and announced, "Ewin asked Isabella to elope with him."

Nicholas's brow lifted. "When was this?"

"Yesterday."

Turning his gaze towards her, the duke said, "I take it that she said no."

"Of course I said no," she huffed. "And, frankly, I find it disconcerting that my family is so cavalier about Ewin asking me to elope with him."

Everett shrugged. "It wouldn't be the worst thing."

"How can you even say that?" she exclaimed. "Just think of the scandal that would ensue if I ran off with an engaged man to Gretna Green."

"Scandals come and go amongst the *ton*," Nicholas remarked. "Besides, no one would dare give you the cut direct because you will have my endorsement. I promise you that." His words were spoken with such a steely intensity that she knew he was in earnest.

"I thank you for that, but Ewin and I will not be eloping," she said.

"But you are going to get married, aren't you?" Nicholas pressed.

She pursed her lips. "As of now, I don't intend to marry anyone," she replied honestly.

Nicholas looked disappointed by her response. "That is disconcerting," he muttered.

Following the duke's response, a silence ensued before Everett interjected, "And with that, shall we adjourn to my study?"

With a nod, Nicholas followed Everett out of the drawing room, leaving her alone in blissful silence. Why did it matter to the duke that she wasn't going to marry Ewin?

Howe stepped into the room, and Isabella's heart began to race at the thought of seeing Ewin again.

But to her surprise, he announced, "Lord Dowding is here to call upon you. Are you available to see him?"

"Just Lord Dowding?" she asked, hoping to keep the disappointment out of her voice.

He bobbed his head. "Yes, milady."

"You may send him in," she replied as she rose and walked the guitar back over to its stand.

A few moments later, Lord Dowding walked into the room with a solemn look on his face. "Thank you for agreeing to see me, Lady Isabella."

"I must admit that I am surprised by your visit," she said, walking over to the settee.

"Yes, it has been a long time since we last spoke."

"It has," she agreed as she lowered herself onto the settee.

She noticed that Lord Dowding perused the length of her, making her feel slightly uncomfortable. He may resemble Ewin, but his eyes were cold, calculating. It was a far cry from Ewin's eyes, which seemed to draw her in, comforting her.

"What can I do for you?" she asked.

Lord Dowding came and sat across from her. "I have come to speak to you about a ticklish subject."

"Which is?"

"Ewin."

She tensed. "What about Ewin?"

"My brother is an engaged man, but I can't help but notice that he spends an exorbitant amount of time over here," he hesitated before adding, "with you."

"Ewin and I are just friends."

Lord Dowding's eyes grew hard as if leveling a challenge. "I think we both know that is not true."

"What is it you want?" she asked boldly.

"For you to refuse him when he comes to call."

She straightened her shoulders. "I will not," she replied. "He is a dear family friend, and I will not insult him by turning him away."

"But he is engaged to Lady Rebecca."

Maintaining his gaze, she asked, "May I speak plainly?"

He bobbed his head. "I wish you would."

"Ewin has no intention of marrying Lady Rebecca."

Lord Dowding sighed. "I'm afraid he has no choice," he said. "If he doesn't marry Lady Rebecca, then our family is ruined."

"Ewin did inform me of your family's financial state, but in the next breath, he informed me that he still refused to marry Lady Rebecca."

"I think we both know why that is."

Despite not wanting to hear his answer, she decided to ask it anyway. "And why is that?"

"Because you are giving him hope that there is a future between you two," Lord Dowding replied.

"I am doing no such thing," she declared.

"Aren't you?" he asked with a knowing look. "Ewin is beguiled by you, by your beauty, and I don't blame him. But by doing so, he is neglecting his duty to his family."

"I'm afraid we are at a stalemate, Lord Dowding," she said, rising. "I will not turn Ewin away when he comes to call."

"You would jeopardize his chance for happiness, then?"

She huffed. "I would not."

"Then let Ewin and Lady Rebecca marry," he pressed.

"If Ewin did decide to marry Lady Rebecca, then I would support the union."

"I am relieved to hear you say that," he remarked, "because they are on their way to Gretna Green as we speak."

"They are?" she asked, lowering herself back onto the settee.

His eyes flashed in triumph, and he smirked. "I saw Ewin stepping into a hackney on his way to rendezvous with Lady Rebecca."

"But..." Her words trailed off, unsure of what to say.

"You are not the first woman to fall prey to my brother's flowery words," Lord Dowding said. "He is a known rake amongst the *ton*."

She brought her hand up to her forehead, attempting to make sense of what he was saying. "But this is impossible," she breathed. "He doesn't care for Lady Rebecca."

Lord Dowding chuckled. "Since when did men and women in our positions marry for love?" he asked. "They marry for security, you foolish girl."

"But Ewin was adamant that he wasn't going to marry Lady Rebecca," she argued, lowering her hand.

Lord Dowding rose and tugged on the lapels of his riding jacket. "It matters not," he declared. "They are on their way to Gretna Green and there is nothing you can do about it."

"We have to stop them," she said. "Ewin is making a horrific mistake."

"Absolutely not!" Lord Dowding exclaimed. "You will let them be."

"But…"

Lord Dowding advanced till he loomed over her. "I am warning you," he growled, "you will not attempt to stop this union. Or else."

Isabella rose slowly, not cowed by his threat. "Or else what, Lord Dowding?" she asked, her own words taking on an edge.

"You will be sorry."

They glared at each other for a moment before she broke his gaze and walked swiftly over to the door. "Everett! Nicholas! Come quickly!"

She had barely turned back to face Lord Dowding when Everett and Nicholas raced into the room, their breathing labored.

"What is wrong?" Everett asked.

She placed her hand out towards Lord Dowding. "Lord Dowding has threatened me."

Everett's eyes narrowed dangerously. "He has?"

"He has," she confirmed.

Lord Dowding put his hands up in front of him. "This is all just an unfortunate misunderstanding," he said. "Lady Isabella must have misconstrued my words."

"Pray tell, what were you referring to when you said I 'would be sorry'," she asked directly.

Nicholas growled, and his hands clenched to his sides. "I strongly urge you to apologize to the lady for this misunderstanding and never speak to her again. *Ever.*"

"Of course," Lord Dowding responded quickly. "My apologies, Lady Isabella. I assure you that I meant no harm."

"But you did," she corrected.

Lord Dowding frowned, his eyes growing fearful. "And that was wrong of me." He started edging towards the door. "If you will excuse me, I shall take my leave."

As Lord Dowding fled from the room, Nicholas muttered, "Coward."

Isabella turned to face them. "I think Ewin is in trouble."

"Why do you say that?" Everett asked.

Isabella started pacing as she explained, "Lord Dowding informed me that Ewin is on his way to Gretna Green with Lady Rebecca, but I suspect that Ewin didn't go willingly."

"You think he was abducted?" Nicholas asked.

She stopped pacing. "I do," she said, wincing. "Is that foolish thinking on my part?"

Everett shook his head. "No, I do not think so."

"Can we go after him?" she asked hopefully.

Nicholas and Everett exchanged a look before Everett replied, "No need for you to put yourself in danger, Isabella. We will take care of this ourselves."

"I want to go, as well," she stated firmly.

"I don't think that is a good idea," Nicholas remarked. "It could be dangerous."

Isabella squared her shoulders; her jaw was set. "I am going, whether or not you agree," she said determinedly.

Everett humphed. "I'm not going to be able to talk you out of this, am I?"

"No," she replied with a shake of her head, "and you are wasting time trying to convince me to stay."

"I assumed as much," he sighed.

She smiled victoriously. "I have always wanted to save a gentleman in distress."

Nicholas chuckled. "Let's hope Ewin doesn't hear you say that."

❦ 18 ❦

EWIN WOKE UP WITH A HEADACHE THAT RADIATED FROM THE back of his head. He groaned as he reached up and touched his head. He could feel dried blood caked in his hair. As he moved to sit up on the bench, he seemed to feel every wheel rotation of the coach as it moved at a rapid clip.

"Oh, good," Lady Rebecca said cheerfully. "You are finally awake. I was worried that ruffian had hit your head too hard."

He blinked his eyes as he tried to bring Lady Rebecca into focus in the darkened coach. "Where am I?"

"We are on our way to Gretna Green," she answered, smiling. "Remember?"

He closed his eyes as he felt his stomach start to churn. After the feeling abated, he breathed, "I still have no intention of marrying you."

"But you will."

"I would rather die first," he contended as he opened his eyes.

"That could easily be arranged," she snapped. "I already have many people willing to testify we are traveling to Gretna Green to be wed, including your own brother."

"They would be lying."

She shrugged. "That matters not."

"Why are you doing this, Lady Rebecca?" he inquired, his head still groggy.

In a sultry voice, she asked, "Would you believe it if I said I fancy you?"

"No, I wouldn't."

"You are smarter than I have given you credit for," she remarked. "My original plan was relatively simple. I marry you, and after George kills your father, then I slowly start poisoning him with arsenic." She put up her hands in a flamboyant manner. "Then, you would become the new duke and I would become a duchess."

"I thought you cared for my brother?"

"I did, at one point," she admitted, her eyes growing reflective. "But my affection wanes easily, much more than my ambition."

"And now?"

Lady Rebecca smiled cruelly. "You have forced me to change my plans."

"In what way?"

"Sadly, you shall have to die in the new scenario," she said without a hint of remorse.

That doesn't sound too promising, he thought. "And why is that?"

"Because you know too much," she shared. "After I kill you, then I will begin to poison Jane with arsenic. It produces the same result, really. When she dies, I will wed George and become a duchess."

"But, by law, George cannot marry you," he argued. "A brother cannot marry his brother's widow."

"We've already anticipated that hurdle, and we can easily skirt around that law by marrying in France," she announced proudly.

He felt the need to point out the obvious. "But we are at war with France," he said. "You can't just jaunt over the channel."

She waved her hand dismissively. "I am not concerned by that," she stated. "I won't be able to kill Jane right away. If I did, it would arouse too much suspicion."

"So, you have thought of everything?"

She smiled smugly. "Yes, I believe we have."

"And what is my incentive for not fighting back," he asked, clenching his fists to his sides, "especially since you already intend to kill me?"

Lady Rebecca shifted her gaze towards the window, clearly not concerned with his growing agitation. "If you don't go through with the wedding, then I will ensure that Lady Isabella will be killed, in as gruesome a fashion as possible."

He shot up in his seat, ignoring the pounding in his head. "You wouldn't dare!"

"I would," she replied. "In fact, after you left your Albany apartment this morning, George paid a visit to see your Lady Isabella."

With a clenched jaw, he asked, "For what purpose?"

"To threaten her, of course," Lady Rebecca said lightly. "His task was to kindly ask her to stay away from you, or else there would be consequences for her." She paused. "Dire consequences."

"But Lady Isabella is an innocent in all of this," he asserted.

Lady Rebecca arched an eyebrow. "Is she?"

"She is!"

"That chit beguiled you, encouraging you to turn your back on your family and your duty."

He shook his head and immediately regretted that action. "You are wrong," he replied. "Isabella did none of that."

Lady Rebecca shot him a look of disbelief. "You are blinded by love, I see."

"Perhaps, but it is better than being blinded by greed and

ambition," he countered.

"It is a shame, really," she began. "We could have been good together."

"I disagree."

Leaning forward, she reached out and ran her finger down his jawline. "This is your fault, you know."

"In what way?" he asked, jerking his head back.

"I came to you and offered to let Lady Isabella become your mistress, but you refused," she said, lowering her hand and leaning back. "Why was that?"

"I would have never dishonored Isabella in such a horrendous fashion."

There was a fixed smile on her lips, but her eyes were mirthless, almost vacant. "Your honor does you a disservice."

"Again, I must disagree."

"It is a pity that I will have to kill you," she said, cocking her head. "I have enjoyed our short time together immensely."

"You are mad."

Shrugging her shoulders, she replied, "I won't entirely disagree with you."

A muffled shout came from behind the coach, and it started picking up speed. Ewin braced himself as the coach began weaving back and forth.

"Highwaymen," he shouted. "Do you have a weapon?"

"I do." Lady Rebecca reached into the pocket of her riding habit and pulled out an overcoat pistol.

He placed his hand out. "Give me the pistol," he ordered.

She huffed, pointing it at him. "Do you take me for a fool?"

"I do, vehemently," he said, "but I am trying to protect you."

"Well, sir, I do not need your protection," she declared, lowering the pistol to her side.

He put his hands up in surrender. "Fine. By all means, protect yourself." He pulled back the curtain and saw three riders, low in the saddle, gaining on the coach.

"There are three of them," he informed her. "How many men do you have?"

He saw a trickle of fear come into her eyes. "Two," she replied.

"Just two?"

She nodded. "A driver and an additional guard."

"What happened to the other men?"

"I sent them away," she replied. "I didn't think they were necessary."

Ewin watched as one of the riders broke free from the group and was quickly approaching the coach on a white horse. As the moonlight hit the rider's face, his heart leapt with recognition. *Isabella*. It was a face that he had memorized.

What in the blazes was she doing here?

She rode past the coach without sparing him a glance and started riding next to the driver. She pointed her pistol at the driver and shouted, "Stop, or I will shoot!"

Immediately, the coach began to slow down, and Isabella kept her pistol trained at the driver without wavering. The other two riders came to ride next to her, and he recognized them as Everett and Nicholas.

He closed the curtains and announced, "It is highwaymen. Just do what they say, and we will be on our way."

Lady Rebecca nodded, and he almost felt bad for lying... almost.

After the coach came to a complete stop, the door was flung open, and Nicholas held a pistol in his hand as he stuck his head into the coach. When his gaze landed on Ewin, a look of relief flashed in his eyes.

"I found him!" the duke announced over his shoulder.

Nicholas lowered the pistol to his side. "Would you both mind stepping outside?" he asked in a firm tone. "We have much to discuss."

"I should warn you that the lady has a pistol on her person,"

Ewin informed him, causing Lady Rebecca to stare daggers at him.

The duke brought his pistol back up and pointed it at Lady Rebecca. "Kindly hand your pistol to Ewin, or I will kill you." The way he spoke his words, Ewin knew he was in earnest.

"Well, I never," she huffed as she slowly raised her hand up and extended the pistol towards him.

Nicholas took a step back. "Now step outside," he barked, extending his other hand to assist her out of the coach.

Once Lady Rebecca was on solid ground, Nicholas dropped her hand and took a step back, his alert eyes focused on her.

Ewin stepped out and his eyes sought out Isabella, who had dismounted and was guarding the two ruffians with her pistol, alongside Everett. He couldn't help but notice that she was dressed in dark trousers and a dark shirt. Her blonde hair was pulled back into a low bun at the base of her neck, but tendrils had escaped and were framing her face. He had to admit that Bella had never looked more beautiful than she did at this moment.

He wanted to run to her and pull her into his arms, but, fortunately, sanity prevailed. This was not the time or the place.

Everett's voice broke through his musings. "Are you all right, Ewin?"

He nodded. "I am, thanks to you," he replied, hoping the relief was evident in his tone.

"No thanks are necessary, especially since it was more of a team effort," Everett said. "Besides, it was Isabella's idea to come after you."

"It was?" he asked, turning his attention back towards Isabella.

She glanced briefly over at him but continued to guard the men. "It was." She smirked. "I have always wanted to save a gentleman in distress."

Everett groaned. "We went over this, Isabella, multiple times, in fact," he began, "that joke is not humorous and never will be."

"And I still contend it is quite witty," she bantered back.

"Well, you would be wrong," Everett jested.

Nicholas chuckled. "I must side with Everett," he said. "That joke is awful, and no man wants to admit that he is in distress."

"You are both half-wits," Isabella teased. "What do you think about my joke, Ewin?"

Ewin smiled. "I think it is rather clever."

Lady Rebecca interjected, "If you ask my opinion, it is terrible."

"No one asked for your opinion," Ewin stated, "and I most assuredly never will."

Nicholas spoke up. "Now, will someone kindly explain to me what the blazes is going on?"

Without hesitation, Ewin stepped forward and announced, "Lady Rebecca abducted me."

Isabella had never felt such relief as she did at this moment. She had been right that Ewin had been abducted by Lady Rebecca, and he didn't willfully elope with her to Gretna Green. She wanted to step into his arms, to ensure he was all right, but she knew that it was not her place to do so. She had rejected his offer, something she was beginning to acknowledge might have been a mistake.

With a watchful eye on the ruffians, Everett asked, "How could Lady Rebecca have possibly abducted you?"

"I was abducted when I stepped into a hackney and was taken out of Town," he explained. "Lady Rebecca was waiting for me and threatened to kill Isabella if I didn't go along with her sinister plan."

Everett's eyes narrowed as he glared at Lady Rebecca. "Did she now?"

Ewin nodded. "Furthermore, Lady Rebecca and my brother, George, made plans to kill my father, Jane, and me."

Isabella arched an eyebrow. "Why would she want to kill you?" she asked.

"If I married Lady Rebecca, then her father would pay off a large portion of my father's debts," he shared. "So, my usefulness would expire the moment I married her."

"That is horrible." She turned her gaze towards Lady Rebecca. "You should be ashamed of yourself."

Lady Rebecca was standing in a defiant pose. "I am not," she declared. "I should have been the one to marry George, not Jane. But Ewin's father, His Grace, foiled that plan. It is the duke's fault, not mine, that I had to resort to such underhanded tactics."

Nicholas spoke up in a steely tone. "From here on out, I will do everything I can to ensure that you and your family will be outcasts amongst Society."

"You wouldn't dare, Your Grace," Lady Rebecca exclaimed, but her eyes showed her uncertainty.

Nicholas took a commanding step towards her, causing Lady Rebecca to shrink back in fear. "What you were planning to do was disgraceful and would have gotten you hanged," he asserted, "which is no less than you would have deserved."

Tears welled up in Lady Rebecca's eyes. "I just wanted to be a duchess," she declared, stomping her foot. "Father promised me that I would be!"

Feeling no sympathy for Lady Rebecca, Isabella asked, "What do we do with her now?"

Everett lowered his pistol to his side. "We let her go."

"We are just going to let her go?" Isabella asked in astonishment.

"Yes, but I have a condition," Nicholas growled. "You will

retire to your country estate, not daring to show yourself in Town, and remain there for many, many years."

"Then I shall be destined to be a spinster," she cried out.

"Frankly, I don't care what you are," Nicholas stated dryly. "You are just lucky we are not turning you over to the magistrate." He paused, turning his attention towards Ewin. "Unless you would prefer us to do so?"

When Ewin didn't respond right away, Lady Rebecca's eyes grew wide. "You... wouldn't dare. I am a lady, daughter of an earl," she cried, her words panicked.

Ewin turned to face Lady Rebecca. "No, let's keep the law out of this for now. I do not want Lady Isabella associated with this scandal," he said. "I shall extend mercy to you, which is something I suspect you would have never bestowed upon me."

"Thank you, Lord Ewin," Lady Rebecca murmured, lowering her gaze.

"But I don't ever want to see you again," he pressed.

"I understand."

"Nor will you ever speak to George again."

Lady Rebecca nodded weakly.

Ewin tucked the overcoat pistol into the waistband of his trousers. "And, lastly, I believe you owe Lady Isabella an apology."

Lady Rebecca pursed her lips together. "I'm sorry," she muttered under her breath.

Ewin turned his attention towards her with a hint of a smile on his lips. "Do you accept Lady Rebecca's apology?"

"I do," Isabella replied, "but only because I wish to be rid of her."

Ewin chuckled. "You heard the lady, be off with you," he said, waving his hand towards the coach.

Lady Rebecca didn't hesitate as she stepped into the coach and slammed the door behind her. Within a few moments, the coach was rolling down the road.

Isabella was still watching the coach ride away when Ewin approached her and said, "Thank you for coming after me."

Turning to face him, she tucked the tendrils behind her ears. "You would have done the same for me."

"Make no mistake about that," he answered quickly. "But how did you know I was in danger?"

A smile came to her lips. "Your brother paid me a visit and vastly underestimated me. It was quite shameful on his part."

He returned her smile. "I have no doubt."

"He informed me that you were traveling with Lady Rebecca to Gretna Green and warned me not to interfere in your relationship or else."

"Or else, what?"

She shrugged one shoulder. "He didn't elaborate, and I didn't give him time to," she replied. "I immediately called for Everett and Nicholas and informed them that Lord Dowding had just threatened me."

"I take it that didn't go well."

Nicholas spoke up from behind him. "It did not. He ran like the coward that he is."

Isabella reached out and placed her hand on her horse's neck. "I just felt the whole situation was fishy, especially since I knew you abhorred Lady Rebecca."

"That is true," Ewin acknowledged.

"So, I confirmed my suspicions with Everett and Nicholas, and they were gracious enough to allow me to come along with them to rescue you."

Everett cleared his throat. "I wouldn't say we were gracious in allowing her to come. She issued what can only be called a command."

"That doesn't surprise me very much." Ewin smirked. "Although, just so we are clear, I could have rescued myself."

Isabella gave him a look that implied she didn't believe him, but graciously replied, "I have no doubt."

"It is true," he pressed. "I was just biding my time before I escaped."

Everett placed a hand on his shoulder. "I'm afraid you won't live this one down for quite some time, mate," he expressed. "You were abducted by a lady."

"Who hired ruffians!"

Nicholas shook his head. "Two guards and a lady wouldn't have stopped me."

"When I was first abducted, there were four ruffians," he said, "and they all had pistols pointed at me."

Everett gave him a look of pity. "I didn't see four men."

"But the fourth was there, and he even hit me over the head, rendering me unconscious," he shared, bringing a hand up to the back of his head.

Nicholas smiled. "I'm sure he was," he remarked complacently. "But just so you know, my weakest crew member could have fought off four men and a lady."

Isabella decided to come to Ewin's defense. "Leave poor Ewin alone," she chided gently.

"Thank you, Bella."

Tipping her head at him, she replied, "You are welcome."

Ewin grew solemn, stepping closer to her. "And thank you for saving my life." His voice was hushed, oddly intimate, and she felt her heart soaring.

"You are welcome."

"But I wish you hadn't put yourself in harm's way for me," he said. "I couldn't have lived with myself if anything had happened to you."

"As I have told you before, I can take care of myself." She meant her words to be firm, but they only came out as a whisper.

"I know, my dear Bella," he breathed. "However, that doesn't mean I won't ever stop worrying about you."

As she opened her mouth to respond, Everett interjected, "I believe we helped, as well. Didn't we, Nicholas?"

Nicholas nodded. "We did. We stopped that big, bad, scary lady from forcing Ewin into marriage," he replied humorously.

Ewin sighed as he turned to face his friends, and his shoulder brushed up against Isabella's. "And I thank you two ninnyhammers for accompanying Isabella to rescue me."

"You are welcome," Nicholas and Everett said in unison.

"It might be best if we head back to London now," Ewin suggested.

To Isabella's disappointment, Everett replied, "Good idea. I shall ride with Isabella and you can take my horse."

"I don't mind riding with Ewin…" she attempted.

Her brother cut her off. "Nonsense. It is only proper for me to ride with you."

She waved a hand over her boy's clothing. "But there is nothing proper about this entire situation."

"Be that as it may, you shall ride with me," Everett declared.

Knowing that she was fighting a losing battle, she conceded, "As you wish."

She glanced down and saw that Ewin's hand was right next to hers. All she had to do was move her fingers slightly to touch him. But was she brave enough?

Isabella held her breath as she slowly extended her pinky finger and touched his, hoping he wouldn't find her too brazen. Her heart pounded in her chest as she waited for him to make a move to reciprocate her gesture of affection, but when none was forthcoming, she felt only embarrassment and dismay. As she withdrew her finger, to her great pleasure and relief, he moved his hand to gently encompass hers.

Sadly, it was short-lived, because Everett approached her horse, causing Ewin to drop her hand and step to the side.

"We have wasted enough time," Everett said. "It is time to depart."

✣ 19 ✣

THE SUN WAS HIGH IN THE SKY AS EWIN STOOD OUTSIDE OF Stanwich House and debated about even running this errand. Perhaps it would be best if his father didn't know that his own son had been plotting his demise. No. His father needed to know. But he took no pleasure in this.

He walked up the stairs slowly as if his Hessian boots were made of lead and knocked on the door.

It was quickly opened, and Dunn greeted him. "Good morning, milord." He stepped to the side to grant him entry.

As he stepped into the entry hall, he asked, "Are my father and brother home?"

Dunn nodded. "They are."

"I have an important matter to discuss with them," he said. "Inform them that I will be waiting for them in the drawing room."

Dunn tipped his head. "As you wish, milord," he replied before spinning on his heels to do his bidding.

Ewin walked across the expansive entry hall towards the drawing room. When he stepped inside, he was pleased to see that his mother was sitting on a settee, reading a book.

"Good morning, Mother," he greeted as he walked further into the room.

Her eyes lit up. "What a pleasant surprise." Esther lowered the book to her lap. "But may I ask what you are doing here?"

"I have a pressing matter to speak to Father about."

He saw the disappointment flash in his mother's eyes. "Did you change your mind about marrying Lady Isabella, then?"

"Heavens, no," he declared. "Make no mistake that I intend to fight until my last breath to secure her love."

"Oh, good."

He came to sit on the settee next to her. "How have you been?" he asked, noticing for the first time the dark circles under her eyes.

"I am well."

He lifted his brow. "Are you?"

Esther's eyes darted towards the door before admitting, "Your father has found a new mistress to entertain."

With a clenched jaw, he asked, "Is that so?"

"She even stays over on occasion."

Ewin reached for her hand in her lap. "You must leave Father and come live with me when I move to Kent."

"I wouldn't want to intrude."

"It isn't an intrusion if I am offering."

Her gaze lowered to their hands. "Do you suppose Isabella would feel the same way?"

"I have no doubt, but you should know that I still haven't convinced her to marry me yet."

"Are you so sure that she will say yes?"

The memory of Isabella reaching for his hand the night before came to his mind, banishing all his doubts. "I believe she will."

"I am so glad to hear that…"

Her voice was cut off by his father's. "I only can presume

that you have finally come to your senses and have decided to marry Lady Rebecca."

Ewin rose from his seat. "I have not, Father."

The duke came to stop in the center of the room. "Then why are you here?" he asked with annoyance in his tone.

"I have a pressing matter I wish to speak to you about."

"And why do you suppose I should care about this so called 'pressing matter'?"

"I believe you will care greatly about it."

His father humphed. "I doubt it," he said. "You have only been a disappointment to me since you were born, and I care little for what you think is important."

"Alfred," her mother chided. "That was uncalled for."

Ewin put his hand up. "No, it is all right, Mother," he said. "I am sorry that you feel that way, Father."

Before his father could respond, George walked hesitantly into the room and met his gaze. "What are you doing here?"

"I asked the same question," his father muttered under his breath.

Ignoring his father's snide comment, he directed his attention towards his brother. "Your plan didn't work."

"What plan?" Esther asked.

"George and Lady Rebecca concocted a plan that would have forced me to marry her had I not been able to escape," he shared.

"Bravo," his father said, turning towards George. "At least one of my sons has a lick of sense."

"Fortunately, I was rescued by the Duke of Blackbourne and the Marquess of Northampton as we were traveling to Gretna Green."

George's eyes grew wide. "The Duke of Blackbourne rescued you?"

"He did," he replied, "and he was very displeased when he found out what your part was in the plan."

His mother turned her attention towards George. "What is Ewin talking about?"

"Nothing," George growled out. "Lady Rebecca and I may have spoken about abducting Ewin, but I didn't think she would actually go through with it. It was sheer lunacy on her part."

"Not only did she go through with it," he began, "but I think we both know there is more to the story."

George frowned. "It matters not," he said. "You managed to escape, unharmed, I see."

"I did," he replied. "But do you want to tell Father what you intended to do after Lady Rebecca and I were wed?"

George's face grew pale. "I…um…don't know what you are talking about," he stammered.

"No?" he asked. "Then please allow me to inform father of your devious nature."

His father interjected, "What are you talking about, son?"

Ewin met his father's gaze and said, "After Lady Rebecca disposed of me, George was supposed to kill you."

"*What?!*" Alfred shouted as he glanced between his two boys. "You can't possibly be serious!"

Ewin stood his ground, his gaze never wavering. "But I am."

"George would never do such a thing," his father exclaimed. "How could you even accuse him of such a slanderous accusation?"

George crossed his arms over his chest. "Ewin is just jealous of me," he declared. "He always has been, and he always will be. He will claim anything in an attempt to win your affection, Father." He huffed. "It is pathetic, really."

Not deterred by their glowering looks, Ewin pressed, "Lady Rebecca confessed the whole scheme to the Duke of Blackbourne and the Marquess of Northampton, and they are both willing to testify against you."

"But it would be their word against mine," George remarked smugly.

Ewin smiled. "I daresay their word means more than yours, dear brother."

His father turned towards George with a stern look on his face, a look that was generally reserved for him. "Ewin is right, son," Albert said. "Which makes me wonder if there is any truth behind his accusations."

Fear flickered in George's eyes before he rushed out, "I wouldn't have done it, Father. I would never have killed you. Lady Rebecca wanted me to, but I refused."

Albert's brow shot up. "You had even discussed the possibility."

"It was Lady Rebecca that was behind all this," George proclaimed. "She was determined to marry Ewin, and she hatched a scheme so sinister that I was afraid not to go along with it."

"And what about poor Jane?" Ewin asked.

Esther rose from the chair, the distress on her features. "What about Jane?"

Ewin shifted to face his mother. "Lady Rebecca intended to kill Jane so she and George could eventually be wed."

"But that is impossible," his father contended. "A brother cannot marry his brother's widow."

"Lady Rebecca and George intended to marry in France to avoid that pesky law," Ewin explained.

Tears came to Esther's eyes as she stared at George. "You would have had Jane killed," she breathed.

"No," George exclaimed. "That was Rebecca's plan. Not mine."

"But you would have let her?" she asked.

George shook his head vehemently. "No, no, no…" His voice trailed off. "Rebecca was obsessed with me, with becoming a duchess. I tried to stop her, but she wouldn't listen to me. She went—"

His father spoke over him. "Enough!" he shouted. "No one is buying your lies. You must think we are all simpletons."

George closed his mouth as he dropped into an upholstered chair.

Alfred gave George a disgusted look before he turned to face him. "Apparently, I have been wrong about a few things."

"A few things?" Ewin mocked.

His father frowned. "I deserve that," he said. "Fortunately, because of Lady Rebecca's horrid actions, I have no choice but to terminate the contract between myself and Lord Frampton, leaving you free to marry Lady Isabella."

"Thank you, but I wasn't looking for your permission to marry Lady Isabella," he asserted.

"But, Father," George whined, "what are we going to do about all your gambling debts?"

Alfred glared at his son. "Do shut up," he exclaimed. "This is your fault, you incompetent nincompoop."

Ewin was tired of his family's squabbles and he decided to take his leave. "If you will excuse me..."

His mother spoke over him. "I have decided to move in with Ewin."

"Are you in earnest?" Alfred asked.

Esther straightened herself to her full height. "I am tired of you parading your mistresses around the townhouse," she said. "I will reside with Ewin from now on."

Alfred lifted his wrinkled brow. "You wish to live in poverty, do you?" he asked. "Because Ewin's manor is smaller than the dowager house at our country estate, and it is located in a hamlet."

"Any place is better than living with you," Esther declared.

His father waved his hand dismissively. "Fine by me," he encouraged. "But if you do go, you won't be receiving an allowance from me. Not anymore."

Ewin came to stand next to her mother and slipped his arm around her shoulder. "We shall see to her needs."

Alfred chuckled dryly. "Let's see how long you last on Lady Isabella's dowry," he said. "You will be back, begging for money, and I shall take great joy in turning you away."

"No, Father," Ewin replied. "I hope not to see you or George again after today. Our time has come to an end, and I feel it is best if we part ways."

For the briefest of moments, he thought he saw his father's face softened a tad bit, but then it grew hard again.

His father shrugged his shoulder. "I shall not lose any sleep over it."

Ewin removed his arm from his mother's shoulder and informed her, "If all goes according to my plan, I shall post the banns tomorrow, and Isabella and I will be wed in three weeks' time. Then, we shall all depart for Eathorne Manor."

Esther beamed up at him. "I shall be looking forward to it."

Ewin turned his attention back towards his Father. "Goodbye, Father. I hope you find joy in this life."

Alfred grunted something incoherent in response as he glared at him.

"Goodbye, George," Ewin said.

George met his gaze, but he didn't acknowledge him.

As Ewin walked out of the drawing room, he felt freer than he had in years. He may have grown up with opulence, but that didn't mean he craved it. He knew he would be content at Eathorne Manor, accompanied by Isabella and his mother. The two women that he loved the most.

Now he just had to convince Isabella to take a chance on him.

Isabella stared out the window as she wondered when Ewin would come to call on her today. They had hardly spoken while they journeyed home last night, since the only opportunity came when they rested their horses. However, he had made a point of telling her that he would come visit her today. And she knew he was a man of his word.

Her mother's amused voice came from behind her. "Staring out that window won't make Ewin arrive any faster, you know."

"What makes you assume that I am waiting for Ewin?" she asked innocently, turning around to face her mother.

Mary smiled as she continued focusing on her needlework. "Pardon me. I had just assumed," she responded. "Was I wrong?"

Isabella walked over to the settee and sat down. "No, you were right," she replied. "I was waiting for Ewin."

Lowering the needlework to her lap, her mother asked, "May I ask what you have decided to do about Ewin?"

"If Ewin does offer for me again," she said slowly, "I am of the mindset... that I will be... inclined to accept it."

A bright smile came to her mother's face. "That is wonderful news."

"That is *if* he offers again, Mother," she pointed out.

"He will."

She bit her bottom lip. "How can you be so sure?"

"Just a mother's intuition, I suppose."

Isabella reached over to the table and picked up the handkerchief that she had just finished working on. She ran her fingers over her initials. "I have decided I am going to give Ewin one of my handkerchiefs."

"I have no doubt that he will treasure it."

She placed the handkerchief back down on the table. "And if he doesn't?" she asked fearfully.

Her mother's kind eyes watched her for a moment before

asking, "I assume that you aren't speaking about the handkerchief anymore."

She shook her head.

"Just as I suspected," Mary sighed. "I suppose you will just have to ask yourself if your love is greater than your fears."

"But I will be giving up everything to marry him, Mother," she stated.

With a shake of her head, Mary replied, "No, you are wrong. You are gaining *everything* by marrying Ewin."

"How can you be so sure?" She paused, smiling. "And don't say 'a mother's intuition'."

Her mother laughed. "Well, it is true."

Howe entered the drawing room and announced, "Lord Ewin is here to call upon Lady Isabella."

"Send him in," Mary said.

Isabella rose swiftly and smoothed out her white gown with a round neckline, attempting to ignore the fluttering in her stomach.

"Nervous?" her mother whispered.

She swallowed down her trepidation and admitted, "Dreadfully."

Mary grinned. "There is nothing to be nervous about."

She opened her mouth to respond when Ewin walked into the room, looking devilishly handsome. He was dressed in a blue riding jacket, an ivory waistcoat and matching cravat, and caramel colored trousers.

When he met her gaze from across the room, she found herself drawn to his greyish-hazel eyes, unable to formulate a greeting.

"Hello, Bella," Ewin said in his deep, baritone voice.

She finally found her voice. "Hello, Ewin."

Ewin turned his gaze towards her mother, and she immediately missed the loss of contact.

He bowed. "It is a pleasure to see you again, Mary."

"Likewise, Ewin," her mother replied, her eyes darting between them. "Does it feel drafty in here?"

Ewin shook his head. "It does not."

Mary turned her head towards the window. "I'm afraid I feel a draft," she said decisively. "If you will excuse me for a moment, I shall go retrieve my shawl from my bedchamber."

Isabella watched as her mother exited the room before she turned her gaze back towards Ewin, who was staring at her intently.

Unsure of what to say, she walked over to the table and picked up the white handkerchief. "I made you a handkerchief with my initials on it," she said, extending it towards him.

"You did?" Ewin asked.

She nodded. "I am not entirely useless with a needle."

Ewin walked over to her and accepted the handkerchief. "Thank you for this gift," he said as he ran his fingers over her initials, much like she had. "I shall treasure it always."

"It isn't much…"

He spoke over her. "It means more than you know."

"Perhaps you can make me one with your initials on it," she boldly asked.

His lips quirked to one side. "It would be my pleasure."

As he slipped the handkerchief into the pocket of his riding jacket, she attempted to think of something clever to say. "Did you sleep well last night?"

Drats. That wasn't very clever, she decided.

"I did," he replied. "Did you," he hesitated, "sleep well?"

She bobbed her head. "I did. Thank you for asking."

"Of course," he murmured.

They both stood there in awkward silence for a moment, staring at one another, before Ewin revealed, "I stopped by Stanwich House to visit my father today."

"Oh," she said. "How did that go?"

He shrugged. "About as well as I imagined it would go," he

confessed. "From here on out, I don't intend to waste any more of my thoughts or energy on my father or my brother."

"I can understand why."

Ewin took a step closer to her, and his eyes seemed to implore hers, a mix of hope and agony mingling there. "I'm hoping that you have had a chance to reconsider my offer?"

Clasping her hands in front of her, she replied, "I have, and..."

He spoke over her. "There are a few things I would like you to consider before you give me your answer."

"Which are?"

He appeared reluctant, a far deviation from his typical confident demeanor. "I am not a rich man. The only thing I have to my name is a minor estate in a hamlet in Kent," he said. "The manor is small and is in no way as luxurious as what you are used to."

"That matters little to me..."

Ewin interjected, "I intend to start a stud farm on my estate, but it will take hard work to get it up and running."

"You do?" she asked, feeling pleased by this unexpected news. "That is wonderful."

He winced slightly. "Furthermore, you should know that I have invited my mother to live at my manor, partially because my father is the most despicable of men."

She waited for a moment before asking, "Is that all?"

"No," he said with a shake of his head. "There is just one more thing that I would like you to consider before you give me your answer."

"And what is that?"

He reached for her hands, as the intensity of his gaze made her tremble inside. His voice was low, intimate. "That I am madly, deeply, and irrefutably in love with you."

"You are?"

"I am," he replied. "I have been in love with you since we

were children, and my love for you has only grown stronger as we have gotten older." He swallowed slowly. "Please, my dear Isabella, say that I have a chance at securing your love."

Isabella smiled genuinely and unrestrained, feeling overwhelmed at the happiness she felt. "Yes."

He stared at her with a bemused look on his face. "Yes, I have a chance at securing your love?"

"No, silly, you already have my love," she said. "I meant I accept your offer to marry you."

His brows shot up. "You will?"

She bobbed her head.

A wide smile came to his lips as he brought his hand up to cup her cheek. "You have made me the happiest of men."

Ewin tenderly ran his finger over her cheekbone as she revealed, "Just so you know, I would have married you even if you didn't have a farthing to your name."

"Does it bother you that I don't meet every requirement from your list?"

She giggled. "That list was ridiculous," she declared. "It was meant to dissuade you from finding me a suitor."

"It didn't work."

"I know, and I am so glad."

Ewin slowly lowered his head until he pressed his lips against hers, causing all of her doubts and fears to melt away. He gave her one kiss, then a second, then a third. Each one was a little longer than the one before, each one touched her a little more deeply.

He leaned back slightly and whispered against her lips, "You don't know how long I have waited to do that, my love."

"I wouldn't mind doing it again."

He chuckled. "Life with you will never be dull or predictable."

Deciding she was done with talking, she went up on her tiptoes, and kissed him. He immediately responded by gathering her close and deepening the kiss, making her feel cherished. She quickly decided that kissing Ewin was her new favorite pastime.

Everett's stern voice caused them both to jump apart. "I truly hope I don't need to challenge Ewin to a duel."

Ewin ran his hand over his lips before saying, "No need. Isabella has agreed to my courtship."

Everett smiled broadly. "That makes me immensely happy to hear, especially since that means I won the bet."

"What bet?" Isabella asked.

"After I made the bet with Ewin that he couldn't find you a potential suitor by the end of the Season, Nicholas and I made a bet on when you two would get engaged," Everett explained, rubbing his hands together.

Isabella cast him a look of disbelief. "You made a bet with Ewin about finding me a suitor?"

Everett nodded. "If you selected a suitor by the end of the Season, then I would pay him ten thousand pounds," he shared. "That was the best money that I have ever spent since I knew you two would eventually end up together, and that money would go to good use in securing your futures."

"You did?" Ewin asked.

Everett nodded. "It has always been evident that you held my sister in high regard."

Isabella turned towards Ewin. "You only offered to help me find a suitor because of a bet?" she asked incredulously. "You failed to mention that part before."

Ewin had a baffled look on his face. "Does it matter?" he asked.

"Of course it matters," she said, tossing up her hands. "You lied to me."

He put his hand up. "No, the truth is, I offered to help you before Everett suggested the wager. It was a pointless bet, so I didn't feel a need to say anything about it."

"Are you actually attempting to justify your actions?" she questioned, creating more distance between them.

Isabella watched as Everett quickly fled from the room, closing the door behind him. She turned her heated gaze back towards Ewin.

"Has this all been some type of game for you?" she asked as she blinked back the unwanted tears that were starting to form in her eyes. "Something to amuse you?"

He shook his head. "No, it hasn't."

"Then why would you have taken the bet?"

Ewin smiled, and even now, her heart leapt at the sight of it. "It was never about the money, Bella," he asserted. "It has always been about winning your heart."

"Why didn't you tell me the truth?"

Ewin took a step towards her. "I am sorry that I hurt you, but I am not sorry that I made the bet," he said. "Because everything I have done up to this point, every decision that I have made, has led me to you. I wouldn't change anything. Frankly, I wouldn't dare, for fear of a different outcome."

She pressed her lips together, knowing that he made a good argument.

"I will gladly spend the rest of my life atoning for my mistakes," he stated as he started walking towards her, "if you would just find it in your heart to forgive me." He stopped in front of her and continued. "I love you, Bella. I always have, and nothing will ever change that fact. I agreed to that bet because it was pointless. I was planning to help you, anyway. I knew I couldn't lose you, so I wanted to be the one to prove how well we suit."

"I suppose I could overlook this misstep," she started, "assuming you promise never to leave something out again."

"I can agree to those terms."

She reached for his hands. "But next time, I won't be as forgiving."

"I can assure you that there won't be a next time."

"Smart man."

Ewin leaned closer until his forehead was resting against hers. "I promise you, Bella, that you will never regret your choice to marry me. For I will cherish you, love you, and protect you always."

"You don't wish to change me?"

She felt his brow lift at her question.

"Change you?" he asked in astonishment. "Why would I wish to change something that is already perfect just the way it is?"

Any doubt or hesitation that she had melted away at his words, and she knew that her heart would always belong to Ewin.

EPILOGUE

Ten years later

Ewin glanced up from the ledgers on his desk when he heard his six-year-old daughter, Emma, giggling from the doorway.

"May I come in, Father?" she asked.

He closed the ledger that was in front of him and nodded. "You may, but I must wonder why you aren't in the nursery?"

Emma hurried over to the desk and whispered, "I need to hide from Mother."

"Why is that?"

She grinned. "Because we are playing a game."

"Ah," he replied. "Where do you wish to hide?"

Emma's eyes scanned his study before they landed on the drapes. "I will hide behind the drapes," she announced proudly. "Mother will never find me there."

"That could work."

She skipped over to the window and stepped behind the

large, maroon drapes. "Do you see me, Father?" she asked in a hushed voice.

"No, but I can hear you," he replied in an amused voice.

"Then I am going to stop talking," she revealed. "That way, Mother won't be able to hear me, either."

"That sounds like a good plan."

Ewin had scarcely turned back to his ledgers when he heard Emma ask, "Is Mother out there?"

"No, she is not."

He heard Emma sigh. "It is rather warm behind these drapes. Perhaps this wasn't the best hiding spot." She stepped out from behind them. "I need a new hiding spot, and quickly."

"You could hide under my desk," he suggested.

She bobbed her head. "That would work." He moved his chair back, and Emma quickly ducked under his desk. "Can you see me, Father?"

"I can," he replied, "but your Mother won't be able to."

"That is good."

He opened the ledger when Emma spoke up. "It is dark and cramped under your desk."

"I imagine that would be the case."

"What are you working on, Father?"

He chuckled. "I am working on the ledgers for the stud farm."

"Oh," she replied. "I have my riding lesson later today."

"Is that so?"

"Will you come watch me?"

"I suppose I could make the time for that."

He could hear the smile on Emma's voice as she said, "I am so pleased. Sometimes I think my horse behaves better when you are watching."

"Truly?"

"Daisy can be quite vexing," Emma shared. "Just last week,

she refused to leave her stall until I gave her two apples. Two, Father. Can you believe it?"

"It sounds like Daisy has trained you," he remarked.

"That is what Mother said, as well." She paused. "This is a really good hiding spot. Mother will never find me here."

"I wouldn't be so sure," he said. "Your mother is quite clever."

"She is the smartest Mother in the whole world."

He smiled. "That she is."

Isabella's cheerful voice broke through their private interlude. "I knew you were an exceptionally smart man."

He glanced up and saw his wife leaning up against the doorway, smiling. Even now, just the sight of her brought a smile to his lips.

"Have you seen a little six-year-old?" she asked, holding out her hand. "She is about this tall."

Ewin brought his hand up to his chin and rubbed it thoughtfully. "Can you be more descriptive?" he asked as he heard his daughter giggle in response.

Isabella straightened from the doorway and walked further into the room. "She has blonde hair, blueish-grey eyes, and she is a terrific hider."

"That doesn't sound familiar," he teased.

His wife stopped at his desk. "What a pity," she pouted. "We were going to go into the woods and look for flowers soon."

Ewin heard his daughter gasp.

"I suppose I will just have to take Edward with me."

Emma crawled out from under his desk and jumped up. "Don't take Edward," she groaned. "He just likes to pick everything."

"Well, he is only three," Isabella remarked, smiling. "I could take Katherine, but your sister is on a riding lesson."

Emma turned to face him. "We could take Father with us."

"No, your father is extremely busy," Isabella said with a shake of her head.

"Nonsense," he declared, closing the ledger. "I have time to take a stroll through the woods."

Emma put a hand on her hips. "We don't stroll, Father," she rebuked him, "we are looking for plants that help with medicinal purposes."

"Well done on saying 'medicinal'," Isabella praised.

A knock came at the door before his butler, Cluett, walked into the room with a silver tray in his hand. "A missive just arrived by messenger, milord. It is from London."

Ewin came around his desk to retrieve the communiqué. It was from his brother's solicitor. He ripped open the envelope and started reading, his eyes widening with each pass.

"What is wrong?" Isabella asked, stepping closer to him. "Your face has gone pale."

He lowered the paper down to his side. "George is dead," he breathed.

In the next moment, he was wrapped up in Isabella's comforting embrace.

"Who is George?" Emma asked from next to him.

He closed his eyes as he felt the tears begin to form. "He was my brother."

"I didn't know you had a brother," she commented.

Cluett spoke up. "If it is permissible, may I take Miss Emma into the kitchen for a biscuit?"

Emma clasped her hands in excitement. "May I, Mother?"

He could feel Isabella nod. "Yes, but only one biscuit."

After he heard Emma run from the room, he felt Isabella reach for his hand. She led him over to the settee and sat down.

"How are you faring?"

He folded the missive and placed it back into the envelope. "I know we have been estranged for some time, but I hadn't expected him to die so young and so soon after my father passed away."

"How did George die?"

"Influenza," he replied. "A few members of his household staff also perished."

"How awful."

Reaching forward, he placed the envelope onto the table. "You know what this means since George has only fathered sons illegitimately," he said reluctantly.

"I do," she replied.

He let out a deep, heartfelt sigh. "I never wanted to be a duke."

"I know, dear," she said, tightening her hold on his hand.

His eyes roamed his small study. "Our children will grow up vastly different than how I envisioned they would." He hesitated before adding, "How I hoped they would."

"They will adapt," she replied encouragingly.

Ewin met his wife's concerned gaze. "I shall have to ride out to London immediately, but I don't dare leave you and the children."

"We will be fine," she assured him. "Besides, I have your mother here to help."

He leaned forward until he rested his forehead against hers. "I won't be able to do this without you," he murmured.

"It is a good thing we are a team then."

"That it is."

Isabella brought his hand up to her lips and kissed his knuckles. "Just think of this as a new adventure."

"The whole idea of being the Duke of Glossner is daunting," he admitted.

"I have no doubt that you will handle it spectacularly."

He leaned back and stared deeply into her blue eyes. "How do you have so much faith in me?" he asked in astonishment.

"Because I know you," she replied. "You are brave and strong, and the finest man that I have ever known."

"Only because you are in my life."

She smiled tenderly at him. "No matter what we do in this life, we do it together."

Ewin lowered his head until his lips hovered over hers. "I couldn't agree more. You are my love, my everything," he murmured, then kissed her tenderly and sweetly.

The End

ABOUT THE AUTHOR

Laura Beers is an award-winning author. She attended Brigham Young University, earning a Bachelor of Science degree in Construction Management. She can't sing, doesn't dance and loves naps.

Besides being a full-time homemaker to her three kids, she loves waterskiing, hiking, and drinking Dr. Pepper. She was born and raised in Southern California, but she now resides in South Carolina.

f ⊙

Made in the USA
Columbia, SC
05 July 2025

60380928R00143